MW00719009

Endorsements of The Envelope

"A masterful use of clarity and detail provide an exciting and authentic look into the world of counterfeit medicine and money laundering. I highly recommend this exciting and enjoyable book that gives insight into the funding of terrorist organizations and the scope of their reach here and around the world."

—**WILLIAM R. ANDERSON**, US Customs Service Special Agent (Retired) and former member of the Joint Terrorism Task Force.

"DHS, Mafia, ICE, and more will keep you looking over your shoulder as you get inside Jake Palmer's head, so be prepared to binge-read this brain-splitting international mystery."

—**TOM WISE**, author of *Life on Base: Quantico Cave*

"*The Envelope* kept me in suspense from page to page following Jake. The plot and character development made me feel I was on this journey, too, which included a romance in the middle of the action. A thrilling, enjoyable read!"

—**BARBARA MCNALLY**, author of *Wounded Warrior, Wounded Wife*

"Jake Palmer is back on the job in this action-packed thriller from Ron McManus. When counterfeit drugs take the life of a mafia don's nephew and possibly that of his own mother, Jake cannot resist jumping headlong into the case to find the culprit. Following a trail that leads him from Philadelphia to London and the Amalfi Coast, what Jake uncovers may well put the lives of his father and his own girlfriend at risk. A fast-paced adventure set in some of the world's most picturesque places, *The Envelope* is a book that you simply cannot put down."

—**DARIN GIBBY**, author of *Gil* and *The Vintage Club*

"Ron McManus has blessed us with another Jake Palmer high adventure. *The Envelope* is a tense, taut roller coaster ride from its appetizing beginning to its satisfying end. Torn between two continents, ex-Navy SEAL Palmer is put through the wringer on this one, testing both his own physical prowess and his relationships with his family and his lover. Exceptionally well-written and several notches beyond exciting, *The Envelope* will open your eyes to a new and potentially devastating world of greed and evil. A warning though . . . Make sure your docket is free for the day, because once you pick up this beauty, you're hooked."

—**LARRY LINDSEY**, Retired Naval Officer, Vietnam Veteran, and Author of *Stump!*

The Envelope
A Jake Palmer Novel

by Ron McManus

© Copyright 2016 Ron McManus

ISBN 978-1-63393-379-8

All rights reserved. No part of this publication may be reproduced, stored in a retrieval system, or transmitted in any form or by any means – electronic, mechanical, photocopy, recording, or any other – except for brief quotations in printed reviews, without the prior written permission of the author.

This is a work of fiction. The characters are both actual and fictitious. With the exception of verified historical events and persons, all incidents, descriptions, dialogue and opinions expressed are the products of the author's imagination and are not to be construed as real.

Published by

 **Bay Beach Books**

Virginia Beach, Virginia

in association with

◣ köehlerstudios™

www.koehlerstudios.com

THE
ENVELOPE

A JAKE PALMER NOVEL

RON MCMANUS

VIRGINIA BEACH

To my wife, Mildred

1

A STEADY STREAM of vans stopped in front of the Welwyn Heights Medical Clinic and dropped off their passengers. Each driver waited. After several minutes, those same people, each carrying a small paper bag, got back in the van and left. The clinic was housed in a large, single-story, wood-frame structure with barred windows and doors, but those were for show. A hand-scrawled gang symbol on the front and sides of the building was the real deterrent to drug addicts and petty thieves desperate for pharmaceutical samples or anything else they could use or sell. The message that symbol communicated was clear: This clinic is protected, and punishment for break-ins will be swift and vicious.

I monitored the activity while leaning against a boarded-up building across the street, my hands crammed in the pockets of my coat. My left hand brushed against my Sig Sauer P938 Nightmare. A Sig P226 9mm was in a shoulder holster nestled under my coat.

Although some areas of this north Philadelphia neighborhood showed signs of renewal, Welwyn Heights remained dangerous—a place where guns were easier to come by than jobs, and a six-foot-two-inch, two-hundred-ten-pound male of Scottish descent, like me, felt like a lost tourist in an inhospitable land. In my feeble attempt to fit in, I had worn a pair of tattered jeans, a sweat-stained Phillies baseball cap with the frayed bill pulled low, and a coat that was one winter short of the Vietnam Veterans' yellow donation bag.

I'm Jake Palmer, investigative consultant under contract with Pennsylvania's Medicaid Fraud Control Unit, or MFCU, to gather evidence involving Dr. Wilson Abercrombie, the clinic's owner.

I was about ready to call it a day when another van pulled up. As with the others, I braced a camcorder, small enough to conceal in my hand, against the building, using the camera's LED screen to view what I was recording. Four elderly women and two elderly men were engaged in conversation as they walked to the clinic entrance, while a disinterested teenage male tailed behind. I zoomed in on them and panned the camera over to the driver, a twenty-something male on his cell phone and looking in my direction. In less than ten minutes, his passengers emerged with their paper bags in hand. I kept recording as the van rolled by. The driver glared at me and pressed his extended middle finger against the window. It was time to go before his friends showed up.

The MFCU's investigation file made for some interesting reading. Abercrombie had graduated from a small liberal arts college in Pennsylvania. He wanted to be a doctor but his grades were not good enough to get him into medical school. So, he applied to a medical school in Mexico and was accepted. I'm sure there are many highly qualified and caring physicians in Mexico, but if I'm really sick—say anything more severe than hay fever—I'm staying well north of the border. To his credit, Abercrombie returned to Pennsylvania after medical school and jumped through all the hoops to obtain his license to practice medicine in the state, including the completion of a hospital residency program. As soon as he had his license, he opened the clinic. According to his tax returns, in the past few years, his reported income skyrocketed from forty thousand a year to over a half million last year.

Abercrombie had billed Medicaid, the state-run program providing healthcare for the poor and disabled, for over two million dollars the last three years, most of it in the past eighteen months. That set off some alarm bells and flagged him for audit. Dr. Abercrombie had leapfrogged onto Pennsylvania's top-ten list of highest paid Medicaid physicians and top-five list of prescribers of oxycodone, a powerful and addictive painkiller. He had dispensed enough oxy to numb the entire population of the state. To top it off, every ambulance-chasing attorney in Pennsylvania had him on speed dial. He may not have been the smartest man wearing a stethoscope, but he wrote medical reports worthy of a Pulitzer Prize, transforming minor injuries into critical, debilitating conditions that garnered large settlements from insurance companies eager to avoid the case going to court. Most were back or neck injuries—easy to fake and hard to prove. State investigators had interviewed a random sample of his patients. All of them confirmed they received the care for which Abercrombie billed Medicaid and raved about his caring, attentive manner. Frustrated by the inability to document any illegal activity, the director of the MFCU turned to me.

Head down and hands in my coat pockets, I walked to my rental car, a barebones sedan with less than five hundred miles on the odometer and the acceleration of a cheap, riding lawn mower. No problem. It was transportation, and there was no way I would leave my own car unattended in this neighborhood.

Two large men standing across the street looked at me and then at the car and laughed. I'd seen smaller men on the Eagles offensive line. *Laugh all you want. I'm outta here.* As I inserted the key in the ignition, I heard a noise behind me and glanced in the rearview mirror. A pickup truck was barreling toward me. I turned the ignition key; *click, click, click.* I turned it. "Oh crap!" The truck was accelerating. A man jumped out and rolled away from the speeding truck. I opened my door, and did the same, rolling onto the pavement. The truck slammed into the rear of the car, pushing it forward about fifty feet. Steam rose from the front end of the rusty pickup, where the radiator had been crushed.

Popping up from the pavement, I extracted the Sig 9mm from my shoulder holster and grabbed the P938 from my pocket. The kamikaze driver ran off, but the two oafs from across the street seemed suspiciously unfazed.

"Don't try anything, assholes. I'm too good a shot, and you're way too big to miss," I yelled to them.

"We saw that pickup was gonna hit ya and came to help. We're good Samaritans," shouted the man on my left, shrugging his shoulders.

Good Samaritans, my ass. I backed away from them. "I appreciate the offer, but really, I'm fine." I moved my head back and forth. The man on my right continued to move away from the other one.

"What waz you takin' pictures of? Give us your camera, and we'll leave you alone," one of the men said.

A black Chrysler 300 with chrome alloy rims and the bass of a song vibrating its dark, tinted windows screeched to a halt in the middle of the street. Two men got out, unhurried and deliberate, and walked straight toward me, stopping about ten feet away. The driver was tall and slender, with a cap on backwards. His passenger was shorter and stocky, built like a fireplug. The driver had a baseball bat extended up and out to the side, his hand about a third of the way up the length of it. The fireplug had a crowbar, a hand grasping each end. I assumed that all four thugs were packing.

"I don't want any trouble. Just go back where you came from," I shouted.

"We from here, cracker," said the one with the bat. "You need to go back where you come from. 'Cept you ain't got no ride. We'll be glad to give you a lift." The other men laughed. Bat guy held up his left hand. The laughter stopped. "Now let's have that camera."

"I don't think so." I stepped back, keeping all four within my field of vision. To my left, out of the corner of my eye, I saw one of the men standing on the sidewalk reach behind his back and pull out a pistol. Before he could bring it to bear, I swung the 9mm in my left hand toward the bat guy to keep him honest and swept the P938 Nightmare in my right toward man with the pistol and fired, striking him in the fatty part of his upper arm. He dropped the gun and looked at his massive arm like a mosquito had bitten him. For good measure, I swept the P938 toward the bat guy and fired again. The bat splintered and flew out of his hand.

"What the hell!" he said, shaking the sting from his hand.

"You're lucky. I was aiming for your knee."

He took a step toward me and extended his hands out to the side, signaling the others to stand down. "Shit! Who da hell are you, man? Some kinda sharpshooter?"

"I'm the man who'll put all four of you down if you don't do what I say. The city of Philadelphia won't waste a dime searching for the killer of four drug-dealing gangbangers, and you know it. Give me the key." I stepped forward until I was within a few feet of him.

"You ain't gonna take my car."

"Move away," I said, aiming both pistols at him.

He stepped back to where the others were standing. Never taking my eyes or aim off them, I moved close to the car and took a quick look inside. The key was in the ignition. I slid in butt first, swung around and started the car. A hip-hop song sprang to life.

"I'll find you, asshole," the bat guy shouted. "You got no clue who you dealin' with."

"Neither do you. Your car will be at the airport—short-term parking. Now, all of you—around the corner." I motioned the direction with one of my pistols.

Concerned that the gunshots would bring reinforcements, I looked around, but in Welwyn Heights, when gunshots are heard, everyone disappears. No one wants to get hit by a stray bullet, and no one wants to be questioned by the police, should anyone bother to call them. I set the pistols on the passenger seat, and sped away with the bass of the hip-hop song booming and my head bobbing to the beat.

I parked the bat guy's car at Philadelphia International and left the key under the visor. Fortunately, I had put the rental car documents in my inside jacket pocket rather than leaving them in the glove compartment of the rental car. If I had left them in the car, he and his friends would have found them and seen my name, address, and phone number. I took a shuttle from the airport parking lot to a terminal and another one to National Rental Car where I reported the accident, thankful that I had made a rare exception to my rule and purchased the full package of insurance. Even the rental agent was surprised. After all, who purchases that? The MFCU was paying my expenses, so I figured, *why not?*

When I got home, I sent the time-stamped digital copies of the videos to the MFCU. After I returned from my father's wedding in New York, I would follow a couple of those vans to see where they picked up and dropped off the patients. Eventually, the MFCU would decide whether the clinic was very efficient, gaming the system, or committing fraud of a government program. I had my opinion. That done, I packed for the morning train from Philadelphia's 30th Street Station to Penn Station in midtown Manhattan.

2

AFTER MY TRAIN pulled into New York's Penn Station, I hailed a cab for the short ride to my hotel. I was full of nervous energy, not because of yesterday's misadventure, but because of my eagerness to see my girl, Fiona Collins. Fiona was en route from London to accompany me to my father's rehearsal dinner and wedding. Being in a relationship with someone on the other side of the Atlantic presented challenges. Even with the various means of electronic communication available to us, our work schedules and the five-hour time difference made it difficult to stay in touch. Spending time together in New York with neither of us distracted by our work was what we both needed and wanted.

After checking in, I changed into my workout clothes and headed to the hotel gym. I had just finished my workout and showered when my cell phone chirped. It was Fiona. Her British Airways flight from Heathrow had landed and was taxiing to the international terminal. An hour and a half later she arrived in a tizzy and in no mood for the passionate welcome to America I had imagined. "Later," she promised, "after dinner." We made small talk while she unpacked. It soon became obvious that she needed some quiet time to get ready. When she suggested I pop down to the bar for a drink, I was out the door before she finished the sentence.

The bar on the second floor had a view of Sixth Avenue, a slow-flowing river of buses and yellow cabs. The sun had set and the tall buildings, which had blended into the gray evening sky, were alive with lights. Manhattan was busier than usual. Vacationers and shoppers crammed into the city to soak up the holiday atmosphere and do some Christmas shopping. Most of my fellow happy-hour patrons, however, were young to middle-aged businessmen with a precarious grasp on the next rung of the corporate ladder. They sat, backs hunched over the bar like commas, staring blankly at the television tuned in to ESPN or fiddling with their cell phones. I wouldn't trade places with them for all the money on Wall Street. A few couples were having drinks at the tables, probably going out to dinner and a Broadway show, putting aside the problems that burdened them at home. Maybe someday I'd have a family waiting for me, a lawn needing to be mowed and a dog wanting to play—maybe a golden retriever, like the one I imagined but never had growing up. Being with Fiona for a few days will be good, and she'll help get me through the farce of my father's wedding. I'll certainly be more pleasant to be around with her there.

I drank the last of the Scotch and set the empty glass on the bar. Only fifteen minutes had passed since I left the room. Fiona needed more time; I was sure of it. I was about to order another drink when I looked at the reflection in the mirror behind the bar. A man wearing an unbuttoned overcoat, dark suit, blue-striped shirt, a mismatched tie, and an ear-to-ear grin walked toward me. *Could it be?* I cocked my head and squinted. *Dennis Goodman. What's he doing here?* I caught the attention of the bartender, held up two fingers and tapped the bar in front of me and in front of the empty chair beside me.

The fifty-four-year-old Homeland Security Investigations agent tossed a large envelope on the bar, draped his overcoat on the back of the chair, and sat beside me as the bartender set a glass of scotch in front of each of us.

Without acknowledging each other, we took a drink.

"Palmer," he said, still looking straight ahead.

"Special Agent Goodman," I said, looking at him in the mirror.

Goodman held the glass out in front of him and looked at the contents. "You don't know how badly I needed this. Your usual, Glenmorangie?"

"The twelve-year-old. Can't afford the eighteen at these prices."

"What'd you expect? It's Manhattan. Everything's twice the price. What brings you to the city that never sleeps?"

Goodman, whom I hadn't seen in over two years, had a five o'clock shadow, and his nose and cheeks were bright red from the cold wind. In spite of the smile, his eyes were those of an overworked man with a lot on his mind. This was no chance meeting.

"I could ask you the same thing. Aren't you still working out of the Philadelphia office? And, if I'm right, you already know why I'm here."

"Yes I'm still in Philly. And I read that your old man, Edward Palmer, president of Palmer Global Investments, is marrying an Italian lingerie model 'bout half his age this weekend. Lucky bastard. Who says money can't buy you love?"

The comment stung. Until a few months ago, when my brother Patrick told me that our father was engaged to Michelle Petrochelli, I could have cared less whom my father married, if anyone. But even my Wall Street broker-of-greed father didn't deserve the misery this gold-digger was destined to rain down. They make lots of money, but sooner rather than later, they land someone who can support them and their lifestyle after their short career ends.

"How's the family?" I said.

"Great. Sarah started at Villanova this year. She's majoring in criminal justice." Goodman beamed. "She's arriving home for the holiday break tonight. Can't wait to see her."

"Like father, like daughter. And the wife?"

"Spending every freakin' dime I earn. Between her spending habits and Sarah's college tuition and eventual wedding, I'll be working 'til the day I die."

"Okay. You didn't track me down for a drink and a chin-wag. I won't ask what I can do for you because that would imply I was willing to do something, which I'm not."

"All right, I know you were a little upset after the bust in Philadelphia a couple of years ago," Goodman said.

"Upset? I did all the legwork and alerted you to that operation. But when the show started, I cooled my jets by my car a half a mile away while you stormed the castle. I had wanted in on the bust, even if you wouldn't allow me to carry a weapon."

"Need I remind you that you were and still are a civilian? You were being paid by a drug company to investigate a counterfeit medicine operation involving one of its branded drugs. We have rules, and having a civilian participate in a bust is *verboten*. You could've been shot."

"I've been shot at before and since."

"Excuse me for not looking surprised or impressed. Still, you managed to take down the suspect, the one who jumped out the warehouse window."

"The dumbass was going to steal my car." I took another drink to hide my smile.

"I need your help."

I choked and coughed. "You're kidding, right?"

Goodman's eyes darted to his right, toward the bar's entrance. He lowered his voice to just above a whisper. "I'm working on a case in Philadelphia that really got to me, the kind of thing that keeps you up at night. I'm here to meet with someone at another agency who's doing some technical work for me. When I'm in town, I work out of the Homeland Security Investigations office at Federal Plaza. Anyway, I told my boss, the Philadelphia special agent in charge, about the case you and I worked on and about the terrorist cell you busted in Virginia a couple of years ago. He gave me authorization to bring you on board."

"Why me? What can I do that someone in your shop can't?" I asked.

"We're short on manpower and, well, there's something else." Goodman stopped and looked behind us, not in a casual way but as if he were looking for someone in particular. "I need a man who knows the law, has pharmaceutical industry experience, and doesn't back down if things get physical. You're an investigative consultant, ex-Navy SEAL, and former big pharma regulatory attorney. If you were any more qualified, you'd have my job."

"Thanks for the compliment, if that's what it was, and as for having your job—no way." I swiveled in my chair and faced

Goodman. "Look, any other time I'd consider helping you. But there's a beautiful woman upstairs, whom I plan to entertain for the next few days. I've screwed up every chance I've had with women in the past. I don't intend to do the same with her."

"You don't have to decide now." Goodman placed his hand on top of the sealed, nine-by-twelve Tyvek envelope he had thrown on the bar and slid it in front of me. "Take this. Look it over after your young lady returns to London." He held his hands out in front of him, palms up. "That's all I'm asking."

Something was eating at Goodman, and whatever it was made the self-confident, federal agent hesitant and anxious. "I get the feeling there's something you're not telling me."

"Of course there is. I can't tell you everything until I know you're on board."

"Okay. After I've gone through it, I'll call you."

Goodman handed me one of his business cards. "Only call me on the cell phone number. If I don't hear from you within the next few days, I'll call you," Goodman said. He tossed back the rest of his scotch, pushed his chair away from the bar and grabbed his overcoat. "Thanks for the drink, Jake. I owe you one. Talk to you soon." Goodman patted me on the back and left.

Goodman had taken a couple of steps, when I said, "Hey. What if I don't hear from you?"

Goodman kept walking but looked over his shoulder and smiled. "Seek Jesus, my friend. Seek Jesus."

I drummed my fingers on the bar and tried to ignore the sealed envelope a foot away from my hand. *Seek Jesus? What's that about?* I stared at the envelope and pulled at my chin with my thumb and forefinger. Goodman would not have tracked me down and given me the envelope if he didn't believe the case would pique my interest. And I doubted Homeland Security Investigations had a manpower shortage. It's part of Immigration and Customs Enforcement, or ICE, for goodness sake, one of the most well-funded government agencies. I fought the urge to open it. Maybe I'd wait until after Fiona and I returned from dinner or tomorrow after breakfast. *No.* This was her first trip to New York. Whatever was in the envelope would be a distraction. Goodman said he would contact me in a few days.

I signed the check and tucked the envelope under my arm.

About a hundred of my father's friends and business associates would be at this dinner party. We were staying several blocks from the exorbitantly expensive hotel where the dinner was being held and where my small family and the wedding party were staying.

I only had a few days to reconnect with Fiona. It was time to fish or cut bait. She was my plus-one, and she was excited and maybe a little on edge about meeting my family. I will not allow my feelings about my father and brother to ruin this for her. *If only we were alone, someplace where the sun is warm, the drinks are cold, and the sea is turquoise.*

The elevator doors were starting to close when I stepped in, causing them to reopen. A man in the rear of the elevator exhaled loudly. "Sorry," I said, pressing the elevator button for the eleventh floor. Then I heard three gunshots pop in rapid succession and people screaming.

3

NO. IT COULDN'T be Goodman. A feeling of dread overcame me. I squeezed sideways out of the elevator doors before they closed, once again causing them to reopen. This time there were no groans of impatience. Instead, my fellow occupants squeezed tight against the sides of the elevator while craning their necks, looking in the direction of the gunshots. One repeatedly pushed the button to close the doors.

The muffled shots had come from outside the hotel, close to the entrance. Rushing into the lobby, I stayed close to the wall, away from the people running away from the lobby and out of the line of sight from the hotel's entry doors. A few had crouched behind furniture. The hotel employees behind the registration desk had dropped down and were peeking over the top of the counter.

I pushed through the hotel's revolving door. Some bystanders, who fled the scene when the shots were fired, had already returned and were gathered three-deep on the sidewalk around the victim. I shoved through the crowd, disregarding the profane protests of those thinking I only wanted a better look.

The victim was a male wearing an overcoat. He was lying on his back with one of New York's forty thousand police officers kneeling beside him. Another officer, standing a few feet away, was calling for an ambulance and backup while attempting to keep onlookers back. A woman standing next to the officer pointed down the street and gasped a breathless, almost incoherent account of what she had seen.

I stood over the victim, the envelope tucked under my arm. It was Dennis Goodman.

"Get back," the policeman, who was tending to him, commanded without looking up.

I knelt beside Goodman and said to the policeman, "I know him."

"Who are you?" the officer said. "How do you know him?"

I ignored the policeman. Goodman turned his head and looked at me, his eyes only slightly open. Grasping his hand, I lowered my head near his. "The ambulance is here. Don't you die on me. Who did this?"

He reached for the envelope under my arm, his hand moving in a slow, jerky motion. "In there. White Jesus," he whispered. His arm dropped.

Again he had mentioned Jesus. *Had he seen Jesus?*

Who would have shot him and why? Random shootings and robberies don't occur outside expensive Manhattan hotels at this time of day. Too many witnesses. Too many wannabe heroes.

The police officer put on a pair of latex gloves and opened Goodman's overcoat, pulled back his suit jacket, and ripped open his shirt. There were three bullet wounds. One was near the center of his chest, one lower and on the right side, and one on the left side of the abdomen. Blood was pooling on the pavement underneath him. Goodman was struggling for each breath and fighting to remain conscious. A sucking sound was coming from his abdomen. A bullet had punctured a lung.

"He's Dennis Goodman, an HSI special agent—Homeland Security Investigations," I said to the policeman. "What happened?"

"A man shot him, dropped the gun and ran. According to the witnesses, he was a white male in his thirties, wearing jeans and a grey hoodie."

A police car and ambulance with sirens blaring and emergency lights flashing screeched to a stop at the curb beside us. The crowd parted for the two paramedics.

The policeman and I moved away so the paramedics could do their job. With three gunshot wounds to the chest and abdomen, the paramedics would try, but the damage to his organs was most likely too traumatic, the blood loss too great. Goodman's only hope was for the paramedics to keep him alive long enough to get him to a trauma center.

The policeman pulled off the latex gloves, careful not to come in direct contact with the blood. "How did you know the victim?" he asked.

"We worked a case together a couple of years ago. We ran into each other in the hotel bar, had a drink, and he left. Then, I heard gunshots from outside the front entrance. I had a bad feeling and came outside to see if it was him. That's all I know."

"Don't leave. I need to ask him some questions before they take him away."

The policeman spoke to Goodman while the paramedics continued to work; he was not responding. After a few minutes, one of the paramedics looked at the policeman and shook his head.

I could not believe it. Dennis Goodman was dead. Before the policeman came over to me, I disappeared into the crowd. I hated to leave, but I needed to get back to Fiona. Other than what I had said, there was nothing more I could tell the police. And if they wanted to track me down, they could. All they would have to do was go to the hotel bar, talk to the bartender, and check the room charges for the drinks.

4

TO A PASSERBY on the crowded New York City street, Viktor Utkin was just another businessman—late forties, wearing a jacket and tie, a full head of dark hair with a smattering of gray, and a neatly trimmed goatee that partially covered acne scars. The one characteristic that separated him from the others was his imposing size. He was six feet six inches tall and weighed around two hundred and seventy-five pounds.

Utkin took a long drag from his unfiltered cigarette and exhaled, twitching his eye as the wind coming through the alley blew the smoke into his face. The cigarette only partially masked the smell of urine and rotten garbage in the alley. He turned up the collar on his brown leather jacket to keep the wind off his neck.

Utkin had heard the faint sound of gunshots in the distance, followed by screams, then sirens. If the man had done his job, he would be here soon to collect his payment. He cursed under this breath. *Should have handled this myself and would have if I had received the assignment soon enough.* Killing someone was one thing; killing an American federal agent was quite another. Proper foresight and planning ensures no witnesses and little or no evidence. With today's forensics and technology, eliminating all evidence from a crime scene was no simple matter. The smallest of trace evidence could convict you. This hit was sloppy, carried off by an amateur, who would piss himself at first question the cops asked.

Utkin's man in New York had located a Bulgarian named Hristo Adonov at a food bank. Not that Utkin wanted to know the man's name; he didn't. Adonov was just another immigrant who had arrived in New York searching for the American dream and discovering the American nightmare. Adonov had lost his job and was a couple of nights away from being homeless in New York in the winter, the end of a downward spiral, from which only a few recovered. According to Utkin's man, Adonov had never shot anyone, yet he had given Adonov the loaded, unregistered gun and pointed out the agent he was to shoot. Utkin didn't care about the identity or unfortunate history of the man who killed the agent, or even how the hit was carried out. The only things that mattered were that Goodman was dead and the package retrieved. Adonov would be by any minute now, looking for a man named Joe.

Utkin stood in the shadows. He watched people walk by on the street, not a single one taking even a quick glance into the alley. They were in one of the wealthiest parts of one of the world's wealthiest cities and did not want the experience tainted by looking into an alley. There was nothing there they needed to see. *A perfect place to meet,* thought Utkin.

A man entered the alley and walked toward Utkin, stopping a few steps away.

"Are you Joe?" the man asked.

"Yes, I'm Joe," Utkin said.

"I'm Hristo Adonov."

"Is he dead?"

"I shot him three times in chest. Nobody can survive it," Adonov said in broken English with a heavy eastern European accent.

Utkin took a long drag from his cigarette and threw it on the pavement.

"Did you drop the gun, like you were told?"

Adonov twisted his head around, checking the entrance to the alleyway. "Of course. I wore gloves, too. Give me money. I go."

"Where's the envelope?"

"No envelope. I looked. Was in hand when he went in hotel.

Not there when he came out. Must have given it to someone. Don't know but not in hand when I shot him."

Utkin slowly shook his head. *Idiot. No envelope. Unbelievable. At least, Goodman was dead.* He reached into his left jacket pocket.

Adonov tensed and took a couple steps back.

Utkin extracted a stack of bills and extended his hand.

"Better count it."

Adonov grabbed the money from Utkin's hand and stepped back. His eyes widened, and a nervous smile came on his face. He turned away from Utkin, flipping through the stack of hundred dollar bills, quickly the first time and then slowly, counting aloud.

With Adonov's attention focused on the money, Utkin eased behind him and clasped Adonov's arm from behind, jerking Adonov toward him, and wrapping his large hand around Adonov's mouth. Utkin dragged him behind a garbage dumpster, and then leaned back and pulled him upward, lifting Adonov off the ground. Adonov, who had been clutching the money, dropped the bills. With his free hand, Utkin pulled a switchblade from his pocket and pressed the button, releasing the long, finely honed blade. He sliced across Adonov's exposed neck in one swift motion that made a deep ear-to-ear cut. The weight of Adonov's body caused the cut to open wide. Utkin shoved him away to avoid getting blood on his clothes.

Adonov fell to his knees and looked up at Utkin. He grasped his throat with both hands, trying to stop the blood spurting from his neck. He attempted to speak, but no sound came out.

Utkin wiped the knife off on Adonov's hoodie, sweeping it across two or three times until it was clean. He folded the blade back into the handle and returned the knife to his pocket. While Adonov was bleeding out, Utkin gathered up the money, some of it spattered with blood, and picked up his cigarette butt so as not to leave any trace evidence for the police. He gave the area another quick check and calmly walked away.

5

BACK IN MY hotel room, I slumped down in the chair, staring at the blank television screen. Fiona was in the bathroom humming a tune to a song I didn't recognize. Her mood had improved. Mine had worsened.

"I'm back," I said loud enough for her to hear me.

"I'm about ready. Five more minutes. I promise. What were all those sirens?" Fiona asked.

"It's New York. There are always sirens."

What, if anything, should I say to Fiona? What would it accomplish, other than to upset her? She was flying home in a couple of days. Goodman was an acquaintance of mine, not a close friend. She had never met him. There was no reason to tell her. I would wait to open the envelope until after she left for London. I looked at the envelope in my lap and again thought about Goodman bleeding out on the sidewalk, moments after we were having a drink and talking. If I opened it, I wouldn't be satisfied until I read every word—twice. I slid the envelope into one of the hotel's plastic laundry bags where I had stowed my sweaty gym clothes and threw it in the back of the closet.

By the time we left for the rehearsal dinner, the emergency vehicles and crime scene investigators were gone. Before stepping into the taxi for the short ride to the hotel where the dinner was being held, I shifted my eyes to the spot where the policeman and paramedics tried to save Dennis Goodman's life. The only clue that something had happened was a bloodstain on the sidewalk. No one on the busy street seemed to notice as they hurried by. By tomorrow it would be gone, buried under the dirt and grime of the city. How many similar spots existed in Manhattan, where the affluent and privileged lived alongside the desperate and disadvantaged?

Fiona slid close to me and put her hand on my leg. "Is something bothering you?"

I forced a wide smile and put my hand on top of hers. "Just thinking about the dinner and you meeting my father and his fiancé and my brother and his wife."

"Actually, I'm a little nervous."

I twisted in the seat and faced her. She was stunning in her black cocktail dress. I had never seen her wear makeup. She had applied some tonight, along with eye shadow, drawing my attention to her bright and alluring eyes. "They'll love you. Why wouldn't they? I'm just glad you're here to help get me through this charade."

Fiona moved closer and kissed me softly on the lips. "There's no place I'd rather be."

"Likewise." I pulled her to me and kissed her until she protested that I'd ruin her lipstick. I wanted more than kisses.

It was the first time in a long while that we had been together in the US. She had made frequent trips to the States with her job as a clinical research auditor for the British company, B&A Pharmaceuticals. But at the time, I had either been with her in England, where she lived and worked, or in Italy. Having her all to myself without distraction from either her job or mine made me smile.

We had met a couple of years earlier when I was investigating the death of a physician in Cornwall in southwest England. He had been enrolling ineligible patients in a B&A clinical research study. Fiona was the clinical research auditor assigned to work with me. What began as a reluctant partnership resulted in our falling in love. Now she was B&A's director of the clinical auditing worldwide.

"Don't be offended if Dad and Patrick don't spend much time with us," I said. "They'll be working the crowd most of the night. For them this weekend is as much a business function as it is a wedding."

"You haven't told me much about your father or Patrick. From what little you've said, you're not at all close."

"As Leo Tolstoy said in the opening line of *Anna Karenina*, 'All happy families are alike; each unhappy family is unhappy in its own way.' Let's just say that I'm very different than either Dad or Patrick."

"Don't let their problems or drama cause you to lose sight of who they are. Be glad for the family you have while you have them," she said.

It was a slap-on-the-forehead moment. Fiona's parents had been killed in a car accident. How petty any expression of bitterness between me and my family must seem. "You're right. Sometimes it's difficult to like those you love. We were very close at one time. I've just taken a different path than my controlling, manipulative, disapproving father would have liked. It's the source of a lot of friction."

∧∧∧∧

The taxi drove up to the hotel where a valet opened the door. Fiona and I stepped onto the red carpet that led to the hotel entrance and the grand lobby. There a wedding concierge directed us to the ballroom. A man dressed in tails announced the arrival of Mr. Jacob Palmer of Philadelphia and Ms. Fiona Collins of London. Upon hearing the name Palmer, heads turned to see who had arrived.

Fiona leaned over and whispered as we followed the man to our table. "Very posh."

"What's the expression you use? OTT?"

"Over the top," Fiona replied.

"Right. Very OTT."

A server offered us flutes of champagne on a silver tray. I declined, saying I was holding off for something stronger. We strolled to the front of the ballroom, where a string quartet was playing and guests were mingling while having drinks. My father and Michelle Petrochelli met us on our way to the bar.

He extended his hand to me and I shook it, and then, almost as an afterthought, he hugged me. "Good to see you, Jake."

He introduced me to Michelle, whom I had met once before, and I, in turn, introduced them to Fiona. He told us that Michelle would be retaining her maiden name, Petrochelli, because it was so strongly associated with her commercial brand.

"I am pleased to meet you, Fiona," said my father, beaming.

"Likewise. I've been looking forward to meeting you and Miss Petrochelli ever since Jake invited me to attend. I'm honored and excited to be here."

"Jake said you're an auditor for B&A Pharmaceuticals," my father said. "Did the two of you meet there? I know he was in their legal department for a year or so before he gave it up to become a...." He looked at me, palms turned upward.

"Investigative consultant," I added. My father had no idea what I did for a living.

"No. We met a while back when B&A brought him in to do some contract work."

"I've been trying to lure him into the exciting world of finance to work with Patrick and me. But he thinks we're all a bunch of greedy, unethical bastards."

"I'm sure he is as proud of you as you are of him," Collins said.

The truth was quite the opposite. My father had told me I was throwing my life away. He measured success by the amount of money you accumulated and how powerful you were. Being neither rich nor powerful earned me none of my father's pride or respect.

"How long will you be in town, Fiona?" Michelle asked. "Maybe we can go shopping after we return from our honeymoon."

"Oh, I'd love to. Unfortunately, I fly back to London in a couple of days. Where are you going for your honeymoon?"

"Actually, we're stopping in London—Eddie has business there—then we're off to Italy for two weeks."

"Really? I live just outside London and work at B&A's London office. My mother was Italian, and my father British. My full name is Fiona Isabella Collins. Where in Italy will you be?"

"We're going to Rome first for a reception for my friends and relatives who were unable to come to the wedding. After that, we're staying in Positano on the Amalfi Coast."

I listened to the two women talk, as they occasionally switched back and forth between English and Italian. They were close enough in age to be sisters. Michelle could have just stepped off the cover of *Vogue*. Her dress fit her like the expensive couture creation it was, and her diamond and emerald necklace drew one's eyes to her famous bustline, displaying what the press deemed the "breasts that sold a million bras." She caught the eye of every man who passed by.

Love not withstanding, my father and Michelle seemed to be a good match. He was handsome and charming and had amassed a small fortune, enough to support her lifestyle. She attracted a great deal of attention from the paparazzi and press, garnering publicity for my father's business. Likewise, I felt Fiona was a perfect match for me. Her natural beauty overshadowed her simple black cocktail dress, and her only jewelry was a small, ornate gold cross necklace she told me she had purchased while on holiday in Cephalonia, one of the Greek islands. She was hardworking, intelligent, and refined. She was just what I needed and wanted in my life.

My father leaned over and whispered to me, "I need to talk to you."

The two of us took a few steps away from the ladies.

Here it comes. He's going to say something negative about Fiona and me.

"Julia, your mother . . . she died last night. Matt called this afternoon and told me."

Although I had not seen my mother in years, the news hit hard. When Patrick and I were children, our mother had an affair with Matt O'Malley, the pastor of our church. After the affair became public, she left my father and us, and O'Malley left the church. They moved to Florida. When the divorce became official, about a year later, O'Malley and Mother were married. Although Patrick and I spent some time with them in the summer in the following years, our visits became shorter and soon stopped altogether.

"Had she been ill?"

"Matt said Julia's health had declined over the past few years—complications of diabetes. The reason I'm telling you this is that I can't attend the funeral even if I wanted to, and I don't. And Patrick refuses to go. If you can and want to attend, here's

the information about the funeral arrangements." He handed
me a sheet from the hotel notepad with the details written on it.

"My initial reaction is not to go."

"It's your decision. No pressure. I only wanted to let you
know she has passed away and give you the option to attend the
funeral or not."

I took a step to return to Fiona, but my father grabbed my
arm.

"There's one more thing," my father said, removing a white
business envelope from his inside jacket pocket and handing it
to me.

"What's this?" I said.

"Our itinerary and contact information. I want you to have
a copy."

"Why do you want me to have a copy of your itinerary?" I
asked, cocking my head. You've never bothered to tell me before.
What's going on?"

"I gave Patrick a copy, too. There's something else I need to
tell you, Jake."

We talked for several more minutes. When we returned to the
ladies, my father and Michelle moved on to talk to other guests.

"My God. She's drop dead gorgeous," Fiona said. "And
she and your father are so pleasant. Definitely not what I was
expecting based on what you had said."

"He's on his best behavior tonight."

"You look strange. I glanced over to see what you were doing.
You both looked very serious. What were you talking about?"

"I'll tell you later," I said, forcing a smile. I wasn't going
to throw a wet blanket on the evening by telling her about
my mother's death. First it was Goodman's murder and now
Mother's death. The bad news was mounting up.

We made our way to the bar. Fiona, who had finished her
champagne, ordered a chardonnay, and I ordered a Bombay
Sapphire gin and tonic with lime, telling the bartender to go easy
on the tonic and ice. My brother Patrick and his wife soon found
us. I was grateful Patrick didn't mention Mother's death. He only
asked if Dad had spoken to me. When I said yes, Patrick changed
the subject. After the least socially acceptable time with us, he
and his wife begged off, saying they needed to mingle.

I talked Fiona into an early exit after dinner. It didn't take much to convince her. She confessed that she was a little jet lagged in spite of the excitement of the occasion. Guests had surrounded my father and his bride-to-be, and I didn't want to waste time chatting with people I neither knew nor cared for. I would rather go back to the room and enjoy Fiona's company. Still, I was preoccupied with conflicting thoughts about Mother. *Should I go to the funeral or not? If I don't go, I'll send flowers. Maybe that's all I need to do.*

On the way back to our hotel, Fiona asked again, "What did your father pull you aside to tell you? I saw him hand you something, and you had a rather serious look on your face."

"My mother died last night."

Fiona's jaw dropped. "Oh Jake, I'm so sorry. What happened?" She slid close to me in the taxi and put her hand on top of mine. I had told her about my mother and our strained relationship.

"Complications of diabetes. The funeral is the day after you leave."

"I know you weren't close, but you're going, aren't you?"

"Hadn't planned on it."

"Your father obviously can't go. How about your brother Patrick?"

"He could go but isn't."

"You should go, Jake. Funerals aren't for the deceased. They're for the living, to bring closure to the loss. If you don't go, I'm afraid you'll regret it later."

"She started a new life and new family. There are children, grandchildren, friends I've never met. I wouldn't know anyone."

Fiona rested her head on my shoulder and said nothing more. I appreciated her not nagging me about the funeral. It had been a long day. I would decide in the morning after a good night's sleep.

We were back at the hotel before ten o'clock, earlier than planned. I inserted the room key card into the door lock and stopped—voices inside the room.

6

WITH A WAVE of my hand, I motioned for Fiona to step away from the door. As she did, she made the sign of a telephone with her hand, her little finger and thumb extended away from her fist and held it to her ear, mouthing "front desk." Using her other hand, she pointed to the hotel phone on a table by the elevators. I nodded.

I stood close to the door and listened—two male voices, one man telling the other to hurry. Fiona was on the hotel house phone at the elevators. *Wait for hotel security or go in?* The men could be armed but better to be on offense and have the advantage of surprise than to find myself on defense against two or more armed men. I inserted the key card again and withdrew it. A green light appeared. They had not locked the deadbolt. I turned the door handle and charged into the room.

The two men jerked their heads toward the door. One had been looking through our suitcases, which were open on the bed, and the other had been searching the closet. Clothes were strewn everywhere. The doors to the nightstands and dresser were open. The man at the bed, who was less than six feet tall with a medium build, rushed me. I met him with an extended leg thrust to the midsection. He doubled over, stumbling backwards. I stepped toward him, drew back my right arm and threw an uppercut that connected with his jaw. The man crashed to the floor and did not attempt to get up. The second man, who was a few years older and fifty pounds overweight, ran past me toward the door. Fiona, who had been peeking around the doorjamb, extended her leg. As he fell, she pushed him with both hands, causing him to hit the floor with a thud. She reared back and kicked him in the head. I jerked up the groggy but still conscious man by the shirt collar and belt and slung him into the wall. He collapsed onto the floor.

"Well done," I said, massaging my knuckles.

"I've been taking a self-defense course for the past couple of years, ever since that night in Hyde Park," she said with a gleam in her eyes.

"Good to know." She had not mentioned that night in a long time. I'd leapt from the cold water of Hyde Park's Serpentine Lake in London and killed her abductor, a known murderer, with my bare hands.

The noise had aroused the attention of the other hotel guests, some of whom opened their room doors slightly and peered out. I dragged the man in the hallway into the room, laying him beside his partner, and flipped through the contents of their wallets. If their driver's licenses were authentic, they were William Jamison and Samuel Riley. Both had Brooklyn addresses. Both had come around and were sitting upright.

They were not going to tell me anything, but I had to ask. "What were you looking for? Who sent you?"

Neither responded. When I heard the elevator bell chime, I gave Jamison and Riley their wallets. Two hotel security men entered the room.

"When we opened the door to our room, they were going through our things. They came after us, and we defended ourselves," I told them.

I handed one of them my driver's license to verify my identity. He looked at the license and at me, and then nodded to his partner, who phoned the night manager and told him to call the police.

The police arrived, took our statements, then handcuffed the two intruders and led them away. An apologetic hotel manager arrived with a couple of bellmen. He handed me the key cards for another room and asked if we needed assistance in packing up our belongings and moving them to the new room. I said yes. Fiona, however, insisted on gathering up her own clothes and packing them. The bellmen loaded our things, including the hotel laundry bag with the envelope hidden among the dirty clothes, and left with Fiona for the new room. I said I wanted to check over the room and would join her in a few minutes.

After they left, I sat on the bed and let everything sink in. *It has to be the envelope. But how would the men know I have it?* Whatever it contained had gotten Goodman killed and two others arrested within a matter of hours. The only explanation is that someone at the murder scene saw me with it and followed me back to the room.

^^^^

When I got to our new room, Fiona was unpacking her luggage for the second time that day. The hotel manager had upgraded us to a suite.

It was time to come clean. "We need to talk," I said.

"Yes we do," she said, sitting straight up. "You've been in a weird mood ever since before we left the hotel tonight. First, I passed it off as your apprehension about the rehearsal dinner, then the news about your mother's death. Now this. What's going on, Jake?"

I told her about Dennis Goodman and the envelope. The envelope probably contained the background information on the case. Fiona listened without commenting, nodding every once in a while. When I told her about the gunshots and finding Goodman shot dead outside the hotel, her eyes widened and her mouth gaped open.

"That's why the sirens sounded so close. They were at the hotel entrance. Why didn't you tell me?"

"I didn't want to upset you and ruin your night."

"You waited to tell me about your mother's death and now this. In the future, let me be the judge of what upsets me."

Her eyes were burning a hole in my face. I decided the best response was none.

"Where's the envelope?" Fiona said, more like a demand than a request.

I went to the corner of the room where the bellman had put our luggage, and turned the laundry bag upside down. My sweaty gym clothes spilled out onto the floor along with the envelope. I picked up the envelope and handed it to her.

"Is this what they were after? How did they know you had it?"

"I'm guessing someone saw me with the envelope when I was with Goodman after he had been shot. They must have followed me back to the room. Usually, I would be aware of someone getting off the elevator on the same floor and walking behind me down the hall, but I was preoccupied. These men were not petty thieves. Petty thieves go for the quick hit, laptops, jewelry, and prescription drugs, whatever they can turn around for a quick profit. They're in and out in minutes. These two were searching for something. Either they overlooked the laundry bag or were put off by the smell of my gym clothes."

"Quite right, too. You said the shooting might have been unrelated to what's in the envelope, yet you hid it. You must have suspected it was somehow connected to his death."

"Before Goodman died, he reached for the envelope I had tucked under my arm and said, 'It's there.' So, yes, I believe that whatever is in this envelope is somehow related to his death. I need to return it to Homeland Security Investigations before anything else happens. I told Goodman I wouldn't have time to look at it until after you left. I should have told him I wasn't interested and given the envelope back to him. We'll go to the local HSI office at Federal Plaza tomorrow and be done with it."

She turned the envelope over in her hands, then got up and walked toward the bathroom.

"Where're you going?"

"To get some scissors."

7

FIONA RETRIEVED A small pair of scissors from her toiletry kit and returned to the bed. She cut through the end of the tear-resistant envelope and poured the contents onto the bed. A white business envelope was on top of the stack. She read the handwritten note on the front, "Jake Palmer: Open if you don't hear from me in five days. She handed it to me."

Outside of a séance, Goodman was not going to contact me, so I ripped open the envelope and read the handwritten note aloud.

> "Jake, if you've waited the five days to read this, and I haven't contacted you, I'm probably dead or wishing I were. I didn't want to talk to you about the details of the case until you had read the documents and committed to work with me. An important piece of evidence is hidden away. I can't say where in case someone, other than you, ends up with this letter. You're a smart guy. You'll find it.
>
> "I am the Homeland Security Investigations case agent for this investigation and have been compiling evidence for the Assistant US Attorney. Another federal agency in New York has been assisting me. When I'm in New York, I work out of the HSI office at Federal Plaza. This envelope contains medical records

and documentation related to the death of a young boy in Philadelphia. You know your way around medical records and counterfeit medicine. Follow the breadcrumbs. This is only the beginning.

"Because you have this envelope, your life might now be in danger. Sorry about that. I hope you pursue this case, but even if you don't, be careful. Contact Special Agent Jim DuPont at Homeland Security Investigations at the HSI Philadelphia office. His cell phone number is 215-555-4962."

"You need to go home," I said to Fiona.

"She squinted her eyes and pursed her lips. "I am. On my scheduled flight in a couple of days."

"No. Now." I held up the note and shook it at her.

"I'm not going home. I love you and everything that comes with it. I'm not running away from you or from the trouble that always seems to surround you, Jake Palmer."

Fiona, bless her soul, was as hardheaded and stubborn as I was. Arguing with her was pointless. "Okay then." For the next hour, we passed documents back and forth.

We were nearing the end of the stack. The information gave me a good feel for the case. Like the one Goodman and I worked on before, it was a counterfeit medicines operation, albeit a substantially different one. In retrospect, the earlier case had been straightforward, involving a shipment of counterfeit medicines that originated in China and smuggled into the US aboard a cargo ship. The counterfeits were destined for an illegal drug wholesaler. I had put Goodman in touch with an informant. The bust took place at a warehouse where the wholesaler was taking possession of the shipment. Although outwardly identical to the branded medicine, analysis subsequently showed the medicine contained no active pharmaceutical ingredient, only inert fillers, some of which were toxic.

This case began with the death of a teenage boy, Pietro Calabrese, following a kidney transplant. His body rejected the kidney. His distraught, frustrated parents refused to accept their child's death. His doctors had told them that the high degree of compatibility with the donor kidney almost guaranteed a successful outcome. They wanted answers. The physicians were unable to explain what had happened, other than to say Pietro's death was unexpected and related to the risks associated with kidney transplants. The boy's father, Paul Calabrese, insisted on an analysis of all the drugs his son had received. When, without any reason to suspect the drugs related to his death, neither the hospital nor the boy's doctors would agree to do the drug analyses, Paul Calabrese paid to have an independent lab test them. The results showed that one of his son's drugs, B&A Pharmaceutical's brand, Transpro, had far below the labeled amount of the active drug zufridone.

"Fiona, what do you know about Transpro?" I asked.

"Transpro, our brand name for zufridone, is a novel drug with a unique mechanism of action. Unlike many drugs used in transplant patients, zufridone's therapeutic index, the difference between efficacy and serious side effects, is wide. Other drugs have a narrow therapeutic index and therefore, require regular monitoring of drug levels during therapy. If the drug level in the blood is too low, the drug is not effective. If the level is too high, serious side effects and transplant rejection are likely to occur."

"So, drug monitoring is not required with zufridone?" I asked.

"That's right. It's highly effective with a very small risk of side effects and rejection. After Transpro was initially marketed, transplant physicians monitored drug levels of zufridone anyway. However, once they gained confidence in its efficacy and safety, they stopped. Sales of Transpro and our sales revenue took off like a rocket."

"There's a lot riding on this for B&A Pharmaceuticals and for transplant patients," I said.

"And, Goodman states the Calabrese boy was not the first transplant patient who died while taking Transpro. There have been other reports," Fiona said.

"That doesn't prove anything. Patients taking the drug have had transplants. A percentage of those will have died."

Fiona held out the report for me to see. "Look at the lab analyses of Pietro Calabrese's drugs."

I took the report from her and flipped through the pages. From my perspective, it was almost impossible for anyone without a degree in pharmacology or chemistry to interpret. "Give me a hand here. What am I looking at?"

Fiona pointed to the analysis of the Transpro. "The amount of zufridone found in the Transpro Pietro was taking was a fraction of what it should have been, enough to have only a small clinical effect, if any at all. Other excipients, inert ingredients that combine with the active pharmaceutical ingredient—in this case zufridone—to make the formulated and approved drug, are also listed in the report." Fiona flipped to the last page of the report, the summary of findings.

We read through the summary and conclusion section. All of Pietro's medicines tested were confirmed to be the drugs as labeled, except for Transpro, where the concentration of the active pharmaceutical ingredient, zufridone, was four percent of the labeled amount and included amounts of unapproved excipients, including drywall and floor wax.

"Drywall and floor wax?" I said.

"I've seen it in other cases we discussed in our audit management meeting. Counterfeiters sometimes use drywall to make tablet formulations. Floor wax is used in the coating, giving the tablet the appearance of being enteric-coated."

"Deaths associated with patients taking Transpro should have been reported to B&A's clinical safety and pharmacovigilance group. Had you heard anything about them?"

"Our manufacturing and security groups manage counterfeit medicine reports and investigations, including analyses of drugs. I'm not directly involved in that process. My role is limited to audit of clinical research studies of our investigational drugs or investigational uses of our marketed drugs. However, those reports are usually vetted and shared with the compliance and audit management team, of which I'm a member."

Fiona picked up several of the papers from the stack on the bed. "Here's something else I noticed." She set the papers beside her, picked up another handful and fanned through them. She shook her head and handed them to me. "The hospital reports and doctors' notes. How did Goodman get the records? I don't know how your government agencies work, but in the UK he would not have been able to obtain them without a court order because of our patient privacy laws."

She was right. "If Goodman was not authorized to investigate the case, he would have been unable to get a court order to release the records," I said. "Under ordinary circumstances the hospital wouldn't have allowed Goodman to review the records without consent, much less copy them, which would have required a court order and the approval of his supervisor, the special agent in charge at the Philadelphia office."

Fiona rubbed her forehead. "I don't understand. Under what circumstance would the hospital release the records?"

"When Goodman gave me the envelope, he told me not to call him. He said he'd be in touch in a few days, after my young lady returned to London. How did he know you had flown in from London? I didn't tell him that. And why didn't he want me to call him?"

"You're scaring me."

I shuffled through the documents. I was being drawn in along with Fiona. I should return this to HSI and end it now. Goodman was their agent, and he had been killed. This was not my case. Decision made. Turn the envelope and contents over to ICE, and then Fiona could follow through with B&A. That was the extent of her obligations and mine.

I took my phone from my pocket and searched for the address for the New York office of the Homeland Security Investigations. "The local HSI field office is at Federal Plaza. The wedding is late tomorrow afternoon. There's plenty of time to go in the morning. It shouldn't take long. Would you like to go with me after breakfast?"

"Shouldn't you take this to DuPont?" Fiona asked.

"Good point."

In spite of the late hour, I phoned Special Agent Jim DuPont. After several rings, he answered. I introduced myself and told him how I knew Dennis Goodman. I went into some detail about the meeting at the bar and being with him when he died. I told him about the envelope and Goodman's note to me and said that I had no interest in working on the case.

DuPont thanked me for staying with Goodman after he had been shot. He said they had been friends for many years. Goodman had phoned him earlier in the week and said I might be calling—but didn't say why. Goodman was the case agent and therefore had sole responsibility for developing the case for the assistant US attorney. DuPont said he had not been involved or kept informed of what was happening. All he knew was that it involved counterfeit medicine, one of Goodman's areas of expertise, and that a child who had taken the counterfeit had died. DuPont said I should give the documents to Mark Brantley, special agent in charge of the HSI New York office

"Tell Brantley to send them to the Philadelphia office. Make me a copy, and don't tell Brantley that we spoke."

I ended the call and told Fiona what DuPont had said.

"Sounds like you've made your decision. You're not taking the case."

"That's right. So, are you going with me tomorrow morning?"

Fiona's eyes brightened and her smile returned. "Go to a government agency in New York to discuss a murder and counterfeit medicine case? I wouldn't miss it for the world."

I gathered up the documents.

"What are you doing?" Fiona asked.

"I'm going to the hotel business center to copy these for DuPont and make a copy for me."

"Why do you need a copy? You're washing your hands of it."

"I'd like to have a backup, just in case. I won't be long."

"I'm coming with you. You're not leaving me alone."

8

FIONA AND I made love, slow and sensuous, yet ending all too quickly. We went right to sleep afterwards; the back of her naked body spooned into mine, my arm wrapped over her and my hand resting on her breast. A short while later, I awoke and lay awake for a long time, listening to the rhythm of her slow, deep breaths. She was exhausted. It had been a hell of a day, and her body was operating on London time, five hours ahead of Eastern Standard Time. I tried to relax and get back to sleep, but my mind jumped back and forth between my mother's death, Goodman's murder, my father's wedding, and the men who had broken into our room. It was well past three in the morning when I finally went to sleep with the only thing on my mind being the warmth of the beautiful woman beside me.

We were up early and at Federal Plaza by 9:00 a.m. I told the receptionist we needed to see the HSI Special Agent in Charge about the death of Dennis Goodman, an HSI special agent. Fiona sat in the waiting area and read a magazine, while I paced back and forth until a woman came to escort us to the office of Special Agent in Charge Mark Brantley of ICE's Homeland Security Investigations in New York.

The walls were lined with photos of presidents and senior directors, interspersed with framed patriotic photos and slogans, not a piece of decorator art in sight. Work cubicles were crammed into a central area designed to accommodate about half as many.

Individual offices lined the exterior walls, an antiquated design that reduced the amount of natural light shining through to the cubicles.

Brantley was seated at his desk, checking something on his cell phone when our escort dropped us off at his office. He appeared to be in his mid-fifties, wearing a light blue shirt and navy blue tie that was an inch wider than the current style. His sleeves were rolled up to compensate for an office that was a few degrees too warm. After introductions, Brantley wasted no time getting to the point.

"Thanks for coming in. What do you know about the death of our agent Dennis Goodman?"

"Dennis and I worked on a case a while back," I said. "Yesterday evening I was at the hotel bar when he walked in and sat beside me. He wanted me to work with him on another case. I told him I wasn't interested."

"Did he discuss it with you?"

"No. We had a drink, and he left this envelope and asked me to go through the contents. He said he would be in touch in a few days, if he hadn't heard from me." I handed Brantley the envelope, excluding the handwritten note Goodman had written to me.

"Three or four minutes after he left, I heard gunshots. By the time I got to the hotel entrance, the police were already there. The paramedics arrived and did what little they could, but Goodman died. Later that night, two men broke into our hotel room. I believe they were searching for that," I said, pointing to the envelope.

"Dennis was based in our Philadelphia field office, but another federal agency here in the city was doing some work for him. He used our office as his base when working in New York. His death hit us hard."

"Which agency was working with him?" I asked.

"I can't say."

"Can't or won't?" I said.

"Doesn't matter. You have no need to know."

"Any leads on the man who killed him?" Fiona asked.

"The NYPD found the suspect's body in an alley near the hotel. His throat had been slit."

"Who was he?" I asked.

"Hristo Adonov, a Bulgarian immigrant. He fit the description that witnesses gave to the police. A hotel bellman, who was standing close by when Goodman was shot, also confirmed Adonov was the shooter based on a photo of the corpse. The police believe it was a hit for hire."

"What's so important about the contents of this envelope? Why would someone want Goodman dead and then ransack our room looking for it?"

Brantley leaned forward and put his elbows on his desk. "I don't know why Dennis was killed. Neither do the police. There's certainly no proof it was because of the contents of this envelope. Also, I wasn't aware your room had been ransacked. What makes you think the men were looking for the envelope?"

"When we returned to our room after dinner, two thugs were going through our belongings. Ms. Collins and I subdued them. The police hauled them away."

Brantley gave Fiona the once over, perhaps doubting she was physically involved in the fracas.

"Do you really believe these events were random and unrelated?" I said. "And what hotel robber takes the time to go through everything in a room? They grab and run to lessen the chance of being caught. They were looking for the envelope."

"Why didn't they find it?"

"Maybe we interrupted them before they did."

"Was it sealed when Dennis gave it to you?" Brantley poured the stack of papers from the unsealed envelope onto his desk and thumbed through them.

"Yes. I wanted to see what was inside and assess whether or not I would be interested in working on the case."

"That's unfortunate. It seems you opened it after Goodman's death. Any request he may have made before his death would be null and void. Therefore, you had no reason to open it other than to satisfy your curiosity."

"Unfortunate?" I said, raising my voice. "I didn't ask for this; Goodman left it with me. Goodman *asked me* to read the contents."

"It is documentation related to a counterfeit medicine report," Fiona said. "A teenage boy died following a kidney transplant.

When his parents couldn't get any sound explanation for his death from his physicians, they paid to have his medications analyzed. Based on the lab analyses of his drugs, the anti-rejection drug he was taking, Transpro, was counterfeit."

"One of your company's products, isn't it, Miss Collins?" He pointed a finger at her. "B&A Pharmaceuticals."

"Yes, it is. How did you know I work for B&A?"

"Before you were escorted to my office, we ran a quick background check on both of you. Quite a coincidence, a former B&A Pharmaceuticals regulatory attorney and a B&A research auditor meeting with one of our agents regarding the counterfeiting of one of B&A drugs."

Fiona leaned in toward Brantley. With eyes narrowed, she said, "I never met or saw Mr. Goodman, and I don't like what you are implying, Mr. Brantley."

"I was a B&A regulatory attorney a long time ago and only for about a year before I quit and became an investigative consultant," I said. "Ms. Collins and I met when B&A contracted with me to work for them. Goodman found me—not the other way around. He said he needed someone with my qualifications and experience."

"Thank you for returning the envelope. That was the smart thing to do. I'm sorry you got involved." He stood, signaling the meeting was over.

"Well, I'm sorry, too," I said, still sitting.

"If we need any information from you or want your assistance, we'll be in touch," Brantley said. "My secretary will escort you to the lobby."

"Let's get out of here," I said to Fiona. I had worked with lots of law enforcement officers and had great respect for them. Maybe Brantley was just having a bad day. Regardless, he didn't want me involved, and that was fine with me because I didn't want to be involved.

The secretary escorted us out, making certain we signed out on the visitors log before she left.

"Guess they're glad to get rid of us," I said, still mildly agitated. "Not that I expected Brantley to greet us like a long lost relative, but he knows more about this case than he's willing to tell us. It's not like we were asking for classified information."

"I got that, too," Fiona said. "When I get back to London, I'll look into any reports of counterfeit Transpro we've received."

"We were right to return the envelope to ICE," I said. "They can do what they want with the case. Life's too short for that kind of aggravation. I'll give DuPont his copy and shred mine."

9

I FLAGGED DOWN a taxi and held the door open for Fiona. A black Mercedes S-Class was double-parked nearby with its motor running. When the taxi pulled away from the curb, I glanced out the rear window. The Mercedes was three cars behind us. Several blocks later, it was still there. I leaned forward, "Take the next right."

"That's not the fastest way to your hotel," said the taxi driver.

"Just take the next right."

Fiona grabbed my hand. "Are we being followed?"

"Probably not," I said, wanting to calm her. Maybe I was being paranoid but it seemed like they were tailing us.

The taxi turned. The Mercedes turned, too, and backed off. "Take the next left."

"It's your dime," mumbled the driver. He took a left. Once again, the Mercedes turned.

"They're following us, aren't they?" Fiona asked without getting an answer.

"Where to now? Want me to keep turning?" said the taxi driver.

"The hotel," I said.

A few blocks from the hotel, the traffic backed up. The Mercedes was stopped five cars behind us. "If I'm not back by the time the light changes, go to the hotel. I'll meet you in the room." I handed Fiona a couple of twenties for the cab fare in case she was short on American money.

"Where are you going?"

"To see who's following us."

I got out of the taxi and walked fast to the car. The Mercedes driver was looking over his shoulder, saying something to his passenger. A man in the front passenger seat was watching me. I grabbed the door handle on the passenger side. It was locked. I lowered my head, tapped on the window and shouted. "Are you following me? Open the door."

The passenger lowered the window halfway and nodded toward the back of the car. "He wants to see you." The man stepped out of the car. He was three inches taller than me, at least fifty pounds heavier, and had the look of muscle for hire. The man discretely patted me down, checking for a gun. Once he finished, he opened the rear door. On the other side of the car was a gray-haired man in a suit, a starched white shirt, and a light blue silk necktie tied in a perfect Windsor knot.

"He's clean, sir." The man shut the rear door after I got inside.

"Mr. Jake Palmer, I presume?"

"And who the hell are you? Why are you following us?"

"Yesterday, you received an envelope from Special Agent Goodman, did you not?"

"What if I did?" I said.

"If you want answers, Mr. Palmer, you'll lose the attitude." He took a drink from a crystal tumbler before continuing. "Before he was murdered, Agent Goodman was investigating a counterfeit medicine case in Philadelphia, a child who died following a kidney transplant."

"That's right."

"The name of the child was Pietro Calabrese."

"Right again."

"My name is Anthony Calabrese. He was my nephew."

Calabrese. I had not placed the name when Fiona and I were going through the medical records. But now—the bodyguards, the Mercedes, the man's appearance. This was Anthony Calabrese, the don of one of New York's Mafia families. Perhaps the death two weeks ago of a Mafia boss's nephew had made the local newspapers and television news in Philadelphia. If so, I'd missed it. Sometimes, I let the newspapers stack up. And I rarely watch television except for sports.

"Losing a child is tough, no matter who you are," I said.

"He was my brother Paul's only kid and like a son to me. Paul had the medicines analyzed. One was counterfeit. The hospital and doctors were of no use. They said they would report the counterfeit to the FDA and to the manufacturer. Beyond that, there was nothing they could do. Paul contacted Homeland Security Investigations and turned the information over to Goodman. Goodman recognized how important this case was, but it was more than that. Pietro's death bothered him. The last time I spoke with him, he told me that he wanted to bring you in to work with him. I asked him why. He said you were an investigative consultant and the two of you had worked together before. That's all he would say . . . So, are you going to work with HSI to get the scumbag responsible for my nephew's death?"

"With your influence and connections, you have a much better chance of finding those responsible than I do." Calabrese had ways of finding out things and making people talk. His was not the Mafia of old, but he was still a powerful and influential man.

"Ordinarily, that would be the case," Calabrese said. "But in situations like this, I couldn't make much headway without the feds and Interpol feeding me information."

"The NYPD believe someone paid a Bulgarian immigrant named Hristo Adonov to kill Goodman. Do you know anything about him?"

"We were keeping an eye on Goodman—protecting him. My man saw Goodman give you an envelope at the bar and saw that piece of shit Adonov shoot Goodman outside the hotel. It happened so fast there was nothing my man could do. He ran after the shooter but lost him in the crowd. A couple of blocks from the hotel, he saw a well-dressed man leave an alley and jump into a taxi. Seemed odd in that part of the city, so my man investigated. He found the shooter dead in the alley."

"So your man didn't kill Adonov?"

"No. We can't let some asshole kill someone we're protecting and just run away. It's bad for business. Whoever killed Adonov did us a favor."

"Last night, two men broke into my room. Their names are William Jamison and Samuel Riley. I believe they were looking for the envelope Goodman gave me. Were those your men?"

"Let's just say those are names a couple of my men use. When my man got back to the scene, he saw you kneeling over Goodman with the envelope under your arm. He had no idea who you were. For all he knew, you might have been involved with Goodman's death and had come over to make sure he was dead. We needed to know who you were and see what was in that envelope. He followed you back into the hotel and to your room. Then he went to the lobby and waited until you and Miss Collins left. He had called Jamison and Riley to check your room. He was also there this morning when you and Miss Collins left. He followed you and called me when you went into Federal Plaza."

"How do you know her name?"

"It was on her luggage." Calabrese said. "Riley phoned my man to tell him your names as soon as they got into the room. Riley also told him they didn't see the envelope and would have to search through your things. He said you and Miss Collins were dressed for a party when you left. When I heard you were Jake Palmer, I knew you must be Edward Palmer's son and in town for the wedding this afternoon.

"Guilty on both counts," I said.

"What were you doing at Federal Plaza?" Calabrese asked. "And what was in the envelope Goodman gave you?"

"I met with Mark Brantley, the special agent in charge of the New York HSI office and gave the envelope to him. It contained your nephew's medical records and the test results from the medicines he was taking when he died. An anti-rejection drug they gave the boy was counterfeit. Goodman told me to look over the information and said he would talk to me after the wedding about working with him on the case.

Calabrese gave a subtle nod. "I've seen the records and drug analyses. Paul asked the hospital for a copy of his son's medical records, and they refused to release them. I believe they were worried about a lawsuit. Paul's not used to being told no, so he asked someone with the hospital, who proved more cooperative. When he had the medical records, he contacted HSI and was referred to Goodman. He gave him the records and the drug analyses. I want your assurance that you'll pick up where Goodman left off."

"I'm really sorry about the loss of your nephew, but I'm not getting involved in this. I'm sure the feds will find those responsible. And besides, HSI doesn't want me involved. Brantley all but kicked me out of his office this morning. As you said, on an investigation like this, there's not much that can be done without their help and support. Plus, I already have a backlog of cases. Counterfeit drug cases are complicated. They eat up a lot of time and money."

"Don't work with ICE. You're an investigative consultant. I'll hire you. I'll triple your usual fee, plus expenses, and give you a sizable bonus when you find out who's responsible for the death of my nephew."

"Whoever is behind this is probably operating outside of the country. They import the counterfeit medicine into the US and get it into the legitimate drug distribution system."

"Talk to the boys in the Philadelphia HSI office," Calabrese said. "Tell them you are investigating this for the Calabrese family. If they're uncooperative or if you need anything, let me know. I'll talk to my brother Paul and tell him you're in."

"I don't need or want your help or money. And, I'm not *in*, as you said, and *if* I get involved, it won't be because of you or your brother."

"Enjoy yourself at your father's wedding," Calabrese said. "Family is everything. Never forget that. But think about what I've said. After the wedding, I'll expect an answer."

Calabrese handed me a business card. It was blank except for an embossed telephone number. He shook my hand and said, "If anything comes up or you need something from me, call any time night or day."

10

WHEN I RETURNED to the hotel room Fiona was sitting on the bed with her legs crossed underneath her, wearing the fluffy, white terrycloth robe with the hotel's monogram. In front of her were the documents from Goodman's case file, fanned out chronologically from left to right. Beside the bed was a silver tray filled with hors d'oeuvres, a vase containing a single red rose, a jug of orange juice and open bottle of Vueve Clicquot champagne with a silver stopper in it. Next to the bottle of champagne was an unopened bottle of eighteen-year-old Glenmorangie.

"What too so long? Why didn't you call?" Fiona asked. She took a sip from a champagne flute.

"It's complicated," I said.

"Thanks for the nibbles and champagne. I took that to mean you would be a while. Did you order the bottle of single malt whisky for yourself?"

"I can't take credit for any of it. It's probably from the man who was following us, Anthony Calabrese, Pietro Calabrese's uncle." I picked up a couple of smoked salmon and cream cheese hor d'oeuvres from the tray. Calabrese's man had been close enough to Goodman and me in the hotel bar to overhear our conversation, including our comments about Glenmorangie.

"That was nice of him. Why was he following us?"

"He wanted to talk to me."

"Why didn't he just come by the hotel or call you?"

"I get the feeling he likes to do business on his terms, face-to-face. He asked if I was going to work with ICE. I told him about our meeting with Brantley and said I wasn't interested. He offered to hire me to work on it at triple my usual fee. I told him I still wasn't interested."

"How did he know who you are?" Fiona said.

"One of his men had been following Goodman, to protect him. His man saw Goodman give me the envelope in the bar and saw Adonov shoot him. He claims his man ran after Adonov but lost him in the crowd. He saw a man in a business suit come out of an alley and get into a taxi. When Calabrese's man went into the alley, he found Adonov with his throat cut from ear to ear. He then went back to the hotel and saw me kneeling over Goodman with the envelope tucked under my arm. He followed me back to the room."

"He has men that follow people? What kind of person is he?" Fiona looked at me with her head cocked to the side. "Didn't you notice he was following you? You were a naval special warfare operative, a SEAL."

I exhaled through my closed lips. "That was a long time ago, and I was eager to get back to the room to see you."

"Sure you were," Fiona said.

"Those creeps in our room last night were Calabrese's men. Also, his man followed us to Federal Plaza this morning and notified him we were there."

"Who is he? Some sort of criminal."

"Anthony Calabrese is the don of a New York Mafia family."

If Fiona's jaw had dropped any further it would have been resting on the bed. "What! Don of a New York Mafia family? Are you kidding me? And the men we fought are Mafia?"

"I'd considered not telling you who Calabrese is or about the two men, at least not yet, but you told me I should let you be the judge of what upsets you."

Fiona raked her fingers through her hair. "I need to rethink that. Do you believe him?"

"Do I believe a Mafia don, a man who would do or say anything to get what he wants? He told me what he thought I wanted to hear. There's probably more he didn't tell me. However, until I learn otherwise, I believe him because it involves the death of a nephew who was like a son to him. He wouldn't lie about that. Family is too important to them. He gave me this." I threw Calabrese's card on the bed.

Fiona picked up the card and looked at both sides. "That's it? A telephone number?"

"He told me to call that number, day or night, if I needed anything. Keep it as a souvenir, if you like. I have no intention of calling him."

"I will." She placed the card on her bedside table.

"Find anything interesting?" I said.

"I'm getting a better picture of what occurred. Everything seemed to go well during the surgery and immediately post-transplant. A couple of weeks after the transplant, however, Pietro Calabrese returned with symptoms of acute rejection. The doctors had carefully documented problems from the initial signs that the kidney was not functioning properly. I reviewed the battery of diagnostic tests, including an ultrasound of the ureters, taken to see if there were blockages, and a scan to determine if there were problems with the blood flow to the transplanted kidney. It's sad. They did all they could. High-dose steroids were ineffective in stopping the rejection. One of his doctors noted that Pietro was on the highest recommended dose of Transpro. Someone, perhaps Goodman, had created a spreadsheet of Pietro's medicines, both prescription and over-the-counter. I reviewed the analytical data for each of his drugs. All were within normal limits except for Transpro, where the active drug, zufridone, was a fraction of the required concentration. I'm sure it caused his death or at the very least contributed to it."

I poured myself a glass of the champagne and grabbed another hors d'oeuvre. "Any record that B&A was notified?"

"I phoned the office," she said. "I spoke with our vice president of manufacturing quality. He has responsibility for the investigation of counterfeit medicine cases. He confirmed that the company is aware of the report and an investigation is underway. Our manufacturing quality control group found subtle differences between our packaging and the packaging of the drug administered to the patient, differences only a close examination would reveal. An investigation is ongoing. I'm meeting with him the morning after I return. I wonder why this hasn't been communicated to our audit management team?"

"Probably because of potential legal liability and adverse publicity," I said. "Don't be the bull in the china shop, Fiona."

"I like being the bull in the china shop, replacing complacency with a little constructive chaos. That's what auditors do. This case is no more sensitive or confidential than any of the others we see."

I once again became lost in Goodman's notes and the medical records, not saying anything. She refilled her glass of champagne and orange juice and topped off my glass of champagne. She shrieked and set her glass on the nightstand.

"What?" I said loudly, snapping my head around to see what had alarmed her.

Fiona pointed at the clock. "We're going to be late."

The wedding was at five o'clock and it was a little after three now. We were not in the wedding party, so we did not need to arrive early. A limo was taking us to the wedding, which was at the same hotel where the reception had been last night. I slid close to Fiona. "We have plenty of time." I eased my hand under her robe and up her thigh, while pulling her to me. Kissing her lightly on the lips, I pressed my body against hers. We moved together, our lips almost separating before coming back together. Using my hand that was squeezing her bottom, I grasped the top of her panties. I pulled them slowly down her legs and threw them on the floor. Her breaths deepened.

She moved away and whispered, "No. We can't. I need to shower and get ready."

Fiona sat on the edge of the bed and took a moment, shaking her head as if trying to awake from sleep. She stood and walked toward the bathroom. Halfway to the door, she stopped, dropped her arms and rolled back her shoulders. Her robe slid onto the floor.

Before she reached the door, I embraced her from behind, my arms wrapped around her naked body, my hands cradling her breasts. "No reason we can't do both," she said, turning to kiss me while taking small steps backward across the bathroom floor toward the shower.

11

THE HOTEL NEAR Fifth Avenue and overlooking Central Park was one of the most expensive hotels in the city. The venue befitted the power couple that my father and Michelle Petrochelli had become. The guest list was extensive and included celebrities and public figures, many of them guests at dinner the night before. The paparazzi jammed near the entrance, taking photos of everyone who entered for fear of missing a celebrity unknown to them. My father had insisted on sending a stretch limousine to pick us up. He would be embarrassed if his son arrived in a yellow taxi.

It had been a sunny late December day with temperatures in the high thirties and a brisk northeast wind. A nor'easter had skirted along the East Coast and was now bringing cold Canadian air into the area. Our limo driver maneuvered into the line of other limos waiting to dispatch passengers. Red velvet ropes linked to brass posts separated them from the guests. Some guests, fed up with the wait, got out of their cars and walked down the sidewalk into the hotel. Most, however, remained in their warm chauffeur-driven cars and limos until they were let out at the entrance. A few stopped and posed for the paparazzi.

"This is going to take forever," Fiona said, her head leaned against the window.

I took in her silhouette, her aquiline nose, soft mouth, long curved neck, and her thick black hair in an updo. A dangling chandelier earring sparkled in the late afternoon light filtered by the tinted window of the limo. Even though we had just made love, I had a sudden urge to do more than nibble at her ear.

"I could ask the driver to shut the privacy screen," I said.

Fiona jerked her head around. "Jake Palmer. Is there no satisfying you?"

I laughed and kissed her lightly on the neck.

"Maybe on the way back," Fiona said with a wink and a grin. "When I don't have to worry about my hair and dress."

By the time our driver stopped at the entrance, Fiona had worked out the proper arrival protocol and gave me instructions. A hotel valet opened the limo door. Cameras flashed even before we got out. I, dressed in a black rental tuxedo, got out first and moved to the side, per Fiona's direction. The photographers got the first glimpse of her shapely calf and her pedicured feet, encased in strappy, gold-embossed Jimmy Choo stilettos and began to shout for her to look their way. I had to smile, because it was her calves that caught my attention the day we first met, when she had stretched to get something from a shelf in her kitchen cabinet.

In my eyes, Fiona was movie-star glamorous, wearing an emerald green full-length dress that clung to every inch of her bodice and fish-tailed at the knees into soft folds. She adjusted her mother's mink stole to keep her arms warm before she put her arm through mine, and we began our slow, confident walk to the hotel entrance. The paparazzi shouted for us to look their way. They didn't know or care that I was Edward Palmer's son. They were taking photographs of Fiona. My time in the Navy had conditioned me to be anonymous, neither seeking nor wanting attention. So even though this over-the-top show made me uncomfortable, I would get through it today as I had the night before because being with her and seeing her enjoy the moment made it all worthwhile.

Inside the lobby, Fiona patted her windblown hair to ensure it was still in place. "Whew. I've never ever had that many photographs taken of me."

"None of those photos will ever be printed once they discover we're not A-list celebrities."

"You never know. They might publish photos of Mr. Jacob Palmer, son of the groom, with his lovely English lady friend."

Once inside, we were escorted to the front rows of seats reserved for close relatives and distinguished guests. My father had asked me to be a groomsman, but I declined, easing the path for him to ask my brother, Patrick, to be best man. I caught Fiona looking around the magnificent, neo-Rococo grand ballroom and the women, dressed in their finest *haute couture*, seated near us. She moved her head only slightly, but her eyes were swinging far to the right and left and up and down. I spotted Anthony Calabrese sitting several rows back beside an attractive woman at least twenty years his junior. Our eyes met. Calabrese grinned and slowly nodded his head. *What is he doing here? Not still following me, I hope.*

When the wedding began and Michelle Petrochelli walked down the aisle between the rows of seats, Fiona reached for my hand, interlocked her fingers with mine, and squeezed. During the service, she sniffled once or twice before extracting a tissue from her clutch and wiping her eyes. Call me cold-hearted, but I had attended too many weddings to become emotional or sentimental. At least half those couples had already divorced. Yes, that was a glass-half-empty way of looking at the situation; the other perspective being that half are still happily married. Had I been influenced by the failure of my parents' marriage? Perhaps. But even so, I wasn't optimistic about the long-term survival of my father's marriage. I didn't trust Michelle Petrochelli's heart. I prayed I was wrong.

Thirty minutes later, the ceremony was over. We made our way to the ballroom for the reception. By the time we arrived, a band was already playing. It was a lavish affair. We were seated at the table with the newlyweds and Patrick and his wife. We stayed for the dinner and the toasts and danced a few times before making our move to leave. On our way out, someone behind us said, "Mr. Palmer."

We both stopped and turned to see who it was. I recognized Anthony Calabrese and the woman I had seen him with earlier.

"This is my wife, Victoria," Calabrese said.

I extended my hand to Victoria Calabrese and introduced myself before introducing Fiona to her and to Anthony Calabrese.

"Friends of the bride or groom?" I said to Calabrese.

"Your father manages a few of my investments. I'm also an acquaintance of the bride. Have you decided what you are going to do?"

My father should know better than to manage Calabrese's investments. No good could come of that. "I haven't given it much thought. Fiona and I only have a couple of days before she returns to London."

"If I can do anything to sway your decision, don't hesitate to ask. You have my number. I look forward to hearing from you."

"Regardless of whether I take on the case or not, I'm certain Agent Goodman's colleagues at HSI are far more capable than I at finding those responsible."

"I wish I believed that. If you haven't made dinner plans while you're here, may I suggest a wonderful family-run restaurant in Little Italy? On me, of course. Just tell them I sent you." He extracted one of the restaurant's cards from his jacket pocket and handed it to Fiona.

"Thank you," I said. "We really must be going."

Anthony Calabrese and his wife returned to the ballroom, while we continued on to the lobby.

"I can't believe I just met Don Anthony Calabrese of the New York Mafia," Fiona said, her eyes open wide. "You were very short with him. Was that wise?"

"Although it's not the Mafia it once was, it's still the Mafia. I refuse to work for people like him."

She looked at the restaurant card. "Let's eat here tomorrow night. I suspect the people watching would be as intriguing as the food would be delicious."

"We'll see." I switched on my cell phone. A beep alerted me to a missed call. I didn't recognize the number, but it was a 215 area code—Philadelphia. "Do you mind?"

She rolled her eyes and exhaled a frustrated sigh. "Make it quick."

I took a few steps away and hit the number to return the call.

"Homeland Security Investigations. Agent DuPont."

I handed Fiona the card with the limo driver's telephone number and motioned for her to call him to pick us up. Fiona called him on her cell phone, and then we waited inside, with me still on the phone with DuPont. In a few minutes, the limo pulled up, and I ended the call.

"Who was that?" Fiona said as the limousine pulled away from the hotel.

"Agent DuPont of Homeland Security Investigations. He's going to pick me up at the train station when I get home. He wants to get the copy of the medical records and documents from the envelope and discuss Goodman's death and the case."

"The more you say no, the more someone tries to convince you otherwise. Have you decided whether or not you're going to your mother's funeral?"

"I've thought about what you said—about regretting it later if I don't go. You're right. I need to be there."

"Is that from a sense of obligation that your immediate family needs to be represented, a sense of guilt if you don't go, or is it because you really want to go?"

My unfocused gaze was past Fiona and out the window of the limo. It was a good question, one I was unprepared to answer. To my father's credit, he had not pressured me to go to the funeral. He only wanted me to know Mother had passed away and had given me the opportunity to go. Fiona made me think about how I might feel in the future, not how I felt now. I refused to allow Patrick's decision not to attend influence my decision. "To be perfectly honest—a little of each."

"Whatever the reason, I'm pleased you're going. When is it?"

"The day after you leave."

Fiona grasped my hand. "I'll extend my stay and go with you."

"You not only got me through Dad's wedding, you made it enjoyable. I couldn't turn around and ask you to accompany me to Mother's funeral. No—this is something I need to handle alone, for a number of reasons."

12

I SETTLED INTO my seat on Amtrak's Acela Express train for the one hour fifteen minute ride from New York's Penn Station to Philadelphia's 30th Street Station. Fiona and I had a late lunch before she left for JFK International Airport for her British Airways flight to London Heathrow. I hated to see her leave. She left determined to find out more about the counterfeit Transpro when she got back to the office. She was concerned that the process for communicating reports of counterfeit versions of B&As medicines seemed to have been circumvented. Nothing would deter her from getting to the bottom of it.

Between my father's wedding, Goodman's death, the envelope, the hotel room break-in, and the visit to Federal Plaza, we had only a couple of days to ourselves. We did the usual tourist things, the Statue of Liberty, Metropolitan Museum of Art, and Ground Zero. We also went to a Broadway show and had a couple of fabulous evening meals, including—at Fiona's insistence and against my better judgment—the restaurant Calabrese suggested. I didn't tell the maître d' that Calabrese sent us, and he told us the restaurant was fully booked. He recommended another restaurant down the street. Before I could say anything, Fiona spoke to him in Italian. I didn't understand any of it, except for "Antonio Calabrese." As soon as she said his name, the maître d' ran his finger down the reservation book and this time discovered a table for two was available. I ordered an inexpensive bottle of Montepulciano d'Abruzzo to start off. The sommelier returned, saying they were out of the d'Abruzzo and cradling a bottle of Borolo, which he said was a comparable substitute. One taste and even my untrained palate recognized this was a fine wine, costing twice as much as the twenty-five dollar bottle I had selected. Several times during our meal, Fiona was convinced she'd spotted a mobster.

DuPont met me at the 30th Street Station and dropped me off at my condominium on Rittenhouse Square, a short drive from the station. We had barely scratched the surface of the topic of Dennis Goodman's death, so we arranged to meet a half hour later at Devon, a popular seafood restaurant on the square. I gave him the documents I had copied to look over while he waited. When I arrived, DuPont was sitting at a booth, drinking a beer in the back of the restaurant away from the bar and reading the documents.

"Sorry your weekend with your girlfriend was totally messed up," said DuPont between sips of his beer as I sat down across from him.

"That's okay. It turned out much better than expected," I said.

"How much do you know about Immigration and Customs Enforcement, or ICE, and Homeland Security Investigations?" DuPont asked.

"Enough. You're the investigative arm of the Department of Homeland Security and one of the largest federal government investigative agencies."

"Second largest to be exact. Only the FBI is larger. Homeland Security Investigations is part of ICE, which is part of Homeland Security."

Special Agent DuPont was in his early to mid-forties, wearing a sport coat, no tie, and casual slacks. His black wool overcoat was folded neatly on the seat of the chair beside him. When he raised his glass to take a sip of beer, I saw he was wearing a wedding band.

"What did you do before joining HSI?"

"I was with Army Criminal Investigation Command. Did my time and got out. After that, I worked with the Norfolk Police Department for several years. While there, I got involved in a customs case with some ICE guys at the Port of Virginia.

They talked me into applying. I was hired and went through the twenty-two-week course at the Federal Law Enforcement Training Center in Georgia. After completing the course, I was assigned to the Philadelphia office. Been here ever since—about eight years."

"I don't need to tell you anything about me, do I?"

DuPont grinned. "Let's see . . . UNC football, Navy SEAL, Duke Law School, lawyer at B&A Pharmaceuticals, and now an investigative consultant, concentrating on healthcare cases. You also played a key role in taking down a terrorist cell in Virginia a while back."

"Anything you don't know about me?"

"Very little. Since 9/11, we have the means and authority to get information about anyone and anything we want, but as someone once said, with great power comes great responsibility."

"Voltaire," I said.

"Your undergrad degree really is in English literature, isn't it? I thought it was an error on your transcript."

"Voltaire wasn't English; he was French, aka Francois-Marie Arouet. You were saying?"

"Right," said DuPont. "Sometimes the ability to abuse that power is too tempting. A guy was shit-canned last year for checking out his wife. He thought she was cheating on him."

"Was she?"

"No, but after she found out why he was fired, she left his sorry ass."

"Tell me about this case, the one Goodman was working on," I said.

"To stop counterfeit medicine, you need to go to the source, where it's manufactured. If you don't, it just keeps coming. That's expensive, time consuming, and impractical. Most counterfeit medicine comes from India, China, or one of the African countries. The foreign authorities have responsibility for going after the source of manufacture. The best we can hope for is to prevent entry of the medicine into our country."

I thought about what DuPont had said. Tracing the medicine back to the original source could take months. Drugs do not go direct from the pharmaceutical company to pharmacies, hospitals, and doctors that dispense them to patients. First they pass from the pharmaceutical companies through a complex network of wholesalers and distributors. Hospital and chain pharmacies shop for the lowest price, and prices vary day-to-day. That is why when the pharmacy refills a prescription for a generic drug, it might be from a different manufacturer. In that case, it could be a different shape and color, with different numbers and letters on the tablet or capsule. If the counterfeit Transpro manufacturer was outside the US, which it probably was, and somehow the counterfeit drug got into the global distribution system, the chances of identifying the culprits and bringing them to justice was miniscule. Add a few more months to negotiate with foreign agencies, and by then, those responsible would have closed up shop and moved elsewhere. Even if they were eventually caught, the penalty might amount to no more than a slap on the wrist.

"Were you and Goodman partners?" I asked.

"No. It doesn't work that way. When you take on a case, you're the case agent. There are no assigned partners. Dennis and I worked out of the Philadelphia office for many years. We were close friends and sometimes talked about cases over drinks and bounced ideas off each other. Investigations are initiated in a number of ways, such as getting a tip from an informant, being the initial contact when you're on duty, or having your supervisor assign a case. In this case, Paul Calabrese called with information about the death of his son, which he believed was the result of the boy taking a counterfeit medicine. The receptionist triaged the call to Dennis because he was our counterfeit medicine guy. I don't know much about the case. I do know that this one got to him. A kid died long before his time because someone somewhere wanted to make a buck. He got so wrapped up in it that for weeks I only saw him in passing. He spent a lot of time in New York."

I handed DuPont a copy of the note that was in the envelope Goodman had given me.

DuPont read it and said, "That's odd."

"It says to follow the breadcrumbs, and I'll figure it out," I said.

"Lots of breadcrumbs to follow on a counterfeit medicine case. Most involve a foreign source shipping product into the

US and somehow getting it into the supply chain. Or they're foreign sources with Internet pharmacy sites that look legit. Once customers order a drug on the Internet, be it Viagra, Adderall, or whatever, the seller aggressively follows up for additional orders. Since no one orders anti-rejection drugs on the Internet, this must be a case where the drug got into the legitimate pharmaceutical supply chain."

"What's going to happen to the case now? Has it been reassigned?"

"I asked my supervisor the same question this morning. This is a high profile investigation. Dennis was compiling evidence for the US Attorney. Because the case originated here in Philadelphia, we have jurisdiction; however, Dennis told me that the New York office was making a play for it because the drugs were suspected of coming in through the Port of New York. Also, Dennis was murdered in New York, so the NYPD is investigating. The FBI is also investigating because he was a federal agent. When multiple agencies and offices get involved, it gets messy. As of yet, nothing connects his death to his counterfeit medicine investigation. The Philadelphia Agent in Charge is waiting for the NYPD and FBI to complete their preliminary investigations.

"That could be a long wait," I said.

"Not too long, I hope. In the meantime, the counterfeit medicine investigation must go on. In answer to your question, I'm the case agent now. That's why I'd like you to work with me, so we're not wasting time. I'm authorized to tap into some unrestricted funds to pay you. I'll establish a task force to include HSI agents at our attaché offices once we determine the source of the counterfeit medicine and how it got into the drug distribution system."

"Goodman's killer was found dead in an alley several blocks from the site of the shooting," I said. "A Bulgarian immigrant named Hristo Adonov."

"Adonov was no professional hit man. He was a down-and-out immigrant, probably looking to pick up a few hundred dollars. He was seen talking to someone before the shooting. We suspect that person pointed Dennis out to Adonov before the hit to be certain he shot the right man. Of course, no one's certain he was killed because of this case. If he were, maybe Adonov was also supposed to grab the envelope, but Dennis didn't have it. He had given it to you. The NYPD said another man was seen chasing after the shooter."

I leaned forward. "The one who had been talking to him before the shooting?"

"No, another man."

That was the right answer. That was Anthony Calabrese's man. DuPont's story matched what Calabrese told me in the car. "Who?"

"The NYPD is trying to identify him based on security cameras in the area. So far, no luck."

"What about Anthony Calabrese and his relationship to the boy?"

My mention of Anthony Calabrese caught DuPont's attention like nothing else I had said. DuPont had mentioned that Paul Calabrese had reported his son's death to ICE. However, DuPont made no mention of Paul Calabrese's relationship to Anthony Calabrese and the New York Mafia.

"You know about him?" DuPont asked.

He leaned over the table and listened as I told him about meeting Anthony Calabrese. "If you want me involved, you need to tell me everything," I said. I'm flying to Florida for a funeral tomorrow, and then I need a day or two to wrap up a case I'm working on here. That'll give me some time to think. By the first of next week, I'll be ready to talk. When we do, you're going tell me all you know. Based on what I hear, I'll decide if I'm in or out."

"You should know that we don't have a shortage of resources, especially to work on a case as big as this one. We have over six thousand agents. But there's a reason Dennis wanted you to work with him. Call it a breadcrumb, if you like, but until I know what that reason is, I want you close by. I have a call in to Mark Brantley in New York," DuPont said. "I am going to tell him this is a Philadelphia case, and they need to back off. I'll be polite, of course."

"Good luck. One more thing; when Goodman was leaving the bar, I asked him what to do if I didn't hear from him. He said I should seek Jesus. What does that mean?"

"Seek Jesus? Other than the obvious, I haven't a clue. Dennis was Jewish."

13

THE TRAFFIC ON the M25, London's 117-mile orbital road, was horrid. Fiona was stopped in what many called London's largest car park. She hated the motorway. Her mother and father had died in a car crash at its junction with the M-4 motorway, which she took into London most days. She thought about them every time she passed it. For a year after their death, she went an hour out of her way to avoid the intersection. She had been in Madrid on business when she received the phone call. It was one she would never forget. She remembered nothing about the drive to the Madrid-Barajas Airport to catch the flight home. She did remember looking out of the window of the plane as it crossed the English Channel. A cloud formation reminded her of a kittiwake, a species of seagull, wings extended making a turn toward the plane with its head turned as if it were looking at her. When she was a child, she went on walks on the Coastal Path in Cornwall with her father, who taught her about the birds and would quiz her about them. Whenever they saw a sea gull, he asked her what species it was. When she saw the kittiwake-shaped cloud formation, a sense of calm overcame her, assuring her that he and her mother were at peace with God. Her father's spirit was telling her not to worry.

If she were able to put everything else aside, spending time with Jake was the highlight of her New York trip. After the wedding, he treated her like a queen. She didn't want to leave. When she left for the airport, they hugged and kissed goodbye. She told him she would call him after she found out what she could at B&A, and he promised to stay in touch and let her know about his mother's funeral and his meeting with DuPont.

During their previous long absences, the emotional distance between them had grown. She had wondered if their relationship was winding down. But as soon as they were together, it was as if they been with each other the day before. No awkwardness, no getting reacquainted, and no doubts about how she felt about him. She loved him; of that she was one hundred percent certain. But, was he in love with her? Although he said he was, she wasn't sure. Could she commit herself to him? Yes, he was exciting to be with, at times exhilarating. But being with him had meant being pulled into some dangerous situations, and that scared her to death. Long distance relationships seldom lasted. Perhaps this one was the exception. She needed it to be the exception.

Finally, the traffic was moving again. She exited the M25 onto the M4 motorway and drove east toward central London. Using her Bluetooth-enabled cell phone, she called Steve Holloway, the vice president of manufacturing quality, to let him know she was running late and that barring another delay she would be in his office in thirty minutes. Holloway had been appointed vice president of manufacturing quality eight months earlier, when the former senior vice president retired. Her priority was to find out what she could about the counterfeit Transpro.

When she arrived at the B&A headquarters building, she grabbed a coffee and went straight to Holloway's office on the third floor, bypassing his secretary.

Holloway looked up, his fingers still on his laptop keyboard, and smiled. "Fiona. Welcome back. How was the trip to New York?"

"Tell me what you know about the counterfeit version of Transpro?" Fiona asked, foregoing the pleasantries.

Holloway adjusted his wire-rimmed, John Lennon-style glasses. He was in his mid-forties and his hairline was beginning to recede. He had joined the company twenty years ago as an entry-level quality control technician and had worked his way up.

"What do you mean?"

He was stalling, a tactic any auditor worth his or her salt recognized. Both his question and her answer provided more time for him to think of a way to respond to or deflect the question.

"Why was the existence of a counterfeit version of Transpro in the US not communicated to the audit management team?" Fiona asked again. "There's been at least one death, probably more. Is there some reason this is being kept quiet?"

Holloway leaned back in his chair and interlocked his fingers behind his head. "It's complicated."

"A boy was given a counterfeit version of Transpro following a kidney transplant and died. How bloody complicated can it be? I assume we have a serious adverse event report on file. I'll go to my colleagues in Product Safety and Pharmacovigilance and ask them."

"Transplant patients die. Why would there be an adverse experience report on file?"

"Serious adverse experience reports must be filed for patients who die while taking one of our medicines, even if there is no proven association with the drug. You know that. It's the law."

Fiona could see his leg jumping up and down under the desk. "Close the door and have a seat."

She sat in a nearby chair and took a sip of coffee before setting the cup on his desk.

"The case you mention was our first report of the counterfeit version."

"He's not a case; he was a boy. A teenage boy named Pietro Calabrese."

"The board directed me to keep it quiet. The chairman put a lid on all internal communications. I wish I could tell you more, Fiona, but I'm forbidden to do so. All I can say is it's being managed. Don't worry about it."

Fiona leaned back and crossed her arms. "I thought we trusted each other, Steve."

After an awkward silence, Holloway shrugged his shoulders with his palms up and eyebrows raised, as if to say it was out of his hands. With that, she got up and walked out of his office, the steam still rising from coffee she left on his desk.

14

FIONA WALKED QUICKLY to the elevators. Going to her boss would be a waste of time. He would comply with the chairman's directive to keep the issue quiet and not tell her anything. Quality and compliance types always follow the rules and stay in their own lane. She knew. She was one of them. Maybe she overreacted to Holloway's refusal to open up about the case. He was only doing his job. Her concern was that lives were at stake and keeping the lid on counterfeit Transpro could increase the number of people who would die unnecessarily.

A co-worker passed heading in the opposite direction. "Good morning, Fiona."

Fiona nodded without looking. It was not a good morning, and she was in no mood to pretend otherwise. She loved her job and the company, but it was times like this that tried her soul. The vertical, top-heavy structure was often dysfunctional and slow. However, Fiona knew one senior vice president who challenged authority and sought out opportunities to shake things up, and she was making a beeline to his office.

David Tomlinson, the senior vice president of clinical safety and pharmacovigilance, was standing outside his office, chatting with his secretary. Tomlinson was responsible for the worldwide monitoring and management of clinical safety of all of B&A's medicines, vaccines, and consumer health products. That included monitoring for a previously unreported adverse event or drug interaction, or for an observed increase in the incidence or severity of an adverse event. It was without question one of the most stressful jobs in the industry. Fiona considered Tomlinson a friend and confidant.

"Good morning, Fiona. I'm afraid to ask what you're doing here. It's never good news," Tomlinson said.

"May I have a quiet word, David?" Fiona said.

"Just as I thought."

Fiona followed him into his office and shut the door behind her. Before he could sit, she asked, "Why hasn't the existence of a counterfeit version of Transpro been communicated either internally or externally? Why the secrecy? What's going on?"

Tomlinson stopped in his tracks and faced her. "How much do you know?"

She told Tomlinson about her trip to New York, about the murder of Special Agent Goodman and the envelope containing the medical records. Tomlinson flopped down in the closest chair. Fiona sat beside him and continued, telling him about the meeting with Mark Brantley, the special agent in charge of ICE's Homeland Security Investigations in New York, and Jake's encounter with Anthony Calabrese, the don of a New York Mafia family.

"My God! Jake has a way of stepping into it, doesn't he?" Tomlinson said, shaking his head. "You already know as much as we do."

"I've read the medical records, including the analysis of the Transpro Pietro Calabrese was taking. Steve Holloway told me that the chairman wanted it kept quiet. That is all he would say."

"Steve's right. The pertinent regulatory agencies have been informed and pharmacies in countries where counterfeit versions have been discovered are on alert. We've also distributed a 'Dear Doctor' letter to all transplant physicians in countries where Transpro is marketed, primarily in the US and Europe. Our Audit Committee is aware of it, and the chairman has forbidden any internal or external communication while the authorities are investigating. We're giving them our full cooperation."

Fiona stood and crossed her arms. "Why can't I get to the bottom of this? I came close to losing my life working on a case for this company, a case involving an adverse event B&A was covering up. Had it not been for Jake, I'd be dead."

"I know," said Tomlinson. "I was there that night. Contrary to what you might think, that incident has only made the company more cautious about involving the police."

"You say it's the company. It's *individuals* within the company, senior executives and board members, who are making those decisions. People like you and me, who are not afraid to speak out, ensure that the company and those individuals comply with our ethical obligations, not just the laws and regulations. We're part of the corporate conscience."

"You've been a clinical auditor long enough to know our intention is to always comply with local and international laws and regulations," Tomlinson said. "You should also know that seldom, if ever, do we go beyond what's required. We're doing what we're obligated to do by regulation."

"Tell me what's going on," Fiona demanded.

"This is confidential, between you and me. Right?"

"For heaven's sake, David. It's me. Do I have to promise you I won't tell anyone?"

"The only reason I'm telling you this is so you won't go off half-cocked and do something you'll regret later. Corporate Communications and Legal have drafted a five-sentence response to any question we receive from the press or public. In short, it says that we are aware of the report of a possible counterfeit version of Transpro and are cooperating with regulatory agencies and investigators and are communicating with pharmacies and transplant physicians. Holloway's counterfeit medicines investigator and one of our internal auditors have been tasked with working with regulatory agencies and investigative bodies to find the source of the counterfeit version." Tomlinson paused, as if he had said enough, before proceeding. "The bottom line is that based on our internal investigation, we believe a current or former employee is somehow involved."

"Are you serious? Who would do something like that? How do we know it's an employee?"

"Manufacturing has a suspect under surveillance, but I've been kept in the dark. Our Transpro packaging and the counterfeit packaging are almost identical, in ways only someone on the inside would know. We believe that this individual may be advising the counterfeiters on the packaging and on the manufacture of the active pharmaceutical ingredient, zufridone. The counterfeit version contains a small dose, too small to have much clinical effect, but enough for the culprits to claim it was just a lapse in quality."

"Have the police been told who we suspect?"

"Not yet. Once we received the analysis of the Calabrese boy's Transpro, everything changed. We reviewed every Transpro adverse experience report, thousands of them, in our database. Most were minor; however, there were reports of death following transplant rejection. We had reported these to the regulatory authorities, as is required. But because transplant patients sometimes die and because no direct relationship could be established between the death and Transpro, there was no reason to be unduly concerned. However, on further investigation, we identified a substantial number of cases where Transpro was reported as ineffective. In each of those cases, the physician switched the patient's medication, perhaps saving the patient's life. Had Transpro not been relatively new to market, those cases would probably not have been reported to us."

"We should recall Transpro until this can be sorted out," she said, raising her voice. "This has to stop before someone else dies. Has the suspect been questioned and arrested?"

Tomlinson shook his head. "I hear you. But you know we can't do that. It's a complex situation, and we don't have sufficient evidence to support the accusation. The CEO wants us to be certain before reporting it to law enforcement. Also, I'm sure he's concerned about the media and regulatory authorities' reactions to an employee being involved. Transpro was launched in the US and Europe in January. It's now our top revenue-generating drug. Analysts credit it with saving the company from a hostile takeover."

"I'm aware of the sales figures," Fiona said. "It always comes down to money, doesn't it? The financial forecast has to be met or exceeded—but not so much that it looks like we weren't expecting it. All of this just so the shareholders will receive a good return on their investment."

"Marketing has projected the negative impact that any

announcement would have on sales to be about eighty percent, possibly higher. Physicians, concerned about the risk of administering a counterfeit version, would simply use one of the alternative therapies."

"Do you have a list of the patients who died, ones we believe may be related to the counterfeit Transpro?" Fiona asked.

"I do."

Fiona stood up. "May I see it?"

Tomlinson reached behind him and grabbed a file. He flipped through the pages until he came to the one he was searching for and slid it across the desk.

Fiona scanned down the list. There were twenty-two reports, all on the east coast of the United States. At the top of the list was a boy in Philadelphia, Pietro Calabrese. Her eyes froze on one of the reports—a sixty-seven-year-old female in Sarasota, Florida.

15

I EXITED SARASOTA Bradenton International Airport, my jacket draped over my arm and pulling my carry-on bag. The sunshine, cloudless blue sky, and mid-seventies weather were a welcome change from the frigid, overcast skies I left in Philadelphia. Sarasota was a serene, well-to-do part of Florida's west coast. Although home to some of the country's wealthiest families, most permanent residents were of average means.

I arrived at the funeral home in the business center of Sarasota an hour early for the two o'clock service. When I entered the building, a soft-spoken, overly polite man asked me whom I was there to see, as if my mother was still alive. When I said Julia O'Malley, the man directed me to a room down the corridor to the left. The large room was almost empty, only a few people, talking in hushed conversations, were there. At the center of them was the only person I recognized, my stepfather and former pastor, Matt O'Malley. He made eye contact, walked over and shook my hand.

"Jake, I'm glad you came," O'Malley said. His eyes were bloodshot. He looked like he had not slept in days. "Your father said he would be out of the country on his honeymoon. Is Patrick coming?"

When two people fall in love and run away from their responsibilities and family to be together, it can have a profound effect on others. Two of the people I most loved and trusted, my pastor and my mother, had betrayed me when I was a young boy. I had never forgiven them. But of the two, I placed most of the blame with O'Malley. He had been in a position of authority and trust. He must have understood that, like a doctor and patient, a pastor and parishioner can develop a close relationship, which can progress into an attraction. Theirs did, and the attraction blossomed into an affair. After their affair became public, O'Malley resigned and never preached again. When he and my mother moved to Florida, he became a hospice counselor and she took a position as a bookkeeper.

"No. Patrick sends his apologies. With Dad out of town, he has to run the business. I believe they've sent flowers." I glanced at the sprays of flowers in the room and noticed two that were larger than the others. Regardless of the history, neither would allow themselves be outshined by what they considered to be a bunch of retirees.

"I understand."

"What happened to Mom? Dad said she died from complications of diabetes."

"That's right. Your mother had Type 2 Diabetes. It proved difficult to control and she developed diabetic nephropathy. Her kidneys began to fail, and she was placed on a transplant list. She finally got the call a few weeks ago."

"She should have let us know. Patrick and I might have been matches."

O'Malley's chin quivered. He cleared his throat before proceeding. "I begged her to call you. Not to ask for a kidney, but to let you know about her condition and the surgery. She didn't want either of you to feel a sense of obligation to donate a kidney. She was insistent. As it turned out, the hospital located a match, and she received the transplant late last month. Still she refused to phone you or Patrick until she was certain the surgery and post-surgery therapy were successful."

"What happened?" I asked, fearful of where this was headed.

"Her body rejected the kidney, and she died."

I inhaled before I spoke. *What were the chances? It wasn't possible.* "Was she taking anti-rejection drugs? Was she taking Transpro?"

"I don't know. She was taking so many medicines. The doctor said no one was to blame. Sometimes, in spite of all they can do, it just happens. Everyone dies of something. It was just her time. God called her home."

"Would you happen to have some of the tablets left?"

"I think so. Since Julia died, it's been an effort for me to do anything. Some of the ladies from church are coming over tomorrow and clearing out her clothes and things. I suppose they'll throw away the medicines, too."

"I want to see Mom's drugs. I need to know what she was taking."

O'Malley hesitated and bit at his lip. "The hospital and her doctors were great. I'm not going to be party to any legal action or assist you in doing so."

"No. No. That's not it. I promise. I just want to have them checked."

"Checked for what?"

"I'm involved in a case involving counterfeit drugs. A boy in Philadelphia died after a kidney transplant. His parents had his medicines analyzed and one, an anti-rejection medicine, was counterfeit. It's probably nothing. I just want to have them tested."

"I suppose that would be okay. Can you come by the house first thing tomorrow?"

"I'll be there. I'll explain then."

"I'm glad you're here. The casket is open at the front of the chapel, if you want to see her before the service begins. Also, there's a private room off the chapel foyer. Please meet there so that you can go in and sit with the family during the service."

The family O'Malley spoke of sitting with would be his. I had met a few of them during my summer visits to Florida when I was a boy. They had been nice enough, but after I returned home, there was no effort on either their part or mine to stay in touch. "Thank you for the invitation. I'll feel more comfortable sitting by myself."

O'Malley returned to the couple with whom he had been talking, and I made my way down the aisle. A few people were already seated in the pews, some talking quietly to each other. An elderly couple stepped away from the open casket and walked past me. I stood and looked at my mother. People often say the body looks natural, like the deceased is asleep. To me, the dead look like the lifeless forms they are. I rarely go to church, but I've maintained my faith and believe the corpse is the lifeless, earthly shell of the person. Still, seeing my mother's body caused an unexpected rush of childhood memories, reflections of days when the family was together and blissfully ignorant of what lay ahead. I fought to keep my raw emotions inside. Before I moved on, I wiped my eyes, composed myself and uttered a silent prayer, asking God to forgive me for turning my back on my mother and for not being a better, more understanding son. I had never truly forgiven her, and for that, I was sorry.

∧∧∧

The next morning, I was at my mother and stepfather's house at nine o'clock. O'Malley opened the door before I could ring the doorbell. He stepped outside onto the covered porch to meet me. He was wearing a pair of pleated slacks and a golf shirt, both of which were in need of ironing. His eyes were still red and puffy and the wrinkles on his face seemed to have deepened overnight. O'Malley was clutching two zip-lock bags, each containing several bottles of medications.

"Jake, I've thought a lot about this. You've not been a part of your mother's life for many years. I am not going to be party to any lawsuit against your mother's doctors, a drug company, or anyone. Before I give these to you, promise me that's not your purpose."

"I promise you; that is not my intention. I'm going to have the medicines analyzed to see if any were counterfeit. Any information I find will be used to identify those responsible and to keep others from suffering the same fate as Mom. I swear."

O'Malley's eyes met mine. "I take you at your word." He handed me the two bags.

"I'll let you know what the analyses reveal."

O'Malley took a deep breath and exhaled. "I don't want to know the results."

"Are you sure?"

"Nothing you find will bring Julia back. If you learn she died because she was taking a counterfeit medicine, it would only replace the grief I am feeling now with a burning hatred of those who did this. I need to let go of it. I need to be thankful for the years we had together and the love we shared."

"I understand." As I stepped away to leave, O'Malley grabbed my arm.

"I need to say something before you go. When your mother and I fell in love, we both knew it was wrong. However, there was nothing we could do to stop the feelings we had for each other, and the flesh was too weak not to act on those feelings. It tore her up to leave you and Patrick and move away. Your father had made it clear that he would accept nothing less than full custody, and she knew she had no choice other than to grant it. She felt too guilty. I don't believe you ever forgave either of us. With her passing, I hope you can find it in your heart to forgive."

I let what O'Malley said sink in before responding. "I may not have been the son I should have been, but over the years, I've come to accept that you and Mom were good for each other, perhaps even meant for each other. She was a very different person with Dad. Their marriage might have lasted years longer had you not come along, although I seriously doubt they still would have been married. The things that fulfilled them were not compatible; their temperaments were too different."

We shook hands, and O'Malley went back inside and shut the door.

I had not wanted to attend the funeral, but I walked away from the house thankful that I had. Without Fiona's urging, I would have missed it and also missed the opportunity to speak with O'Malley.

A few blocks away from the house, I pulled over to the curb and went through the medicine bottles. Among them was a bottle of Transpro with several pills inside. I put it back into the zip-lock bag and stuffed them in my carry-on bag on the passenger seat of the car. I would have to check the bag on the trip back to Philadelphia. TSA would not like the fact I was carrying several bottles of medicine, none of which were mine. I would dispose of all the bottles except for the Transpro before I got to the airport. I was about to drive off, when Fiona called.

"Jake, one of the patients on B&A's list of those who died while taking Transpro is a sixty-seven-year-old female in Sarasota, Florida."

"That's Mom. She had a transplant a few weeks ago. I have her bottle of Transpro. I'm taking the tablets to the drug analysis lab in Philadelphia that Calabrese used. I should know the results in a day or two."

"There's more, Jake. A current or former B&A employee may be involved."

16

IN WELWYN HEIGHTS there were no construction cranes, or new condominiums with marble countertops and stainless steel appliances, or upscale shopping malls, or franchise pharmacies on opposite corners of major intersections. People had only enough spending money for the essentials, and the high crime rate made the cost of doing business prohibitive. People who needed medicine and could not get it free through federal or state entitlement programs often went without, or they risked buying it from Internet pharmacies or from dealers on the street, who peddled prescription drugs.

I sat in my car, parked within sight of Dr. Abercrombie's clinic, near where I had stood a few days before. I had already followed two vans leaving the clinic. Both dropped off people at houses within several miles of the clinic, confirming my notion that the vans were a patient shuttle service—nothing illegal about that. I considered calling it a day and wrapping up my contract with the Fraud Control Unit but decided to follow one more van. Within thirty minutes after I parked, a van pulled up to the clinic, and several men got out and went inside.

Strange, I thought. All of the others had transported a mix of men and women, most elderly, like the ones I had videoed during my previous visit. I kept the car running, frequently checked the rearview and side mirrors, and had my 9mm on the console.

I was driving my car and didn't want another pickup truck crashing into it. While waiting, I thought about my mother's death. She had been on Transpro and her death was reported to the manufacturer, B&A Pharmaceuticals, and to the regulatory authority. I had dropped off the Transpro pills at the drug analysis lab and paid extra for expedited processing. Although I would not know for sure until the analysis was completed, my gut told me she was taking the counterfeit version.

The men exited the clinic and got back into the van. I waited until the van was a block away before I followed it. The driver wove through the streets before heading northeast on West Sedgley Avenue and then east onto West Lehigh Avenue, making a couple of other turns before arriving at a building on North American Street. There were several other large buildings on the street, most abandoned or in poor repair. The men hopped out and went inside. I drove by slowly enough to look for any signage, some indication of what was inside. Seeing none, I circled around the block to look at the other sides of the large structure. There were no signs or trucks bearing a company logo.

I had to go. I had just enough time to get to the Philadelphia Museum of Art for my meeting with DuPont.

^^^^

I parked and then hustled to the front of the art museum and up the seventy-two steps, the same steps Sylvester Stallone ran up in the 1976 movie, *Rocky*. I couldn't stop the movie theme from playing in my head. A statue of Stallone as Rocky Balboa had stood at the top of the museum's steps for years. Then some uppity art patrons decided it was more movie prop than art, and the statue was moved to the Spectrum in South Philadelphia where sports fans had a greater appreciation for it. Later, it was returned to the museum and hidden from view at the foot of Eakins Oval next to the steps.

DuPont was waiting inside. I followed him through the museum to one of the large galleries and sat on a bench strategically placed to contemplate the art in front of us. I had a feeling that this wasn't the first time DuPont had met someone here for a private conversation.

"Time for you to tell me what you know," I said.

DuPont edged closer. "Anthony Calabrese is a New York mob boss and has been for the past few years. He's into a variety of nefarious activities, drugs, protection, loan-sharking, and labor, just to name a few. There's not been a notable mob presence in Philadelphia in years, so when Paul Calabrese moved here two years ago, it got the attention of the Philadelphia PD. Paul shifted the family's business here toward less risky operations than in New York, ones where the rewards are great and the risks are small."

"Counterfeit medicine?"

"We don't think so, at least not yet. You've used the term 'counterfeit medicine.' You know the difference between the terms substandard, falsified, counterfeit, and unregistered?"

"I had a brief stint as a pharmaceutical company attorney. I believe I have a good sense of the definitions," I said. "Because Pietro Calabrese's Transpro contained only minute quantities of the active pharmaceutical ingredient it was termed falsified. Because it was sold under the B&A brand name in containers bearing B&A's trademark, it was termed counterfeit. Had the amount of active pharmaceutical ingredient been only slightly below the standard, as might occur during a lapse in the manufacturing process at a pharmaceutical company, it would have been substandard. Or if it were being sold in a country where the regulatory agency had not approved it for sale, it would be unregistered. Neither of those would apply to this case."

"Correct. The Transpro that lead to Pietro Calabrese's death was both falsified and counterfeit. Over 100,000 people worldwide die each year from falsified medicines, where the ingredients are of low quality or the wrong doses or deliberately mislabeled or have fake packaging. It involves criminal intent, *mens rea*—guilty mind—and violates the regulator's quality specification. The justice system prosecutes and punishes instances of falsified medicines as serious crimes, not just regulatory violations or negligence claims."

"If it's both, wouldn't the FDA's Office of Criminal Investigations also be investigating it?" I asked.

"Yes, but we are taking the lead and coordinating with FDA's OCI," DuPont said.

"If it's all right with you, let's just refer to it as a counterfeit medicine."

"Fine with me. Anyway, after the boy's death, Paul Calabrese contacted Goodman. According to Goodman's notes, Calabrese wasn't keen on being seen going in and out of a federal building. So he met him at a restaurant in the Italian Market neighborhood. He gave him the medical records and the drug analysis and told him to find the bastards who killed his son."

"Yeah, he wants you to find those responsible, so he can kill them."

"Without a doubt," DuPont replied.

"B&A Pharmaceuticals has twenty-two reports of patients who died while taking Transpro," I said.

"We have the list, and FDA Office of Criminal Investigation is keeping us updated on any new reports."

One of the deaths was my mother, but DuPont wouldn't know that because the patient names were not included. I'd wait until I had the analysis back before telling him.

"So far, these are the only reported cases," I said. "The actual number of deaths could be higher because not all cases are reported. Proving a medicine caused death is difficult in these cases because other factors could have contributed to or caused rejection of the transplanted organ."

"True. And some physicians may fear that if their patient had taken counterfeit Transpro and died, they could be accused of not adequately monitoring the patient.

"Dennis wanted to prove the deaths were a direct result of the counterfeit Transpro and that whoever manufactured and distributed it did so knowing it would result in the deaths," DuPont said. "I want us to pick up where Dennis left off. I'm sick of the bastards getting away with a fine and few months in the slammer."

"It'll be a tough case to prove. The defense will argue that the physicians had a responsibility to identify the symptoms of rejection and alter the medications. The distributor would argue that it was also a victim, stating they thought the drug was legit. The manufacturer, to use the term loosely, is probably in Africa, India, or China. Finding and convicting them of anything other than a regulatory violation would require that you prove criminal intent, *mens rea*. And, convicting them of the counterfeit labeling would result in a relatively minor penalty in relation to the crime."

"I didn't say it would be easy or quick. I won't stop until those responsible are brought to justice," DuPont said. "Dennis's death is all the incentive I need. The US Attorney is especially eager for us to move this forward. This is a big case for us. I've been given a task force budget to move it forward as quickly as possible."

"What about the other agency that was assisting him in New York. Were you able to find out anything from Brantley?"

"He said Dennis was working with FinCEN."

"FinCEN?"

"The Financial Crimes Enforcement Network, a bureau of the US Treasury based in Vienna, Virginia," DuPont said. "They combat money laundering and have the expertise to collect, analyze, and disseminate financial intelligence. We involve FinCEN whenever money laundering is suspected. Apparently, Dennis picked up on the money laundering and contacted them to do some work for him. FinCEN has a particular interest in counterfeit medicine cases, because terrorist organizations have been known to use money generated by the sale of counterfeit medicines to finance their operations. If FinCEN confirms money laundering, the HSI case agent, like Dennis, is often assigned, along with representatives from other agencies, to provide support to FinCEN. That appears to be what happened in this case. I'll know more after I contact them. I'm hoping that if I head down the same path as Dennis, someone's going to notice."

"Is that the plan? You want them to come after you?" I asked.

"To put it bluntly, yes."

"I like it," I said.

"I've tracked the source of Transpro for each of the hospitals where the counterfeit medicine was administered or dispensed."

"Is there a common wholesaler or distributor?"

"No. But the one that supplied the hospital where the Calabrese kid was treated is here."

"In the US?" I asked.

"In Philadelphia—a small operation on North American Street."

I didn't react to the information. At least I tried not to do so. The address seemed more than a coincidence.

"If you found it that quickly, why wouldn't Goodman have done the same?" I asked.

"I'm sure he did. It's a starting point. He was after much bigger fish. Now, I've told you all I know. Are you going to work with me?" DuPont said.

I stared DuPont in the eyes. "Yes. But if you lie to me or withhold information, I'll walk away and never look back."

The sides of DuPont's lips rose slightly forming a subtle smile. "What changed your mind?"

"Let's say it's personal and leave it at that." My mother's death had made this personal, and regardless of the Transpro lab analysis result, I was in. Now that I was, I told DuPont about the warehouse on North American Street where I had seen the van from Abercrombie's clinic drop off a group of men. His eyes widened as he leaned forward.

17

I PARKED ON the shoulder on the east side of North American Street in Philly, about three blocks from the address DuPont had given me—close enough to see the loading dock and entrance, far enough away not to be noticed. As I suspected, it was the same building where the van had dropped off the men.

I'd watched the warehouse for over two hours and hadn't seen anything since I arrived at midnight. The large brick building's only windows were near the roof; and even though some interior lights were on, it was possible no one was inside. Nothing was going to happen in the short time it would take me to go to an all-night fast food restaurant, use the facilities and get a coffee. As I reached for the ignition key, a tractor-trailer went by and downshifted. The truck passed by the warehouse and stopped. The beep-beep-beep of the reverse warning signal broke the silence of the frigid night as the truck eased towards the loading dock.

The loading dock lights came on, the door rose, and a forklift emerged. Through my binoculars, I watched a man from the warehouse sign some paperwork for the truck driver. The two men stood by and talked while the forklift operator unloaded about twenty large pallets of boxes and moved them inside. There were no logos or identifying markings on the side of the tractor-trailer, and even with the binoculars, I was too far away to read the labels on the boxes.

An hour later, the truck pulled away from the loading dock and drove off. I held the binoculars with my left hand and wrote down the New York license tag number with my right. On the rear door of the truck in black letters was "Empire Transport" and below it "USDOT 739503," the US Department of Transportation identification number. I sent DuPont a text with the information.

DuPont had asked me to do some reconnaissance to see who came and went from the building. He told me only to observe and not do anything else. I recalled his stern warning not to go inside, because anything I did under the color of law would be judged as if I were a law enforcement officer. And, as such, anything I found would be inadmissible. Nonetheless, I had to see what they were doing inside. Just a peek. DuPont would never know.

I drove by the warehouse and parked about a block from the building. Before getting out, I stuffed my Sig Sauer 9mm into my shoulder holster, zipped three loaded magazines in my coat pocket, and put on my Phillies baseball cap. I scanned the backside of the warehouse through the binoculars. There were doors at each end and in the middle and security cameras attached to the two top corners of the building in the front and back, pointing at the doors and the loading dock. There were no cameras on the sides of the building, where there were no doors, only windows on the upper level.

Before leaving home, I'd checked out the building on my computer. Zooming in, I concluded the only safe entry might be through the roof. My drive around the building and the location of the security cameras did nothing to change my mind. Screw DuPont and his recon only. I popped the trunk and grabbed the grappling hook and rope, I had brought along—just in case. Okay, maybe I had planned on going into the building all along. I had intended to pick the rear door locks if the warehouse was unoccupied, but abandoned that plan because of the security cameras monitoring the doors. I sprinted across the street to within a few yards of the building and whirled the grappling hook around in wide circles before releasing it. The hook landed with a thud on the roof on the first try.

I remained still and listened, waiting to see if anyone came outside to investigate. After a few minutes, I pulled until I felt the hook slide across the roof, stopping when it stuck onto something. Like most commercial buildings, the roof was flat and supported the heating and air conditioning air-handling units and ductwork. I tugged on the rope, testing the security of whatever it had anchored onto. Satisfied it was secure, I used the J-Hook technique to lock my feet around the rope and climb up. When I reached the level of the windows, I sidestepped along the wall until I was at one of them. The window was for light only and could not be opened. I searched for a spot clear enough to see through the years of built-up grime. Finding none, I used my coat sleeve to rub off some of the exterior dirt. I could see men moving boxes off the pallets that were in the middle of the floor.

I made it to the top and crawled over the wall onto the roof. Somewhere on the street, men were talking and laughing. I walked toward the rear wall and peeked over. Several men were getting into their cars and leaving. I tried to open a roof access door. It was locked. I pulled a lock pick kit from my inside jacket pocket. In less than a minute, I picked the lock and entered a dimly lit stairwell, the 9mm in my hand. Taking slow, quiet steps I descended the stairs to the ground floor. At the bottom was another door. I listened before turning the knob and inched the door open. The rusty door hinges creaked. I opened it only wide enough to squeeze into the dimly lit room. The angry bark of a dog came next and then everything went black.

18

WHEN I CAME to, I reached up to the source of the pain on my head and felt a warm liquid. Blood. After blinking a few times, a fuzzy image of a man standing over me appeared. A large dog beside him, some type of pit bull, growled.

"Sharpshooter. Wha' da hell you doin' here?"

I recognized the bat guy's distinctive voice before I could make out who it was. "Is that you?"

"Hell yeah. I still got splinters in my leg from that bat. You coulda killed me. What if one of them splinters cut that big artery? I coulda bled to death."

"Sorry about that." I said, wincing from the pain.

"You're lucky I didn't hit that melon of yours any harder." He was standing ten feet away, holding my gun in one hand and a bat in another.

"We're both a couple of lucky sons of bitches, aren't we?" I squinted. "New bat?"

"Louisville Slugger composite metal. Hey man, thanks for gassing up my ride. I was about out."

I had filled up the tank before leaving his car at the airport. "It was the least I could do."

"But why'd you put that crap in my CD player? You're one sick mutha."

I laughed. The gas station had old CDs for five dollars each. I bought a romantic Broadway show tunes CD, put it in the car's player, and queued up one of the songs before I shut off the car.

I was angry with myself for allowing someone to surprise me. I had been distracted by the dog's bark. Rookie mistake. Feeling kind of wobbly, I rose to my knees and stood. He backed away a couple of steps.

"And what exactly is your job?" he asked.

"I'm looking into the murder of my friend, Dennis Goodman, in New York and trying to find out the source of the counterfeit medicine that killed a teenage boy here in Philadelphia."

He shook his head. "Can't help you. Don't know anything about either of them. Why were you videoing the clinic, and why did you break into here?"

"The state paid me to do a routine follow-up on Dr. Abercrombie. His high Medicaid earnings triggered an audit."

"You leave the doc alone. He's the best thing that's happened to the hood in a long time. He's a good man. Really cares about the people."

"You think so?"

"Damn straight I do."

"Then help me prove it," I said.

"What does he have to do with you bustin' in here tonight?"

"People, including my mother and the teenage boy I mentioned, have died because they took a counterfeit drug—a bogus copy of a drug that would have kept their body from rejecting a kidney transplant. The feds believe the counterfeit drug came from this warehouse."

For the first time, my vision had cleared enough to take in the interior of the building. It was part warehouse and part something else. The tables, equipment, and lighting reminded me of a pharmaceutical research and development lab.

"That's bullshit," he shouted. "They're wrong."

"You've got a choice to make. Show me what's here. Convince me they're wrong. Then I'll do what I can to convince the feds your doc's clean. It's that or a SWAT team busting down the door with the news cameras on their heels."

"How about a third option? Put a cap in your ass and dispose of your body." The dog growled, showing its teeth.

I had been around guns most of my life. They didn't frighten me. The people holding the guns did, especially someone inexperienced with firearms or a hardened killer. I studied his eyes, the tension of his facial muscles, the rigidity of the hand holding the gun, and the steadiness of the gun. He was neither. He was comfortable having a gun in his hand, but he was no killer. He held with a firm grip and a steady hand, like someone who had spent some time in the military. Still, my analysis was imperfect and men holding guns are unpredictable. I needed to keep him talking.

"Shooting me won't solve anything. It'll only make matters worse. The feds know I'm here. Work with me. You're on the inside. You can help prove the doc is legit. Tell the feds what's really going on here."

"No way I'm working with the cops. I'm no snitch," he snapped. He kept the pistol pointed at me and without diverting his eyes, leaned the bat against a box.

I had a fraction of a second to decide. Charge him or stand my ground. Less than five feet separated us. If I charged him, the dog would probably go for my throat.

I stood my ground and waited. He lowered the 9mm, ejected the magazine, and then pulled back the slide, ejecting the unspent cartridge in the chamber. He took the pistol by the barrel and handed it to me, and then gave me the magazine and cartridge. "You're one crazy son of a bitch."

"Jake Palmer," I said, extending my hand.

He firmly grasped my hand and shook it. "Moses Jefferson."

"Does this mean you are going to help me?" I said

"Hell no. It means I didn't pop a cap in your ass *this* time. That don't mean I won't the next time. I'll show you around—but I'm not working with the feds. I live here, man. If word gets out I talked to you, I'm good as dead."

"Why don't you leave? You seem like a smart guy. Do something else."

"Don't want to. Born and raised here. As shitty as it is, Welwyn Heights is my home. It's all I got. And besides, what skills does a former Army infantryman have?"

"Come on. That's like saying that my Navy experience only taught me how to drive a boat, which by the way, it didn't. Why protect Abercrombie? He's making a fortune off his patients."

"When I got out of the Army after my third deployment to

the Gulf, I came home. I had some medical issues and went to see the doc. Unlike those overworked and underpaid VA docs, he took a personal interest in me and my problems. We were talking during one of my visits, and he offered me a job, protecting his clinic and warehouse."

Jefferson's demeanor changed. That day at the clinic, his gait, speech pattern, and demeanor were that of a hardened street thug, talking and acting tough. Tonight, not trying to impress friends, he stood more erect, and had dropped some of the tough, urban vernacular. He was a war veteran and when he let down his guard, it showed.

"Are you a gang member? I saw the symbols on the clinic."

"Look around. Would you ask a gang to guard this? The doc has an agreement with the gang. When they get shot, stabbed, or beaten-up, he treats them—no charges, no questions asked, no reports to the police."

"They could get the same at the emergency room. Physicians don't have to report injuries from violence unless it involves a child," I said. "Safeguarding patient confidentiality is more important than reporting the injuries to the cops."

"This is Welwyn Heights. No one trusts the man or the system, including me. I provide the security for the clinic and warehouse. If there's a problem I can't handle, I let the gang know about it."

"What's this warehouse used for?"

Jefferson walked with me toward the center of the building, the dog between us.

"Some sort of pharmacy warehouse. The doc set it up to cut the cost of drugs for his patients. We receive bulk shipments of drugs and put them into small bottles to be given to patients through a pharmacy he runs inside the clinic. His patients pay almost nothing for their medicine. Sales to other pharmacies and to hospitals make up the difference, plus enough to cover his costs and generate a little profit."

"I've watched vanloads of patients come and go from the clinic. They're there for only a few minutes. When they leave, they have a bag. What's in it?"

"Their drugs. The pharmacist processes all the refills and has them ready for the patients when the van brings them by."

"So they're not seeing the doctor, only picking up their prescriptions," I said.

"It's a mix. Some do see the doc for a quick visit while they're there."

That explained it. Abercrombie was not only running a drug distribution business; he was also dispensing medications from his office, a practice that was controversial. In states where it's permitted, doctors need a special permit or license or need to be registered with the state Board of Pharmacy. In Pennsylvania, no permit or license was required, although some regulations governed the practice, including a requirement for physicians to submit information to a statewide database when dispensing controlled substances. There was little government control of the process and no inspections of physicians who dispensed medications to their patients.

Abercrombie was not Philadelphia's Mother Teresa. He was running a clinic, pharmacy, and drug repackaging and distribution center. He was making a lot of money, about a million and a half dollars, according to the Pennsylvania Fraud Control Unit. Maybe he was providing a much-needed medical service to an underserved community in the process, but he was probably committing fraud while he was doing it. It was up to the Pennsylvania FCU to build that case. On the other hand, if Abercrombie knowingly distributed the counterfeit version of Transpro and other drugs through this facility, and patients died as a direct result, he was a murderer.

"The shipment we received tonight is stored there." Jefferson pointed a caged area in the far corner of the building. The metal caging was padlocked. "The medicines come in large containers. The men who work here put them into small bottles or packages that are dispensed to pharmacies, hospitals, and the doc's patients."

The facility appeared clean enough, although I doubted it was up to the regulatory standards for a sterile work environment. The Food and Drug Administration inspects repackaging facilities much less frequently than they inspect pharmaceutical company packaging operations. DuPont could find out if the FDA had inspected this facility since it opened. If they did, I wanted to know what they found.

"Who are the men who work here?" I asked.

"I don't really know them. They speak English with a funny accent. I think they're from somewhere in Africa."

"Where do the drugs come from? Let's see the shipping documents."

Jefferson took me to the far corner of the building. Several gray metal file cabinets lined the wall. An old wooden desk was beside us with the front of the desk flush up against the wall. Jefferson picked up a manifest from the desk and handed it to me. I flipped through the pages.

HealthTech, a drug distribution company, had shipped the drugs to the Port of New York from Civitavecchia, Italy, the port of Rome. The manifest detailed the drug names and quantities. Most were commonly used antibiotics and other drugs that were generic and cheap to obtain through the normal supply and distribution channels. Some were branded drugs, still on patent, unavailable in generic form, and exorbitantly expensive. My eyes lit up when I saw Transpro on the list. This was a key piece of the puzzle, the first step in tracking the Transpro back to the manufacturer. However, there was no way of knowing if this Transpro was the counterfeit version. Even if Jefferson allowed me to take a box, I would be crossing the line as far as evidence and chain of custody is concerned. I took photographs of the manifest pages with my cell phone camera. When I finished, I said, "Give me the tour."

Jefferson walked me around, describing what he had observed the workers doing. I took photos of the equipment.

"How long until the workers arrive?" I said.

"The first shift comes in at seven."

"I'll meet with the feds tomorrow. I won't say anything about seeing you. They'll follow up on the information from tonight's shipment and the photos I've taken. I'd better get out of here."

"How can I reach you, if I need to get hold of you?" Jefferson asked.

I handed Jefferson my card and entered my number into his cell phone and gave the card back. "You're in my phone as Sharpshooter," Jefferson said.

Jefferson gave me his cell phone number, which I entered into my phone. "If you need to contact me, call and hang up after a couple of rings. I'll see it's you and call you back when I'm free to talk."

"Be careful," I said. "Whoever's behind this will stop at nothing to protect it. I'd better go. I'll leave by the roof."

Jefferson seemed like a good guy, but good guy or not, he didn't have a clue about the complex regulatory requirements for pharmaceutical manufacturing and distribution. He was not alone in that regard. People who worked in counterfeit medicine operations were often unaware they were involved in a criminal activity. Quite the opposite, they believed they worked for a reputable company and provided a valuable healthcare service.

I stepped out onto the roof and into the frigid night air. Jefferson followed me and threw down the grappling hook after I was safely on the ground. I saluted him and he returned the salute. One of the many things my years in the Navy, many of which were in combat, had taught me was that trust is never given or assumed; it is to be earned. DuPont had not yet earned my trust or respect. Jefferson had.

19

FIONA COULD NOT shake thoughts of the Transpro deaths even though the B&A investigation was not her responsibility. That belonged to Holloway's counterfeit medicine investigator, Sue Cooper. Until two years ago, when Holloway created the position, Cooper was Fiona's most experienced and best auditor. When Cooper told her she had been offered the job, Fiona could match neither the pay grade nor the salary of the new position, so Cooper took it. Who could blame her? The job was new and challenging and exciting—much more so than conducting clinical research audits.

Although the two of them remained friends, it had been over a year since Fiona had talked to Cooper. Fiona called her and arranged to meet after work at a pub in south London, which was near where Cooper lived. She told Cooper she had a lot to talk about. When Fiona arrived at the pub, Cooper was sitting at the bar, looking at a menu. They embraced and ordered a glass of pinot grigio. The conversation was light, just two people catching up on each other's social life. Fiona told her about the visit to New York to attend Jake's father's wedding.

"Jake Palmer invited you to his father's wedding? When a man takes you to a wedding, especially a family wedding, that's serious."

Fiona's face lit up. In her heart, it was serious even before the invitation. "Time will tell. For now, we're enjoying each other's company."

"If he's the one, don't let him slip away."

Fiona smiled before shifting the conversation back to work topics. She told Cooper about the murder of a US special agent outside their hotel, the counterfeit medicine case, and meeting with HSI at Federal Plaza. Cooper slid her bar stool closer to Fiona.

"Tell me more about the counterfeit medicine case the HSI agent was working on. I investigate B&A's counterfeit medicine cases. How much did you find out before turning the documents over to them?"

"It's a counterfeit version of Transpro. The patient's father had his son's medicines analyzed."

"Are you serious? I'm working on the Transpro case." Cooper appeared to have spit the words out before she could stop herself. She leaned over and put her hand on Fiona's arm. "That's confidential. Keep that information to yourself, if you don't mind. No one's supposed to know."

"I will. Were you aware of the murder of the Homeland Security Investigations special agent Dennis Goodman? He was investigating counterfeit Transpro and the death of Pietro Calabrese, who was taking counterfeit Transpro following a kidney transplant. He was just a child."

"I didn't even know HSI was investigating a counterfeit Transpro case and certainly didn't know an agent investigating it had been killed," Cooper said. "I have the list of deaths and other serious adverse events that occurred in patients taking Transpro. One of them was a child—in Philadelphia, I believe."

"That's Pietro Calabrese. Do you know that he was the nephew of Anthony Calabrese, the don of a New York Mafia family?"

"The Mafia. Are you kidding?" Cooper whispered.

"I understand that we suspect an employee or former employee is involved," Fiona said.

"How do you know about that?" Cooper shook her head.

"Who is it?" Fiona asked.

"I really can't say anything. I'm afraid it's confidential. The Board threatened to sack anyone who leaked information about the investigation."

"Jake is working with HSI to track the counterfeit from the patients in the US to the source. I met with Holloway when I got

back from the States, and he filled me in on the investigation."
Fiona stopped short of telling her a lie. She would let her assume
that Holloway told her about the involvement of an employee.
Tomlinson had told her—not Holloway. And if Cooper thought
Holloway told her, she would be more likely to tell her more.

"Actually, I'm not conducting an investigation," said Cooper.
"I'm B&A's liaison with the Medicines and Healthcare Products
Regulatory Agency. The MHRA is investigating to determine if
the counterfeit has shown up in the UK or if there have been
any deaths or reports of lack of efficacy with Transpro. Thus far,
the deaths are limited to the States, the east coast to be more
precise. We are not aware of any deaths in the UK or Europe that
have been associated with counterfeit Transpro."

"Who's the employee?" Fiona asked.

"We've narrowed it down to one individual. He's . . ." Cooper
took a sudden, sharp intake of breath.

"What wrong?" Fiona asked.

"You didn't get the information from Holloway, did you?
You got it from Tomlinson. Holloway wouldn't tell you anything
if his life depended on it. You and Tomlinson are close. He's the
one who told you."

"I met with both Holloway and Tomlinson today. I might
have gotten it muddled up. What difference does it make? Who's
the employee?" Fiona asked again.

"I can't say, Fiona. I've already said too much."

She couldn't blame Cooper. If the situation were reversed,
she wouldn't have said as much as Cooper already had, much
less give up the name of the suspected employee.

"Did you really want to meet to catch up or was it to quiz
me about counterfeit Transpro?" Cooper said. "I see that look
in your eye, Fiona. This is dangerous work. You almost lost your
life a couple of years ago and then you let Jake involve you in a
US military terrorism investigation that had nothing to do with
B&A. Don't let him do it again. Jake Palmer is dangerous to your
health, my friend."

Was Cooper right? No. It was the other way round. Jake was
ready to take the envelope to HSI without seeing the contents.
She was the one who suggested they see what was inside before
returning it to HSI.

20

THE NEXT DAY, Fiona worked until she was confident almost everyone had left. She exited her office and walked to an empty office that was used by visitors from other B&A sites. Using the unassigned phone, she called Sue Cooper's office. If Cooper answered, she would hang up without saying anything. The phone rang until it went into voice mail. She then called Holloway, whose office was on the same floor as Cooper's. Again, no answer.

Fiona gathered up her things and took the elevator to their floor. She stepped out and walked towards Cooper's office. The office door was closed. She tried the handle, and the door opened. The lights were switched off, but the light filtering in from the central area of the floor was sufficient for her purpose. The information she needed was most likely on Cooper's laptop, which she would have taken home. B&A's clean desk policy required that employees not leave sensitive documents on their desks overnight or if they away from their office for an extended period. Cooper's desk was clear. Fiona looked under the desk and saw two bins, a grey one for routine trash and blue one for confidential trash. Both were emptied each night. The confidential trash was taken to a secure area for shredding and disposal. Fiona pulled the two bins out from under the desk and stuffed the confidential papers into her black leather briefcase. She then emptied half of the non-secure trash into the confidential bin so that it would not seem odd that it was empty and pushed the two bins back under the desk.

Footsteps. If caught, explaining what she was doing there would be impossible. There was only one option. She picked up her briefcase and opened the door. A security guard making the rounds jumped, surprised by the door opening.

"Sorry," said Fiona. "I didn't mean to frighten you. I was just leaving."

The guard glanced at the company ID, hanging from her belt. She moved away from him before he could read her name. "You startled me. I don't usually see anyone this time of night," he said. "The office lights were off." He glanced into the office, as if searching to see if anyone else were there.

"I turned the lights off and was on my way out when I realized I had forgotten something. Have a good evening." She walked away, her heart throbbing as if she had just run a five-kilometer race.

An hour later, Fiona was home in Sevenoaks Weald. She poured a glass of chardonnay, dumped the contents of her briefcase onto the dining room table, and began to go through the crumpled up papers. Most were printed drafts of unrelated reports and communications. Although everyone wrote reports on a computer, when it came to proofreading, many preferred to do it using a hard copy of the document. Fiona did it herself and thought she recalled Cooper doing it as well. Fiona was near the bottom of the crumpled stack and beginning to believe her efforts were for naught when she saw it—Transpro. She flipped through the papers and found several more pages. She arranged them in page number order. It was a draft report Cooper was preparing for Holloway. There were numerous editing marks and revisions scribbled on the document.

Her eyes raced through the document until she spotted what she was searching for, the suspect's name—James Henry Wilcox. Wilcox was a manager in Manufacturing Operations and responsible for product labeling and packaging. Other possible suspects, all current employees, had been investigated and cleared. Several months ago, Wilcox had received notice of possible redundancy as the result of a planned restructuring that would eliminate a large number of positions. He had interviewed for other B&A jobs but received no offers. If he didn't find another position before the deadline at the end of January, he would be terminated and would receive a severance payment sufficient to tide him over until he found another job elsewhere. According to his manager, Wilcox had become increasingly angry and aggressive about the downsizing and job loss. Cooper had included Wilcox's home address in St. Margarets, a borough of Richmond upon Thames in southwest London.

Fiona had no difficulty finding him on Facebook, Twitter, LinkedIn, and Instagram. On LinkedIn, he listed his B&A position as his current job. He had been with B&A for eight years. His current position was distribution manager in Manufacturing Operations at B&A Pharmaceuticals' plant in Hertfordshire, north of London. Prior to that he had worked in pharmaceutical development on the development of the oral and injectable formulations of Transpro. Before joining B&A, he worked for a small biotech company in Manchester. Wilcox was thirty-four years old and single. Most of the photos on Facebook and Instagram were of him in Italy and India. The rest were photos of him drinking and partying in pubs or at soccer and rugby matches. She studied a recent post that showed him leaning against a red, late-model Audi A6.

On Twitter, his most recent tweets, some with photos attached, also boasted about travels to Rome and to India. Fiona sat back and took a sip of chardonnay. Tomorrow she would drive by Wilcox's house.

21

I AWOKE EARLY, had two cups of coffee before breakfast, and then a third for good measure before calling DuPont. We arranged to meet at his office at 220 Chestnut Street at ten o'clock. Before I left, I printed copies of the photographs I'd taken at the warehouse. I was about to walk out the door when I received a text from the drug analysis lab. I clicked on the link provided, entered the PIN code they had given me, and read the results. The analysis showed that my mother had taken the branded product. It was not the counterfeit version. I went to my desk and compared the analysis with that of the Transpro Pietro Calabrese had taken.

I had been certain Mother's Transpro was counterfeit and had caused her death. I was wrong. Even so, I had for a short time experienced the sadness and anger that the Calabrese family had, just like the other families who had lost a loved one because of a counterfeit medicine. I downloaded the lab report and emailed it to Fiona.

When I entered the building, DuPont was pacing back and forth across the lobby like a cat high on catnip.

"You're late," he said.

"Actually, I'm on time," I said looking at my watch.

He suggested we go to a coffee shop two blocks from the office building. *This man does not need any more caffeine, and neither do I*, I thought. We went to the counter where I only briefly considered decaf before ordering a small black coffee. DuPont ordered a large and paid for both.

"You had a busy night last night," DuPont said, sitting down at the table farthest from the door.

"You could say so." I handed him the photographs. DuPont was quiet as he studied each one before setting it face up in an overlapping row on the table, like a blackjack dealer turning up a series of low numbered cards to a player nudging toward twenty-one. When he reached the last one, the photograph of the invoice, he held it close to his eyes, reading all that he could make out. "I'm curious. How'd you get inside?"

"I waited until everyone left and climbed up the exterior of the building. From there I entered through a rooftop door. It was unlocked."

DuPont leaned toward me, his elbows on the table. "Did you see any surveillance cameras?"

"At the front and rear entrances and the loading dock."

"Are you sure there weren't any inside?"

"Yes, I'm sure. It's strange, I know. You'd think there would be."

"If you broke into the warehouse without a warrant, these photographs were illegally obtained and, therefore, inadmissible."

"I didn't break in. The door was unlocked," I said.

"That's still criminal trespass."

Of course, I'd picked the lock, but because no one knew except Moses Jefferson, it was a moot point. "You told me that the drug distribution center at that building is the source of the counterfeit Transpro in Philadelphia. If you have a problem with what I've shown you, go to the assistant US attorney and justify your request for a warrant or a raid based on the information you already have, not on what I've brought you."

"I have no other choice. I got your text about the delivery truck last night and ran it this morning when I got in. Empire Trucking is a contract carrier in New York."

"Did you check the tag number and DOT number?"

"Both are legitimate," DuPont said.

I shuffled through the photographs on the table and slid one in front of DuPont. "How about this invoice?" I pointed to the shipment information.

DuPont leaned back, drummed his fingers on the table and took a drink of his coffee. "I'll follow up on the address in Italy and request the FDA conduct an unannounced inspection of Abercrombie's warehouse operation."

I shook my head. "An FDA inspection? The FDA moves at the speed of cold molasses. That'll take too long."

"Whatever it takes to prove Abercrombie knows he is receiving and distributing counterfeit drugs will be worth the time and effort. We don't have enough evidence to raid the place. An FDA inspection is the next step. I'll expedite the request. It's the difference between a slap on the wrist and some serious jail time."

I tried to shake off DuPont's attitude. Was he trying to convince me that we had nothing to go on? Perhaps I should tell him about Jefferson. Lying or not being completely truthful didn't sit well with me. I demanded DuPont be truthful and not hold back information; I should do the same. Still, Jefferson was putting his life on the line even talking to me. Jefferson saw only the good side of Abercrombie, not the side that was probably skimming millions from federal healthcare programs, like Medicaid, Medicare, and the Affordable Care Act, and who was, perhaps, part of a counterfeit medicine operation. When and if I had complete trust in DuPont, I would tell him more.

"To be honest, nothing we have proves that Abercrombie is aware he's receiving and dispensing counterfeit drugs," I said. "More patients will die while you wait for the FDA to conduct an inspection. You need to do something now."

"What the hell's going on, Palmer? A few days ago, you weren't interested in being involved at all. Now you're pushing me to move faster. You said it yourself. It takes time to track a counterfeit drug to its source. The responsibility to notify physicians, pharmacies, and patients that a counterfeit version of Transpro exists is the responsibility of the regulatory agencies and B&A Pharmaceuticals. They're already doing that."

I had become impatient to get to the source of the counterfeit drugs, and even though the Transpro my mother was taking was not counterfeit, it could have been. I had a burning need to find those responsible and shut down the operation. Pietro Calabrese's death was as much a murder as Goodman's. The only difference was the weapon used.

"And what the hell is going on with you? Do you even want to catch those responsible? Goodman would have raided the damn warehouse by now." I said loud enough so that people in the coffee shop turned their heads toward me. I stood to leave.

DuPont grabbed my arm. "Don't ever accuse me of not doing my job. I'm not Goodman, but I damn well know what I'm doing."

"Then do something."

I sat back down and crossed my arms. The coffee shop's customers, seeing we were not going to throw punches, went about their business.

"Do you know any more about Goodman and his work with FinCEN?" I asked. "Has anyone made a link between this counterfeit medicine operations and money laundering?"

"Nothing specific. However, if FinCEN is involved, it's investigating the possibility of money laundering and attempting to find out where the money's ended up. That, too, takes a lot of time and effort."

"I was under the impression that after 9/11, the federal agencies were realigned and communications between them was improved. Seems to me, nothing's changed. You guys still don't talk to each other."

DuPont sighed. "I'm as frustrated as you are. If we raid the warehouse now without thinking it through, we could screw up the entire investigation and might blow an even bigger case. We've assumed someone murdered Goodman because of his investigation of the counterfeit medicine case and because someone wanted to know what was in that envelope. Maybe they wanted something that wasn't in the envelope. Maybe they didn't want the envelope at all. Hell, maybe he was killed for an entirely different reason."

DuPont was right. The medical records, at least the ones he gave me, and the Transpro drug analysis were not sufficient motive for killing him. Maybe it wasn't the envelope. Goodman said he would tell me more after I signed on. He withheld something until I agreed to take the case. He wanted to wait until I was onboard before he showed me all his cards, giving me only enough to pique my interest. I would have done the same. Whatever he held back would be the most damaging piece of information, the evidence that would potentially incriminate someone powerful and dangerous. What had he withheld? Where is it? What did he really want me to do?

"The medical examiner in New York is releasing Goodman's body the day after tomorrow," DuPont said. "The funeral will be the next day."

"I'd like to go."

"Dennis was Jewish, so the traditions related to Jewish funerals and mourning will be observed."

DuPont proceeded to brief me on the fundamentals of Jewish funerals. First, Dennis Goodman's funeral could not be held within twenty-four hours of his death, as is the tradition, because he had been murdered and an autopsy had to be performed, during which a rabbi was present. The funeral would be held at the Goodman's synagogue in a Philadelphia suburb in what had been a large nineteenth century home. There would be no visitation at the funeral home, as was the tradition with most Christian funerals. Immediately after the funeral, Delores and Sarah, his wife and daughter, would observe a seven-day *shiva*, a period of mourning during which they would remain at home to receive visitors. Under normal circumstances, it would be inappropriate for you to talk to them about the case until the end of *shiva*.

"That complicates things," I said.

"It does. I thought you might want to talk to his wife, so I spoke to her," DuPont said. "Delores can see you tomorrow morning. I told her you were with Dennis when he died, and you're now working with me."

22

ST. MARGARETS IS in the London borough of Richmond upon Thames, where deer graze in Richmond Park, men butt heads at the world's largest rugby stadium at Twickenham, and rush-hour traffic congestion redefines gridlock. Fiona had left work a little early but not early enough to avoid the traffic on her way to St. Margarets. She thanked God she did not have to make this trip every day.

With the help of her GPS, she located James Wilcox's house. It was a three-level dwelling, attached to similar ones on the right and on the left. She drove by at the speed traffic flowed, which was slow enough for her to see that the lights were on in a front room. She wheeled in the first available parking space on the street, a few hundred yards past the house. Her pulse accelerated. She fought the urge to leave and drive home. She'd come this far; she would walk by the house and observe, nothing more.

A light, cold rain had begun to fall. The car lights reflected off the wet road, and cars sent up spray as they passed. Fiona pulled the hood of her Barbour coat over her head and tucked her hands in the pockets. As she neared the house, she slowed her step, turning her head to look in the bay window. Two men were seated inside, one facing the window and the other with his back to the window. She had not expected to see anyone at home because of the long commute from the manufacturing plant in Hertfordshire. Perhaps Wilcox worked the early shift. She couldn't make out if either were Wilcox at first. Then, the man who had been sitting with his back to the window stood and left the room. It was Wilcox. She recognized him from the social media photographs. The other man stood and faced the window. Who was he? A friend? A roommate? She snapped her head forward and continued to walk, looking down at the sidewalk. After passing the house, she circled back. The men stood within a few feet of each other, talking normally, and then the man appeared to shout something, took a step forward and pushed both hands into Wilcox's chest. Caught off guard, Wilcox stumbled backwards, catching his balance before falling.

Fiona needed to be closer where she might be able to hear what they were arguing about. She moved out of sight of the window and near the front door. To avoid arousing suspicion, she opened her pocketbook and fumbled through it. She pulled out her keys and inched forward to where she could hear some of what was being said. At that moment, a car horn blew on the street, and Fiona dropped her keys.

The men stopped talking. One of them shouted, "See who that is." She took the first step toward the street and stopped. She had only a second before she was discovered. She had to do something.

Fiona rang the doorbell. Would Wilcox recognize her? She hoped not. She seldom went to the manufacturing site where he worked.

James Wilcox jerked open the door and looked at Fiona like she was a door-to-door salesman hawking timeshares in Majorca. "What do you want?" Wilcox asked.

"Sorry to be a bother. My name is Gillian Murray. I am looking for friends of mine. They gave me this address."

"What's their name?"

She had to give him the names of someone he would not know, someone from outside B&A. Two of her best friends used to live in St. Margarets before they moved to Yorkshire.

"Peter and Norma Rees."

"Never heard of them."

Wilcox slammed the door. Fiona took a couple of steps back. The other man shouted something to Wilcox. Her pulse was racing. She walked away from the door but had gotten only a few feet away when it reopened.

"I'm such a jerk," Wilcox said much more pleasantly than before. "Maybe I can help you. Please, come in out of the rain." He smiled.

Fiona stayed where she was, not moving toward the door.

"Thank you for you kindness. I'll ring up Norma and get directions. I thought I remembered the address. I should've written it down."

"I insist. Please come in." He stepped outside and toward her.

"I must be going." Fiona started walking toward the car. The door of the house shut behind her. Her heart raced as she listened for footsteps following her. She took deep breaths and exhaled, just as she had been taught to do in her yoga class. Once safely inside her car she locked the doors and twisted in her seat. The man who was in the house with Wilcox was approaching. *Oh God.* Fiona started the car and sped away.

What was I thinking? Going to Cooper's office last night and coming here tonight? They could have pulled me inside. She took a few more deep breaths, inhaling through her nose and exhaling through her mouth to calm herself. She adjusted the rear view mirror, noting the cars behind her. At night, it would be impossible to identify and keep track of the cars. She needed to process what little information she had. Did Wilcox believe B&A was on to him and want to get paid and leave the country? She had to report this to someone, but to whom? Maybe she should talk with Tomlinson. Or should she call Jake? What could he do from the States? Should she contact the UK authorities? Did she have enough information for them to take her seriously? *What have I gotten myself into?*

23

MIKE BAXTER WAS close enough to see the car's license tag number before the woman sped away. He repeated the number to himself over and over until he got back to Wilcox's and wrote it down. He had a friend who could match the tag number to the car's owner. He would contact him in the morning. Soon, he would know if Gillian Murray was the woman's real name. Maybe she really was looking for Peter and Norma Rees and didn't want to give her real name. If that were true, it would have been an unfortunate choice. It was also possible that she was an undercover policeman or government agent or someone working for B&A. He would not waste time finding out why she had lied and why she was at his door. Instead, he was already contemplating how she would die.

A more pressing problem was that his B&A man, Wilcox, was getting cold feet and needed to be dealt with immediately. Wilcox was smart. He had been involved in previous internal investigations of B&A counterfeit medicines, comparing the tablets or capsules and labels or packages of counterfeit drugs with those of B&A or its authorized repackagers. He knew how it was done, and of greater importance, he knew the mistakes made in the past that resulted in the counterfeits being detected. Most were stupid errors, like misspelled words or sloppy printing. Wilcox had spread the word that he had the skills and knowledge to advise on the production of near perfect counterfeit medicines and labels and could help produce zufridone, the active ingredient in Transpro. Including a small amount of zufridone could result in the counterfeit version having a small clinical effect and thus avoid detection by the physician treating the patient, as well as resulting in a less severe criminal penalty than if it contained no zufridone at all. It wasn't long before Viktor Utkin ordered Baxter to contact Wilcox.

Wilcox's incentive had always been financial. As long as the money was good and no one knew he was involved, he was happy. But now that Wilcox believed B&A suspected he was working with the counterfeiters to produce high quality counterfeit Transpro, labels, and packaging, no amount of money was enough to satisfy him.

If Wilcox was right, he needed to be dealt with before the police arrested him.

^^^^

Mike Baxter was born in London's tough East End. His mother had done her best to be a good provider. She seldom mentioned his father, and eventually, Baxter stopped asking about him. She worked two jobs to put meals on the table and provide the essentials. At fifteen, he dropped out of school and took a job washing dishes at a posh West End restaurant. From there, he moved on to busing tables, and then became a waiter. The money was good; however, at the end of the first week, he got into an argument with a customer who had complained about the slow service. The customer turned out to be a friend of the owner. Baxter was fired.

After that, he bounced from job to job, never holding any of them longer than a few months. He turned to petty crime, which escalated to assault and battery and breaking and entering. For the past few years, he had worked for Viktor Utkin, doing anything he was told, including torture and murder. He had no problem with that. In fact, he enjoyed that part of his job.

Baxter had met Utkin at a local pub in the East End, one that Baxter frequented. A twenty-something lout made the mistake of calling Utkin a dumbass Russkie. The fight—if it can be called that—was over before it started. The ambulance took the man to the hospital, while Utkin resumed drinking. Baxter bought drinks for the Russian the rest of the night. The next week, he went along with Utkin on an assignment. Working directly with Utkin for over a year, Baxter gained his confidence and trust. After that, Utkin gave him solo assignments. Still, Baxter feared Utkin, knowing that if he screwed up one assignment he was a dead man. Utkin would never let him walk away. He knew too much.

Utkin's orders were clear—have Wilcox supervise the manufacture of a final shipment, and then eliminate any loose ends. Wilcox and Gillian Murray, or whoever she was, were loose ends.

24

RICHARD DAVID MOORE stood at the floor-to-ceiling window of his HealthTech office overlooking the Financial District of London, his arms crossed over his bespoke Turnbull & Asser striped shirt and silk tie. Underneath the veil of respectability, the massive company, much like its owner, was not at all what it seemed. Moore was the owner and president of HealthTech, one of the largest wholesale drug distribution conglomerates in the world.

The fifty-year-old Moore had studied at Cambridge and the London School of Economics. He had come a long way since he left his position as head of manufacturing for an American pharmaceutical company several years earlier. Although he left on his own accord, Moore's lead-from-the-top dictatorial style had not set well with his staff or Human Resources, which received frequent reports of the senior executive's verbal abuse. The chief executive officer, to whom he reported, tolerated him because he got results. Moore believed that people must be told what to do and punished if they failed to do it in the allotted time. The company had become too soft, too afraid to offend an employee for fear of being sued, and too quick to award pay raises and bonuses for mediocre performance. After he left the company, Moore spent some time at his second home on the south coast in Devon, where he formulated a business plan.

The initial part of the plan involved investing his money in the highly competitive wholesale drug distribution business. Moore purchased a medium-sized, privately-owned company and quickly concluded the only way to succeed was to grow his company—not organically, that took too long—but through acquisitions. For that, he needed more capital. A search for investors led him to Saudi Sheikh Khalifa Isma'il El-Hashem. Under the terms of their agreement, the Sheikh El-Hashem would invest enough cash in Moore's business to allow him to acquire several smaller companies. In return, Moore would funnel a high percentage of the profit back to El-Hashem. Understood, but not in writing, was the requirement for the money that Moore sent the El-Hashem would be untraceable. El-Hashem put him in touch with a drug manufacturer in India that produced medicines at an unbeatable price, no questions asked. In the drug distribution business, where huge sums of money moved based on a tenth of a percent difference in wholesale drug prices, Moore moved quickly to align with the Indian manufacturer.

Although the Indian manufacturer provided only a small percentage of the drugs that moved though HealthTech's warehouses, the profit margin for them was by far the highest. At Moore's direction, one of his managers made certain that the Indian company's medicines were distributed to other drug distributors and not directly to pharmacies and hospitals. He also dispersed the distribution so as not to saturate a single geographic area, which would increase the likelihood of detection. Once in the complex global wholesale drug distribution system, tracing them back to HealthTech and the Indian manufacturer would be difficult.

Now, several years later, HealthTech was the world's largest privately owned wholesale drug distributor and one of the top five market leaders, private and public. Moore had not only met El-Hashem's demands for a return on his investment, he had sent him more than the terms of their contract demanded. El-Hashem, in turn, made his gratitude to Moore known by way of extravagant gifts, such as the thirty-four meter yacht he had given to him outright and use of El-Hashem's Gulfstream G650 executive jet.

El-Hashem told Moore that the operation needed an enforcer or muscle man. Such a man could facilitate negotiations for acquisitions, keep the network of distributors in line, and provide personal protection. El-Hashem gave Moore the name of a freelance mercenary named Viktor Utkin, who, he said, would be contacting Moore on his personal cell phone number.

That night Utkin called Moore and gave him the coordinates for a location off the coast of England and instructed him to anchor there the next night and wait. Moore had his captain take the yacht to the coordinates. Not long after the crew set anchor, there was a knock on Moore's cabin door. It was Utkin. No one knew how he got onboard the yacht without being detected and no one knew how he later left. Moore became Utkin's exclusive employer, although it was more of an understanding between the two of them, because there was no written agreement and payments to Utkin were always in cash with Moore asking no questions regarding the amounts.

Utkin, as Moore learned, was a former Russian Spetsnaz operative. Moore also learned that Utkin had a team of men with similar skills and interests, men whom he had met and trained over the years. Neither Utkin nor these men appeared on HealthTech's books.

HealthTech generated vast sums of money that needed to be laundered for Sheikh El-Hashem. Moore found an American investment firm that was in distress as a result of some misguided investments. The firm's president personally managed HealthTech's short-term investments, ultimately converting them to cash, which could be transferred to El-Hashem. The investment firm was Palmer Global Investments.

25

THE GOODMAN HOME was in Wayne, a community near Villanova University and the main commuter train line into Philadelphia. I drove around the home's semi-circular driveway, stopping where it widened in front of the two-story traditional house. Sarah Goodman opened the front door to greet me. I followed her into the living room where I met Delores Goodman.

"Mrs. Goodman, my name is Jake Palmer. I'm sorry for your loss of your husband. He was a true patriot and served his country with honor."

"Thank you for your kind words, Mr. Palmer. Please call me Delores. Agent DuPont said you were working with him and would be stopping by this morning."

"Thank you for agreeing to see me before the funeral and shiva. I know you have a lot to do before tomorrow. I promise not to take much of your time."

She offered me coffee and a muffin from a tray of them that she said a neighbor had brought over. Delores Goodman appeared somewhat younger than her late husband. Sarah, of course, had the tight-skinned beauty and glow of youth.

"I can't believe he's gone. It all seems like a very bad dream. But I'm so glad someone he knew was with him when he passed," Mrs. Goodman said, her voice breaking up as she spoke.

"I was in New York for my father's wedding. Dennis and I met in the bar at the hotel where I was staying. He wanted me to work with him on a case and gave me some documents to review. He had just left when I heard the gunfire. Fearing the worst, I ran outside. The police and EMTs did all they could. I know this is a difficult time. Are you all right to talk about our investigation?"

Delores Goodman pulled a tissue from the box on the end table beside her and dabbed her eyes. "Yes, I'm fine. I'm not a vengeful person, Mr. Palmer. Ultimately, God will judge the person or persons who did this. However, I want to see those responsible for his death brought to justice."

"I couldn't agree with you more." Turning to Sarah, I said, "Your father said you are majoring in criminal justice at Villanova. He beamed with pride when he spoke about you."

Sarah Goodman smiled. "I was so proud of him, too. Daddy never talked much about his work, but I knew it was dangerous."

"Things that may seem trivial to either of you could provide an important lead in the investigation."

"Some men from the FBI and HSI were here the day after Daddy was shot," Sarah Goodman said. "We told them all we knew. They thought the shooting was related to a case he was working on. They said the man who shot him was found dead in an alley close to the hotel."

"That's right. The authorities believe that someone paid the man to shoot your father." I turned to Delores Goodman. "Had Dennis said anything to you about the case? The one involving counterfeit medicine."

Delores Goodman shifted in her seat and cleared her throat. "He never talked about the specifics of his work, but he did say how terrible this counterfeit medicine business is. He said the people doing it were getting away with murder."

"Did the investigators who came here take his computer or search his belongings for any clues?"

"No. They asked a few general questions. I suppose they were here for less than an hour or so. I can't remember. It's all very hazy."

That gave me pause. Why hadn't they been more thorough? Were they convinced that he, like all agents, didn't take his work home, especially physical evidence, and therefore, there was no need to conduct a search. Maybe he had made an exception to the rule and hidden some information or evidence that would lead to those responsible for the counterfeit Transpro and his death.

"Your husband gave me some medical records related to the death of a Philadelphia boy who had a kidney transplant. The child received the counterfeit version of a drug prescribed for prevention of organ rejection and subsequently died. Dennis said he had more evidence for me to review but wanted to wait until I took the case before he gave it to me. Is there anywhere in the house where you husband kept important papers and documents, someplace where he might keep confidential work files?"

Delores and Sarah Goodman glanced at each other, as if each were waiting to see if the other should answer. Sarah nodded to her mother, a subtle sign that it was okay for her to tell me what she knew.

"We don't have a safe deposit box at the bank anymore. Dennis thought it was an inconvenience to have access to it only when the bank was open. He needed a safe for his guns, so two or three years ago, he had a fireproof safe installed in our bedroom closet. It's large enough to store our valuables—Dennis' guns, my jewelry, some emergency cash, and important documents. If Dennis had something he wanted to protect from fire or theft, that's where it would be."

"I feel bad for asking. Could you check the contents to see if there might be anything that would be pertinent to the case?"

"I suppose so. Follow me," Delores Goodman said.

The master bedroom was on the second floor of the two-story house. I followed them up the carpeted stairs, where they walked through the master bedroom into a large walk-in closet, the type built by a closet specialist. Delores Goodman's clothes and shoes took up approximately three-fourths of the closet, the remaining one-fourth were her late husband's. She extracted a tissue tucked in her long sleeve and wiped her eyes.

"Mom asked me to take Daddy's clothes to a charity shop before I go back to school. It upsets her to see them every day."

I was about to ask where the safe was located when Sarah reached into the rack where Dennis Goodman's clothes were hung and pulled on something. There was a click, and the entire rack swung open, revealing the front of a six-foot high safe with a digital keypad and a five-spoke wheel in the center of the door.

Delores Goodman whispered something to her daughter. I assumed it was the combination to the safe.

"I've not seen the inside of the safe in three years, since the day he transferred everything here from the bank, Delores said. "Dennis was the only one that used it."

Sarah stepped in front of the keypad to block it from my view, entered the combination, and turned the wheel. There was a loud click. She opened the door.

The three of us stared at the open safe, our eyes taking in the contents. Dennis Goodman's guns took up the left side of the safe. There was a Remington 12-gauge shotgun, an AR-15 assault rifle, and several handguns. The space above the guns was filled to capacity with boxes of ammunition. On the right side of the safe were four shelves. The top shelf held a couple of stacks of US bills and small stacks of various other currencies. Three passports leaned against the right side of the space, held in place by a stack of Credit Suisse one-ounce gold bars. I estimated there were twenty or more bars, each worth around twelve hundred dollars at the current price of gold.

"Dennis started buying gold after the last presidential election," Delores Goodman said. "He thought the country was going to hell."

"Gold and lead," I mumbled.

"What?" she asked.

"People who buy gold and keep it at home, tend to also have an ample supply of lead."

On the last shelf, the one at the bottom right of the safe, was a metal box.

Delores Goodman pulled the box, which was about the size of a shoebox, from the safe. She opened it and peered inside before extracting a stack of documents and thumbing through them. As she went through the stack, she said aloud what they were. "Birth certificates, car insurance policies, homeowners insurance policies, car titles, house title, our wills, life insurance policies . . ."

Delores Goodman pulled an envelope from the stack and examined it closely. "It's for you." Looking puzzled, she handed me the envelope. "That's Dennis's handwriting," she said.

On the front of the sealed business-size envelope was written *"For Jake Palmer's Eyes Only,"* and below that was my cell phone number and home address. I tore open the envelope. Inside was a flat key with the number 191 on both sides. There was nothing else.

"It looks like a safe deposit box key. Do you have a safe deposit box at your bank?" I asked.

Delores Goodman shook her head. "After Dennis had the safe installed a few years ago, he removed everything and brought it here. As far as I know, we no longer have a safe deposit box anywhere."

"Where do you bank?"

"Our accounts are all with Liberty Bank & Trust. We use the local branch."

"Do you mind if we take the key there?"

"Dennis went to great trouble for you to have it. If you hadn't discovered it, I would have found it when I got out our will and his life insurance policies. I'd been putting it off. Although I wouldn't have known who you were, I would have phoned the number Dennis wrote on the envelope."

"I'm not authorized to access the safe deposit box because I haven't signed a signature card. Let's assume that he kept paying for the box after he transferred everything here. Did you sign the signature card, Mrs. Goodman?"

"Sarah and I both did. I used to go to the bank to retrieve important papers when we needed them, but he paid all the bills and managed our finances. Dennis wanted Sarah's signature on record, too. He said if we were both killed in a car accident, Sarah could get into the box."

"Can one or both of you come with me to the bank?"

Delores Goodman looked at her daughter, as if silently urging her to go with me.

"I'll go," Sarah Goodman said with a twinkle in her eye.

"I feel like I'm imposing on your good graces, but would now be convenient?"

Sarah Goodman looked at her mother. She was old enough to make her own decisions, but wanted her mother's permission.

"Go ahead, but come straight home."

26

SARAH GOODMAN TALKED my ear off in-between giving me turn-by-turn directions to the bank. No need for a GPS with her in the car. She spoke about her father, her concern about her mother's lack of knowledge regarding personal and household financial management, and how much her mother would be lost now that her father was gone.

"I hope you don't mind that I wanted to come along. I know this is terrible, but I needed to get out of the house."

"Not at all. As stressful as this has been, the real loss hasn't yet set in. The holidays are going to be especially hard for you and your mother. You need each other's support."

"I'm home until mid-January when classes start back. I've been thinking about dropping out next semester and staying home with Mom—you know, start back in the fall."

"You have a couple of weeks to think about it before spring semester starts. I assume you live on campus."

"Yes, Dad said that even though I could commute to Villanova from home, I needed to immerse myself in the college experience and learn to live on my own. I have an apartment within walking distance of the campus."

"Your mom is dealing with a lot right now. Instead of dropping out, have you considered either commuting from home for a semester or coming home every weekend and a night or two during the week, depending on how your mom's doing?"

"The apartment is paid for through the end of the school year. And the weekends are like pretty busy. Maybe I could spend a night or two at home during the week and a weekend every now and then. I could study and be with Mom. Oh, there it is—on the right at the intersection."

I whipped into the Liberty Bank & Trust branch office and parked near the door.

We met with Rick Middleton, a banking manager who knew Dennis Goodman. He expressed his sympathies. Sarah introduced me as a family friend and told him that she needed to get into their safe deposit box. Middleton excused himself, saying he had to make a phone call, and went back to his office. Middleton glanced at us a couple of times during the call. In a few minutes, he returned.

"Sorry about that," Middleton said. "I needed to confirm you are authorized to access the box following your father's death and that there were no legal holds on the contents. Everything's in order."

Middleton was talking to Sarah but kept shifting his eyes toward me. Middleton and Sarah went into the bank's walk-in vault where the safe deposit boxes were located. I stayed behind in the waiting area where I could see into the vault through the thick glass door. Sarah signed the signature card and the manager compared her signature with the one on file before dating and initialing it. She handed him her key. Middleton inserted her key and the bank's key in the small door and swung it open. He pulled out the long flat box and handed it to her. Sarah brought it outside the vault and motioned for me to join her in a small booth. We went inside and closed the door.

"Are you ready?" Sarah said.

"Ready."

She opened the lid that was hinged two thirds of the way back.

"It's empty," Sarah said.

I reached over and tilted the box forward. A computer flash drive slid from the back of the box, where it had been hidden from view, and came to rest against the front. Sarah's mouth fell open. I put the flash drive into a zippered pocket inside my leather jacket and returned to the waiting area. Sarah got

Middleton's attention. They went into the vault and put the box in its slot and locked it.

When we were outside the bank, she asked, "What do you think is on it?"

"I have no idea."

"We'll find out as soon as we get back to my house. I have a laptop at home with USB ports."

I pulled out of the parking lot into the flow of the late morning traffic. Ever since the bank manager stepped away and made the telephone call, something didn't seem right. Why would the manager need to check Sarah's authorization? Why would a bank put a hold on a safe deposit box following the death of one of the three people authorized to enter it? It had to be a common occurrence. A husband or wife dies and the surviving spouse goes to get the will from the safe deposit box where a lot of people keep them. And either you're authorized to have access and your signature is on file, or you're not. Maybe I was overthinking it and it was routine for that bank.

"Do you think the flash drive contains information about the case Dad was working on?" Sarah said. "Will it lead you to the people who had him killed?"

The light ahead changed to green as they approached the intersection. "We'll know the answer those to questions soon enough," I said. Her scream was the last thing I remembered hearing.

^ ^ ^ ^

I slowly regained full consciousness, my vision blurred. The beep–beep–beep of a vital signs monitor was the only sound I heard. A doctor and two nurses stood at the foot of my emergency room bed, whispering to each other.

"Where's Sarah Goodman? Is she all right? Is she here?" I asked, my voice barely audible.

The doctor came to the bedside, held open my eyelid, and pointed a light into my eye. I pushed his hand away. "Is Sarah Goodman all right?"

"Miss Goodman has multiple contusions and abrasions. Other than that, she appears to be fine. We're running a few tests to be certain. You, on the other hand, have a dislocated left shoulder. You may also have a couple of broken ribs."

"I'm fine," I said, even though I wasn't feeling so good.

The doctor rubbed his hand over the back of my head. "I've ordered a CT scan to confirm the concussion and broken ribs. I noticed you have a nasty bump on your head. Have you been hit on the head recently?"

I thought before answering. Jefferson's tap to my head had knocked me out. "I got elbowed while playing basketball."

"Having two concussions in a short period of time is dangerous. We'll keep you overnight for observation. If everything looks okay in the morning, you can go home."

"How about the other vehicle?"

A policeman who had been standing just outside the door entered. "Do you remember anything about the accident, Mr. Palmer?"

"Not really." My clothes were in plastic bag on the chair. I couldn't ask the policeman to see if the flash drive was inside the zippered pocket of my jacket.

"According to the eyewitnesses, you were going through an intersection on a green light when a Chevrolet Suburban ran the light and T-boned you. The force of the impact pushed your car through the intersection. Your vehicle rolled over and came to rest on its side. The men in the other vehicle rushed over and pulled the two of you out. The witnesses said they seemed to be looking for something. I was writing a traffic citation when I got the call. By the time I arrived, the men were gone. The vehicle they were driving had been stolen, so I was the last person they wanted to see. One of the witnesses said when the men heard my siren they jumped into a car parked near the intersection and took off. Funny thing about that is I've been on the force over ten years, and I've never seen or heard of good Samaritan car thieves."

"Hand me that bag," I said, motioning to a clear bag containing my clothes on the chair. "I need to get my phone." The officer shrugged his shoulders and handed it to me.

One of the nurses stepped beside the policeman. "The hospital found your wallet and your insurance information. Nothing should be missing."

"It's not that. I'm looking for my phone."

I fished my jacket from the bag. Before checking for my phone in my front jacket pocket, I unzipped the inside pocket and felt inside. The flash drive was there. I left it there and zipped the pocket shut. The policeman's arrival had disrupted the men's search. One was probably searching me while the other searched Sarah. Given a little more time, they would have located it.

"Your phone is in the bag," the nurse said.

"Now I see it. Thanks." I retrieved it and set in on the table by the bed.

Sarah and I were fortunate. We could have been killed. The men who pulled us out of the car may have saved our lives, but, as the officer said, they were not good Samaritans—quite the contrary. Telling the patrolman that I had driven Sarah to the bank to get something out of her dead HSI agent father's safe deposit box would not go down well. What if Sarah or her mother had told him why we were at the bank?

"Have you talked to Sarah Goodman?" I asked the policeman.

"I have. She's a little banged up. No serious injuries. She said her father passed away, and you were visiting with her and her mother this morning. You had driven her to the bank to make a deposit for her mother."

Smart girl. She didn't mention the safe deposit box key or the flash drive. Time to get out of here.

27

FIONA BREATHED A sigh of relief when she pulled into her driveway at her home in Sevenoaks Weald. She steadied her hand and inserted the key in her front door. Once inside, she flopped onto the sofa. *Why did I go to Sue Cooper's office and take those papers from the confidential bin? Why did I go to Wilcox's home? What's gotten into me?*

Sticking her nose into something that was being managed by B&A's manufacturing organization and the regulatory authorities was out of character. She would never have done this before she met Jake. When she was promoted from clinical research auditor to director of clinical research audits a couple of years ago, she was thrilled and satisfied with her job and responsibilities. Wasn't that enough? But, if she was honest with herself, the excitement of her job had dimmed over time. Managing a department meant administration: meetings, performance plans, performance evaluations, audit report reviews, management meetings, and strategy development. All of that diminished what she had enjoyed about her job—auditing. Auditing was investigation that revealed problems—questions to be answered, those responsible identified, corrective actions assigned. Being with Jake in New York had been wonderful. It had also been an adrenaline rush—the murder, the break-in, the take down of the men in the hotel room, the meeting with a director at HSI at Federal Plaza, and the meeting with a Mafia don.

She longed to talk to Jake. It was half past nine, half past four in the afternoon in Philadelphia. Sure, he would tell her that going to St. Margarets was crazy and going up to Wilcox's door was absolutely insane. He would lecture her on the recklessness of her actions. Lastly, he would say she needed to get out of the house and stay somewhere else until he arrived. And he would be right on all counts. No. She needed to sort this out for herself, not act like a helpless woman needing a man to tell her what to do. She would call him later after she got to wherever she decided to stay.

The man at Wilcox's was a good distance from her car when she drove away, although it was possible his car was close enough for him to jump in and tail her. She had not seen anyone following her. He would have been smart and experienced enough to stay far enough behind her to go undetected. In any case, she had to assume he had her registration number, and with it might be able to find her real name and address.

Now, with a heightened sense of urgency, Fiona rushed to her bedroom and threw some clothes and toiletries into a carry-on bag. Something scraped against the house. She stopped and stood still. A weather system was bringing torrential rain. The forecast was for gale warnings in southern England. The wind whistled through the leafless trees in her back garden. Another noise came from outside—a tree limb scraping against the house? On any other night, she would not have noticed. Tonight she was hearing every creak, groan, and scrape.

She grabbed her carry-on bag, briefcase, and handbag. Pulling the hood of her rain jacket over her head, she waited at the open door for a moment. Everything seemed as it always was. Her car was about twenty feet from the door. She unlocked it with the electronic key fob, took one last look around, and shut the door to the house behind her. The rain pelted her in the face. She opened the rear door, flung her things in the back seat, and jumped into the driver's seat. The town of Sevenoaks was only a few miles away. This time of year plenty of rooms would be available. She would be safe there.

Jake had once told her that he never sought out excitement: it had a way of finding him. That was certainly true, and although she found the adrenaline rush and exhilaration addictive, it was exhausting. She hated the incredible anxiety and fear that stimulated the intense fervor. That was her situation with Jake in a nutshell. Being with Jake was thrilling and exciting, yet she could not imagine a life filled with constant worry, apprehension, and fear. Although he never spoke to her about his time as a Navy SEAL, he must have come close to death on more than one of his missions. She had seen and felt the wounds on his body, never asking him about them. How many more times could he cheat death?

28

I NEEDED TO find out what was on that flash drive, but my first priority was to see Rick Middleton. The bank manager tipped someone off to Sarah's request to access the safe deposit box; I was certain of it. Middleton might lead me to the three men involved in the car crash, the one who had been in the getaway car and the two who had driven the SUV into us, and then searched Sarah and me for the flash drive. I swung my legs off the bed and stood up, holding onto the bed for support. The room whirled around me. I steadied myself and took a deep breath before letting go. Bad idea. I stumbled back onto the bed.

I ached all over and my eyes were heavy. *Damn it. What did they give me? I'll rest a few minutes and try again.* I lay back on the bed and closed my eyes. When I opened them, two hours had passed. Still feeling groggy, I phoned DuPont and told him that I had been in an automobile accident with Sarah Goodman in the car.

"We need to talk," I said. "Get your ass over here."

"I'm on my way."

When DuPont arrived, I was sitting up in bed. My head had cleared, and the room had stopped spinning.

"How's Sarah?" DuPont asked.

"I haven't seen her, but the doctor said she's doing fine. Can you check on her? I assume her mother is with her."

"Why was Sarah with you in the car?"

"I saw Delores and Sarah this morning. Delores told me that no one had searched the house for anything of her husband's that might provide a lead, which I found odd. When I asked her where Dennis kept valuables, she took me to a built-in safe and opened it. Inside was an envelope with my name, address, and phone number on it. There was a safe deposit box key in it, nothing else. Sarah went with me to their branch bank and opened the safe deposit box. A computer flash drive was the only thing there."

"Where's the drive now?"

"I have it. The policeman who was just here said that according to witnesses he interviewed, the men who crashed into us dragged Sarah and me out of the car and were searching us when they heard a siren and jumped into a car that appeared to have been waiting for them. They took off before they could find it. The flash drive was in my jacket pocket. I checked—it's still there." I motioned toward the plastic bag containing my clothes.

DuPont looked at the bag and stroked his chin.

"Don't even think about it," I said. "I'm not letting it out of my sight. This may sound a little far-fetched, but when Sarah asked to access the safe deposit box, the bank manager made a call. He said it was to make sure there were no legal issues with her accessing her dead father's safe deposit box. I don't know who he called, but it was no coincidence that SUV crashed into us. They wanted whatever was in that safe deposit box. Do you know what's on that damn flash drive? You'd better not be keeping anything from me."

"I don't know anything about the drive. You know as much or more than I do."

"Bullshit. You and Goodman were close friends. He wouldn't keep something like this from you," I said, raising my voice.

DuPont shut the hospital room door and sat down in the chair beside the bed.

"Dennis called me one night a couple of weeks ago, said he was making progress on the case, and it was much bigger than he had imagined and involved some important people. He had some loose ends to wrap up before he presented the findings to his boss and the US Attorney's office. That's all he said. Before I hung up, he told me I was a good partner, and he always knew I had his back. It was weird, but in retrospect it was like he knew his time might be short."

"His wife told me that you guys never searched his home or his home computer," I said. "Why not?"

"We never use our home computers for work. Never. Doing so puts the family at even more risk than they already are."

"How about his work computer?"

"Our guys scanned it and came up empty."

"Did you check the results?"

"They know what they're doing, Palmer. I trust them to do their job. It's possible that he didn't put anything on the flash drive. Someone may have given it to him with the information already on it."

"Maybe so. But I still don't believe he would keep the only copy of the information on a flash drive in his safe deposit box that contained nothing else. He would have made another copy—on another flash drive or saved it in one of his computers, perhaps within an innocuously named file."

"All right. If it'll make you happy, I'll have tech-ops check the contents of every file on his work computer and home computer. If Delores is still here with Sarah, I'll ask her if I can come by to get it."

"Thank you. Now, I've got to get out of here, see what's on this flash drive and take care of something."

"You're in no shape to go anywhere, not for a day or two anyway. I'll bring my laptop here and we can check out the contents of the flash drive together. What else do you need to do that can't wait a couple of days?"

"You don't want to know."

^ ^ ^ ^

Convincing the doctor to discharge me proved much more difficult than I had anticipated. I had to sign an Against Medical Advice form. My doctor explained that it released the hospital, doctors, pharmacists, and everyone else who worked there from any liability arising from my premature release from the hospital. It was a long legal form, which I signed without reading. Had the doctor known I was an attorney, they would probably have refused to let me go and placed a security guard by the door.

Before I left, DuPont and I checked on Sarah. She was asleep. Delores Goodman, seated beside her, was holding her daughter's hand. Her smile was gone, and her eyes were even more red and puffy than when I saw her that morning, a combination of a mother's concern and lack of sleep. Delores Goodman's husband had been murdered, and her daughter had been in a serious car crash within days of each other. Both happened in close proximity to me.

"The doctor is keeping her overnight for observation," she said quietly, looking at DuPont and me.

"I'm so sorry this happened. I never saw the SUV," I said.

"It wasn't your fault, Mr. Palmer. Sarah told the police officer and me that the vehicle that hit you had run a red light. Nothing you could have done would have prevented it."

As far as Delores and Sarah Goodman knew, the car crash was an accident. I didn't want them to be even more distressed than they already were. The people responsible would be after me, not them. DuPont drove me home. I booted up my laptop with him beside me, staring at the screen. I slid the drive into the USB port and clicked on the external drive icon. A file folder appeared in the center of the screen. There was only one file in the folder. I opened it. A spreadsheet appeared with information arranged in columns: Country, City, Bank, Account Number, Routing Number, Date of Deposit, Date of Withdrawal, Amount Local Currency, Amount US Dollars. Neither of us were accountants, but it was obvious that we were looking at a complex movement of money. I scrolled through several screens before coming to the end and seeing the totals for the currency columns. The grand total was 558 million dollars.

Pointing to the figure, I asked DuPont, "What do you make of that?"

"I make it to be a helluva lot of cash."

I printed two copies, one for DuPont and one for me. As the printer whirred to life, I ejected the drive and handed it to DuPont. "What are you going to do with it?"

"Dennis told me he was working on something big. He had become rather paranoid and fearful. When I tried to talk to him about it, he said we would talk later." DuPont shook his head.

"Is someone in your office on the take?"

"No way. At least I don't believe so. Regardless, I'm taking this straight to FinCEN."

After DuPont left, I took a long, hot shower and changed clothes. There are a lot of germs in hospitals, and I smelled of antiseptics and alcohol. I slumped down in the recliner and called the insurance company to report the accident and get approval for a rental car. I called a different rental car agency than I had used before. A short time later, a rental car driver phoned from the lobby. I took the keys from him and drove to the bank where Sarah and I had gotten the flash drive from the safe deposit box. The list I had printed was folded in my pocket.

I entered the bank and walked straight to Rick Middleton's office. Middleton glanced in my direction and picked up the receiver of his desk phone. I walked in and shut the door behind me. "Put the phone down."

"You can't barge in here," Middleton said, with the desk phone handset still in his hand.

I took it from him, and pushed the disconnect button. "I just did. In case you've forgotten, my name is Jake Palmer. I'm contracted with US Homeland Security Investigations Enforcement. I'm working with Special Agent Jim DuPont, investigating the murder of Special Agent Dennis Goodman and its connection with a global counterfeit medicine operation that is believed to be funding terrorism."

I had no proof the operation was funding terrorism, but when you mention Homeland Security and terrorism in the same sentence, it gets the attention of the person you're speaking to. Middleton was no exception. His eyes widened, and he sat back in his chair. I slapped DuPont's card on his desk, leaving it only long enough for him to see DuPont's name and title and the HSI symbol.

"Who did you call while Sarah Goodman and I were here?"

"I told you. I needed approval for her to access the safe deposit box. I confirmed there was no bank hold on the contents. I had not seen you before and was concerned about you being with Sarah. It didn't seem right to me."

I could understand Middleton's concern about me being with Sarah. He'd never met me, and I'm not the type who accompanies a college coed to the bank to get something from a safe deposit box. I still couldn't buy his need for approval to access the safe deposit box. "After we left here, an SUV T-boned us. The men in the SUV pulled Sarah and me out of the car and were searching us for something. When the police car arrived, they took off. The investigating officer told me the SUV was stolen. Someone tipped those men off, and the only ones who knew we were here were Delores Goodman and you. You can tell me, or we'll subpoena the phone records and see for ourselves. Even if you called someone within the company, that call can be traced."

That might not be true, but Middleton wouldn't know if it wasn't. He massaged his forehead with the fingers of both hands, as if he were trying to ease the excruciating pain of a migraine headache.

"You're wasting my time," I said. It was time to play my trump card. "Based on what we've seen, this Liberty Bank may have been caught up in laundering money. I'll call Agent DuPont and let FinCEN shine a bright light up your ass."

I rose from the chair and walked toward the door, letting what I said sink in. FinCEN paying a visit to a bank would be to bankers what an IRS audit would be to the average taxpayer. And if Liberty Bank was aware of the money laundering, some people were going to jail.

"No! Wait."

With one hand on the door handle, I stopped.

"Sit down," the manager pleaded, shifting his gaze past me and scanning the interior of the bank.

I sat down and stared into his eyes. "I'm waiting."

"We'd been instructed to notify him whenever Mrs. Goodman or her daughter requested access to the box. They are the only ones with authority to do so. In the event we forgot, there was a notice stapled to the signature card. I tore it off before Sarah signed it."

"Who were you instructed to notify?"

Middleton opened a brochure on home mortgages and pointed at the center of the page, pretending to go over the information. "It's complicated and will take some time to explain. Meet me after work. There's a bar twenty minutes from here, the Cracked Bell. I'll meet you at seven thirty. I'll tell you all I know then. I promise."

"Which car is yours?"

"The white Lexus E350."

"Let me see your car keys. Just set them on the desk."

The manager took his keys from his pants pocket and tossed them on the desk. One of the keys had a forward-leaning "L" within an oval, the Lexus symbol.

"I'll need something from you before I agree to meet—the name."

"OK, but you can't contact him until after we talk. His name is Ray Addison, one of our senior executive vice presidents."

"I'm warning you. If you don't show, I *will* find you," I said, glaring at him.

Once outside the bank, I spotted the white Lexus and doubled-checked to be certain there were no other ones like it parked at the bank. I moved my car beside the Lexus, parking on the right of it and away from the bank building. I grabbed a bag from the back seat and extracted a small black box about the size of a pack of cigarettes, opened the door and got out. I reached above and behind the right rear tire. The strong magnet on the back of the box snapped it against the wheel well. Before driving away, I opened an app on my phone, which showed a map with my current location indicated by a blue dot. The flashing red dot beside it was Middleton's car. The device was working.

^^^^

The Cracked Bell had the vibe of a bar where I would like to hang out. It was dimly lit with two flat screen televisions over the bar, both with the sound muted and closed caption text scrolling across the bottom of the screens. The bar was almost full, and all but a few of the tables were occupied with couples or families eating dinner.

I sipped on a pint of Victory Prima Pils, a local beer. The manager was ten minutes late. *No way he forgot about the meeting. Where is he?* I opened the tracking device app. The red dot was about halfway between the bank and the Cracked Bell in what looked like a residential area. It wasn't moving. I slid a ten under my glass, waved at the bartender and left. I drove toward the dot. The Lexus still wasn't moving. Maybe Middleton removed the tracker. I turned off the main road into a neighborhood and slowed as I neared the red dot's location. There was the Lexus, a few hundred yards ahead. A quick Internet search on my phone confirmed that it was Rick Middleton's home address.

When I walked up the driveway toward the Lexus, a spotlight, triggered by a motion detector over the garage door came on. There were two round holes in the driver's side window about two-thirds the way up. Spider webs of cracked glass radiated outward from them. One was lower than the other. A kill shot and an insurance shot.

"Oh crap," I whispered and eased closer to the car.

A man in the driver's seat was slumped to the right, his body held up by the shoulder harness. There was an entry wound in the left side of the head and another in his chest. I moved to the front to get a better look at the victim's face. It was Middleton.

My first call was to the 911 operator. My second was to DuPont.

29

THE HOMES IN Middleton's suburban neighborhood were of modest size on small lots. It was seven thirty. The lights were on in most of the houses, including the ones on both sides of this house. The shooter would have had a sound suppressor on his pistol; otherwise, the neighbors would have heard the gunshots and investigated. The closest streetlight was a half-block away, providing enough light for what I needed to see. The bank manager's car was not running. Middleton was killed after he got into his car but before he started it and put it into gear.

I removed the tracking device from the wheel well and stuffed it in my pocket. Looking through the driver's side window, I noticed something sticking out of Middleton's jacket pocket. So as not to disturb the crime scene, I slipped on my gloves and tried the passenger's side door. It was unlocked. I slid in, removed the glove from my right hand and felt Middleton's neck for a pulse. As I suspected, he was dead. I extracted a sheet of paper from his pocket. On it was a list of Liberty Bank account numbers arranged in columns. I put the paper into my pocket where I had the printout of account numbers from the flash drive. I didn't have time to check to see if Middleton's account numbers were among those on the spreadsheet. I put my glove back on and backed out of the car and shut the door. Looking down at the driveway, I walked around the car, and then got on my knees and looked underneath. No shell casings. Either the shooter was using a revolver, or he gathered up the spent shell casings. A pro leaves no evidence behind.

I went to the front door and rang the doorbell. When there was no answer, I tried to open it. It was locked. The distant sounds of sirens disturbed the quiet night. Agent DuPont arrived first and skidded to a halt in front of the house.

"Looks like a professional hit," I told him. "Two shots through the windshield, most likely from a pistol with a silencer. Otherwise the neighbors would have heard. No brass either."

"Tell the police what you told me on the phone. You had an appointment to meet with the bank manager. He didn't show so you drove to his home. You found him and, after checking to confirm he was dead, called 911. Did you retrieve the tracking device?"

"Got it."

"Give it to me in case they search you and your car. They don't need to know who I am. That would be tough to explain. I'll play the nosey neighbor. When you leave, I'll follow you."

A police car with emergency lights flashing screeched to a halt on the street in front of the house. Before the two officers got out of the patrol car, the ambulance arrived. Another police car pulled up behind the ambulance. I told my story to one of the policemen while the EMTs gathered around the car. One of them confirmed the bank manager was dead. Within minutes, television and newspaper reporters arrived, and neighbors, who had been watching from their windows, ventured out for a closer look. A television reporter was interviewing one of them.

I repeated my story several times before the police were through with me. When asked why he was meeting with me, I told them about getting T-boned after I left the bank and said Middleton asked to meet at the bar for a drink after work. The police searched my car, with my permission, found my pistols, and much to my annoyance, kept them to run ballistics tests to compare with the bullets recovered from Middleton's body.

They also took gunshot residue, samples from my hands and jacket. Luckily, I was not wearing the same jacket I had worn in Welwyn Heights a few days ago.

DuPont was standing, along with several of the neighbors, outside the yellow crime scene tape that the police had strung around the bank manager's yard. As soon as the police finished with me, I brushed by the TV reporters shouting at me for a comment for the eleven o'clock news. I drove off with DuPont following close behind.

I pulled into a gas station parking lot a few miles from the house. DuPont got in the car with me.

"That went very well," DuPont said, shaking his head. "So that's what you were doing after you left the hospital. You said I didn't want to know. "

I handed him my list of account numbers from the flash drive and the list from Middleton's jacket pocket.

"What's this?" DuPont asked.

"I pulled it from Middleton's pocket. I haven't had a chance to compare it with Goodman's spreadsheet."

DuPont scanned the spreadsheet, looking for the Liberty Bank & Trust account numbers from Middleton's list.

"I'll be damned," DuPont said, tapping the index finger of his right hand on the list I took from Middleton's body. "I'll check it when I get home, but at least some of the Liberty Bank & Trust accounts are on the spreadsheet Goodman had. You need to get on this right away."

"I know," I said.

"Email me a scanned copy of the Liberty Bank & Trust account numbers when you get home. Stay in touch." He handed me the lists and left.

Before I put my car in gear, my phone rang. Thinking it might be Fiona, I answered.

"Jake, do you have a few minutes? I need to talk to you." It was my father. There was an uncharacteristic nervousness in his voice, and he was calling me, which was even more uncharacteristic. Something was up.

"Sure? Everything okay?"

"I've got a bad feeling, son."

"Problems with the new bride already?"

"No. She's amazing. It's the client I mentioned to you. Is it safe to talk over the phone?"

"Where are you calling from?"

"I'm on the room phone in our hotel in London. Michelle is in the other room getting ready for dinner."

"Nothing's ever totally safe, but it should be okay."

My father took a deep breath and exhaled. "I'm not proud of what I've done, but I've laundered money for this client. I told him that what we had done was a federal crime and that we could go to jail, if convicted."

"Stop! Don't say another word. Hang up, go somewhere outside your room, and call me on your cell phone."

My father disconnected the call. I waited for him to call back.

"Okay. I'm in the hallway on my cell phone. Is this really necessary? You said the room phone was safe."

"Yes, it's safe for most things a father would tell his son. It's not safe for admitting that you've committed a federal crime. Who's the client?"

"Richard Moore, president and CEO of HealthTech."

"HealthTech. The drug distribution company?"

"Right. It's a drug distribution conglomerate."

And the same one that had shipped counterfeit Transpro from Civitavecchia, Italy, to Abercrombie's warehouse via the Port of New York. Maybe that wasn't too big of a leap because they ship a lot of drugs to a lot of places, and the counterfeit Transpro may have gotten into HealthTech's inventory without anyone's knowledge. Medicines pass through a complex network, changing hands multiple times between the manufacturer and the patient. There are repackagers, primary and secondary wholesalers, distributors, and retail outlets.

"This morning I met with him face-to-face for the first time. When I began talking to him about what we were doing, he became more and more agitated. Finally, I asked him where the cash was going. He said it was none of my business, and if I wanted out, all I had to do was say so. I said that perhaps that was the most reasonable course of action for us both. He said that was fine. We'd wrap up things over the next couple of months. I've been looking over my shoulder ever since."

"Why the hell did you do it? You should've reported this to the authorities as soon as you realized what he really wanted you to do," I shouted.

My father said nothing in response. He knew he had screwed up. I did not need to remind him.

"I was worried about the meeting with Moore. That's why I

gave you my itinerary, just in case something happened to me."

"But why?" I asked. "Why take him on as a client in the first place?"

"Patrick made some very bad investments. He almost took down the firm. Were it not for Richard Moore and HealthTech, Palmer Global Investments would have gone under. When Moore approached me about managing HealthTech's investment portfolio, it seemed like a godsend."

"Then what happened?"

"It's complicated. I knew the arrangement was somewhat dubious. You know what they say. 'If it's too good to be true, it probably is.' Well, soon after the contract was signed, he asked me to do something I knew was wrong. Initially, it was depositing and moving small amounts of cash between some bank accounts. I knew that was smurfing and highly illegal. However, I believed if I was careful, the feds would never know. In the big scheme of things, it wasn't all that much, a few hundred thousand dollars at most. It's a fairly labor intensive way to launder money. I managed the entire process through our company server, which I now know was stupid, and used some smurfs to make deposits and withdrawals. Then things got worse. He told me to move very large sums between some offshore shell companies. I said no, and he became angry. He said he would report the smurfing activity to the Treasury Department and said I'd done it without his knowledge or permission.

"Shell companies, I understand. What is smurfing and smurfs?"

"It's depositing and withdrawing money in sums of less than ten thousand dollars, so that the bank does not have to report it to the government. However, the US Bank Secrecy Act requires bank officials report suspicious activity, even if the amounts are under ten thousand. Smurfs are the runners used to make the deposits."

I didn't like where this was going. My father was up to his ass in a huge money-laundering scheme for a company that was connected in one form or the other to a global counterfeit medicine operation.

"Do you have a listing of the banks and accounts you used to launder the money?" I asked.

"I don't keep them with me."

"Was Liberty Bank & Trust one of the banks?"

"Most of the banks used for small deposits and withdrawals were in New York, New Jersey, and Pennsylvania. I believe Liberty was one of the banks. I would need to log onto my database and check to be certain."

"Do it. I'll hang on. If it is one of the banks you used, say okay. I'll give a few account numbers. Say only yes or no after each one."

I heard the room door open and shut, and the clicking sound of his fingers hitting the laptop keyboard.

"Okay," my father said.

I read five of the account numbers. There was a pause after each one before he replied yes. I told him to go back into the hallway and waited until he was there.

"The Liberty Bank & Trust account numbers matched. How did you get them?"

"That was only a sample," I said. "There's more. A bank manager in Wayne, just outside Philadelphia, gave them to me."

Of course, he didn't actually give them to me. I took the list off his dead body before the police arrived. My dad was frightened enough already. It was best not to tell him that the bank manager had been murdered.

"I still don't understand," he said. "Why would he give you that list?"

"I'll tell you later. You and Michelle get out of London."

"Our flight to Italy is tomorrow afternoon."

"No Dad, leave now!"

"I can't. We're having dinner with Moore tonight, here at the hotel. He doesn't discuss business in public places, so we should be okay."

"See if you can get on an early morning flight to Italy."

"He'll know we're leaving. He's paying for the room," my father said.

"Don't check out. Just leave."

"Is that really necessary?"

"Yes! And remove the battery from your old phone so there's no possibility he can track you. When you get to Italy, buy a contract phone and call me."

Dad had used Liberty Bank & Trust to launder HealthTech's money. The accounts were in the Palmer Global Investments' system and were on Dennis Goodman's list on the flash drive. I'd bet everything I owned that Goodman's list of banks and accounts matched those my father used to launder the money. Had Goodman tracked HealthTech's laundered money to Palmer Global Investments and my father? Is that why Goodman wanted me on the case? Damn right it was. That would be just like him. I needed to talk to Dad about it when I saw him. Although nothing he had said made me think Moore would harm him, when hundreds of millions of dollars are involved, shit happens that you don't expect. My father was in way over his head and had done things that would land him in jail for a long time. I saw no way out for him. For a man accustomed to five-star hotel suites and restaurants, I couldn't imagine him in jail, even one of the white-collar crime Club Feds. But there was something even more bizarre. My father had confided in me, asked for my help—and called me "son."

∧∧∧∧

Richard Moore was in the rear seat of his chauffeur-driven Bentley making good progress through the evening traffic snarl from his home in Holland Park to the Palmer and Petrochelli's hotel in Mayfair. Unknown to them, the honeymoon suite was bugged. The day before they checked in, three men from Moore's security team went to the hotel, telling the hotel manager they were conducting a check on the hotel room where Moore's guests, Edward Palmer and Michelle Petrochelli, would be staying.

A lone hotel security guard went with them. Once inside, Moore's men split up; one talked with the guard, while the other two, who were experts in audio surveillance, went into the rooms of the suite and planted listening devices. By the time they left, a listening device had been planted in each room of the suite, including the bathroom. Moore's security team monitored the audio day and night. It was not that Moore suspected any problems with Palmer at that time. He believed the monitoring of people who could do you harm was simply good business practice.

When Palmer got cold feet and told Moore that he wanted to terminate his HealthTech contract, Moore alerted his men monitoring the audio to be especially vigilant and report anything unusual or incriminating. It didn't take long. The team picked up a telephone conversation between him and his son Jake, during which Edward Palmer admitted to laundering money. Jake instructed him to go outside the room and call him back on his cell phone. The sound of a door shutting was heard. A minute or so later Edward Palmer reentered the room and was heard saying yes a number of times, presumably in response to questions from Jake on the cell phone. Moore's team had researched Jake Palmer and found he was an ex-Navy SEAL, who was now an investigative consultant and who had recently been involved in a raid on a terrorist cell in Virginia.

Moore contacted Utkin in the US and filled him in on the developments. He told him that Edward Palmer had cold feet, and he was concerned Palmer would go to the authorities. Moore and Utkin had worked together long enough to understand how each other thought on matters such as this. Dennis Goodman had been investigating the counterfeit medicine operation and had to be stopped. Moore had hoped that was the end of it. Now, Edward Palmer had terminated his contract and talked to his son about money laundering. Had he told anyone else?

Utkin told him that his man in Rome would get Palmer and his wife to a safe place and hold them there until he arrived. He said people like Edward Palmer were strangers to pain and did not fully understand its power.

Although Utkin did whatever Moore asked of him, something about this man made Moore uncomfortable, like keeping a wild animal as a pet. It is loyal and friendly until one day it turns on you.

30

I WAS IN the wrong place. With my father, Michelle, and Fiona in London, I needed to be there. First, I had to meet with DuPont, so I called and arranged to see him. He seemed eager to see me. Something was up.

"Before we get started, there's something I want to show you." DuPont, sitting behind his desk, spun his laptop around so we could both see the screen. "I called our liaison in the police department to follow up on the bank manager's murder. After we left, the police did a door-to-door check and talked to Middleton's neighbors to see if anyone saw or heard anything. No one did. However, the neighbor across the street has a security camera. Here's the footage."

Because it was taken at night, the video image was grainy. Middleton could be seen leaving his house. Then the motion detector light over the garage came on. The light washed out much of the image and made individuals unidentifiable. The manager got into his car and closed the door. As he did, a man came into view and walked quickly to the driver's side window. He aimed a pistol and two flashes could be seen, the shots that killed Middleton.

"It's not clear enough to identify the shooter. Keep watching."

I watched as DuPont sped up the video until another figure appeared, and then he hit play.

"That's me," I said.

On the video I could be seen getting the tracker from the wheel well and reaching into the car.

"There's more," DuPont said.

DuPont was seen arriving, talking to me, and walking away before the ambulance arrived.

"The video is being analyzed and enhanced by the police technicians. They can do some amazing things with today's technology. So, when confronted with video, I confessed that the two men seen talking to each other were you and me. They would have found out eventually. I played the federal investigation card and said you were working with me and had placed a tracking device on the bank manager's car. You reached into the car to check his pulse and confirm he was dead. I also told them you phoned me, and I arrived moments before anyone else. As far as the police know, Rick Middleton was involved in a crime that may be connected to the death of Agent Goodman. The police are taking the lead on the investigation of Middleton's death and, at some point, will need to talk to both of us. I've put them off for now."

"I need my guns back."

"I have them," DuPont said. "They ran a ballistics test and confirmed the bullets that killed Middleton did not come from either of your guns."

"Was there ever any doubt? I need them."

"You can have them when you leave."

"Have you had time to determine if the Liberty Bank & Trust accounts from Middleton's list are included in those from Goodman's flash drive?"

"Not yet. I've set aside some time to go over all the data before I meet with the FinCEN guys in New York tomorrow."

In agreeing to work with HSI, I had demanded that DuPont be upfront with me, tell me the truth and withhold no information. The same held true for me. And that was my dilemma. DuPont needed to know that in all likelihood, Goodman had uncovered that the counterfeit medicine operation was generating huge sums of money that my father and Palmer Global Investments was laundering. And one of the banks used to launder the money was Liberty Bank & Trust. The problem was before I could do that, Dad needed to confess what he had done to the feds and report Richard Moore and HealthTech's financial indiscretions. Otherwise, I was ratting out my own father, which from a criminal justice perspective was far worse than him turning himself in and cooperating with the authorities.

"I may have some more information on that front. I need to check it out first."

"Don't wait too long," DuPont said. "Things are moving fast."

"Is it possible the money generated from the counterfeit medicine operation is funding terrorism?"

"Absolutely. Why do you ask?"

"Just curious. That's one of the reasons FinCEN checks out counterfeit drug cases. Most are nothing and they drop them. On rare occasions, they find evidence of money laundering with the cash eventually going to terrorist organizations."

"Ask your spook friends if they've heard any chatter related to a planned terrorist attack or movements of large sums of cash."

"There's always chatter related to a terrorist attack. And the spooks, as you call them, aren't really the sharing type. I'll call my friend at the National Security Agency and let him know what we've found and see if I can convince him to open up."

I leaned back in the chair, my arms folded, tapping my foot, saying nothing.

"What?" DuPont asked.

"What are you waiting for? Call him."

"Wait outside," DuPont said, pointing to the office door.

A few minutes later, DuPont motioned for me to return.

"NSA's heard some rumblings from Pakistan on the dark net," DuPont said. "Nothing specific or particularly worrisome."

"What the hell is the dark net?"

"If the Internet is an iceberg, the small piece above the water would be the information most people access every day. The massive irregularly-shaped piece below the surface would be the dark net, the underbelly of the Internet, accessible only by software programs such as TOR, "The Onion Router," which connects a user to the dark Internet, encrypting the IP address so that it's almost impossible to trace a user's browsing or buying history."

"The damn Internet will be the ruination of civilization," I said.

"I don't know about the ruination of civilization, but it presents new and difficult challenges for law enforcement, as well as some opportunities."

DuPont's phone rang. He answered and pointed to the door. I paced outside his office while I waited. DuPont was on a speakerphone and doing something on his computer. A few minutes later, he motioned me in again.

"This is getting old," I said.

"The police finished enhancing the video of the night the bank manager was shot. They identified the shooter as Viktor Utkin, a former Russian Spetsnaz operative."

"Spetsnaz?"

"Right. What do you know about them?" DuPont asked.

"Spetsnaz is Russian Special Purpose Forces, some say equivalent to the US Navy's SEALs and Army's Delta Force. They are the most ruthless military unit in the world and arguably the best at close quarters combat."

"Viktor Utkin has quite a reputation. The Spetsnaz senior officers couldn't control him, and he was discharged in the late nineties with a chest full of ribbons and more kills than anyone dared count. Utkin put himself out for hire and has had no trouble finding work. Much of it has been within Russia, contract work for Spetsnaz, as well as some clandestine work for Russian Federation's Federal Security Service, or FSB, a successor organization for the KGB. He also did some work for the Russian mafia. Rumor has it that he's contracted himself out full time to a corporate client."

"All the more reason I need to get be in London. You can follow up on Abercrombie's drug distribution facility and the account numbers without my help. Fiona has gotten involved in the counterfeit medicine case, and my father and Michelle may be in trouble. I'm worried about them. Let me know what you learn from FinCEN tomorrow, and if you hear anything else from your NSA buddy or hear anything about Utkin's movements. I'll only be gone for a few days."

"When are you leaving?"

"Tonight, on the British Airways flight to Heathrow. I'll be at the Milestone Hotel in London. You can reach me on my cell."

DuPont scribbled down the name of the hotel. "Jake, don't

get too worked up. Nothing we have points toward anything other than some big-time, white-collar financial crime and some Internet chatter that's probably totally unrelated. Utkin's just a hired gun who's probably the muscle for the counterfeit medicine operation."

"Financial crime is one thing. Financial crime funding terrorism is another," I said. "And with Utkin involved, the stakes just got a lot higher."

"We have no intel to support terrorism, but I'm going to follow through on a hunch today." DuPont scrubbed his face with his hand, looked to me and said, "I'll let you know if I find out anything."

"One more thing, what's going to happen with Abercrombie's warehouse?"

"We're going in."

I left DuPont's office with my pistols. When I got in my car, I called Jefferson.

"What's up?" he said.

"The feds are going to raid the warehouse. Make yourself scarce and be careful. I'm leaving the country for a few days. I'll be in touch when I get back. If you need me, you can reach me on the number I gave you."

"I owe you one, Sharpshooter."

31

THE BRITISH AIRWAYS Boeing 747 took off from Philadelphia International Airport. I closed my eyes and took a few deep breaths, trying in vain to bring my thoughts inward and, if only for a moment, free my mind from worry.

Earlier in the day, I completed my report to the Philadelphia Fraud Control Unit, omitting any detailed information about the warehouse. I wrote that it appeared to be a medicine repackaging and distribution center that Abercrombie had set up to reduce the cost of drugs to his patients and make money through further distribution. I said that HSI Special Agent DuPont was looking into the operation. I told DuPont I had included his name in the report so he would not be blindsided when the FCU contacted him. I also sent Fiona an email with my travel itinerary and attached a copy of the invoice from Abercrombie's warehouse, which identified the origin of the Transpro as the Port of Civitavecchia.

I managed a few hours of sleep on the flight. When the plane pulled into the gate at Heathrow, I switched on my phone and checked my messages. My father had called from his new contract phone number to say he and Michelle had arrived at their hotel in Rome. Fiona left a message for me to call her at B&A's London office. I picked up my rental car and drove to the Milestone Hotel. After checking in, I called Fiona and arranged to meet her for lunch. Then I called my father. He answered on the first ring.

"Did you have any trouble getting out of London yesterday?" I asked.

"None at all. We left without checking out. I phoned the hotel this morning and settled the bill. By now, Moore knows we're gone."

"Does he know you're in Italy?"

"The press release of our wedding stated that we were honeymooning in London and in Italy, but we never revealed any of the specifics."

"Michelle is more newsworthy than you," I said. "One paparazzi photo of her, and your location will no longer be a secret. It's only a matter of time. Stay out of sight."

"We're on our honeymoon, and Michelle's not exactly the stay-in-the-room type. Publicity and public exposure are her drugs of choice. Moore's men won't have to look too hard. The Italian paparazzi have contacts at every hotel and resort, and those contacts know they're in for a big payday if they report our location. We have two bodyguards from a security firm that Michelle's modeling agency has on retainer. When we're in, one stays outside our room and one is posted in the lobby. When we're out, they follow us around like ducks. What else can we possibly do?"

My father was frustrated and tense. He was accustomed to being in control. As much as I needed and wanted to be with Fiona, my concern for my father was increasing.

"Any chance of leaving early and returning to New York?"

His father gave a nervous laugh. "No way that's happening. You know that. We have the family luncheon at her relative's home outside Rome and then a formal party at one of the shops near here that sells the lingerie Michelle models. Then we're off to Positano. There's been no publicity about the family luncheon or about our going to Positano, but the party at the shop is no secret."

"That's not good. Be careful. If you notice anything suspicious, call me. Better yet, check in with me two or three times a day, regardless of what's happening." I took a deep breath. "I have to ask you something, and I need you to tell me the absolute truth."

"Of course. Anything."

"Other than me, who knows about Richard Moore and the accounts list you accessed on HealthTech's system?"

When he hesitated, I knew he had told someone. "Who knows?" I repeated emphatically.

"I swore I wouldn't tell anyone. I could get into a lot of trouble if I do."

"You're already in a lot of trouble. If you want my help, I need to know. Otherwise, you're on your own."

"A few days before the wedding, a man I had never met came to my office. He said he was working with the government agencies that investigate counterfeiting, human trafficking, and financial crime, among other things."

"HSI—Homeland Security Investigations?"

"Yeah, that's it. He talked to me about a case he was working on. There was a young kid with him, who worked at the agency that investigated financial crimes."

"FinCEN? The Financial Crimes Enforcement Network?" I asked.

"That's it. He had been tracking the funds generated by an international counterfeit drug operation. The trail led him to my firm—to me. I tried to put him off, saying my clients were confidential, but he wasn't buying it. He said he was going to serve a warrant if I didn't cooperate. Said he would make a call and sit there in my office until the warrant arrived. That would have been all that my firm needed. If my clients got wind of it, we'd be finished. So I downloaded the account numbers onto a flash drive and gave it to him. I told him I would cooperate, if he could wait until I got back from our honeymoon."

"Was it Agent Dennis Goodman?"

"How did you know?"

"He was murdered outside my hotel the afternoon before your wedding. Didn't you hear about it on the news?"

"No! My God. I didn't have time to read the paper or watch the news. There was the rehearsal dinner party that evening, the wedding the next day, and then we flew to London. Are you sure it was him?"

"I worked with Goodman on a case a few years ago. He showed up at the hotel bar where I was having a drink while I waited for

Fiona to get ready for the rehearsal dinner. When I asked him how he knew I was in town, he said he read that you were getting married and assumed I would be attending the wedding. He talked to me about working on the case with him. I said I would think about it. He was shot outside the entrance to the hotel."

"I thought you worked for pharmaceutical companies."

"You really don't know what I do, do you?"

"Some kind of private investigator. How am I supposed to know?"

"Regardless, the fact you've been in contact with the feds makes this more serious than it already was. Who did you say the young man was, the one who investigated the funding of terrorist organizations?"

"I didn't say. He didn't give me a card. I assumed he worked with Goodman."

"Remember his name?"

"I believe it was van Buren, like the US president. Don't recall his first name. He had long blond hair. Goodman jokingly called him the White Jesus or something like that."

I lay on the bed with my hands behind my head, staring at the ceiling. *Seek Jesus.* Just like Goodman to throw out an ambiguous and misleading clue. *Van Buren, aka White Jesus.* Van Buren had tracked the money to Palmer Global Investments, and he and Goodman went to see my father. During their conversation, the wedding must have come up and Dad mentioned that I was going to be in town with my girlfriend from London. I doubt Dad would have remembered Fiona's name. Goodman didn't let on that he knew me. Sad to say, Goodman knew more about what I did for a living than did my own father. That's how Goodman found me at the hotel in New York and explained how he knew my "lady friend" was from London. As improbable as this mess had become, the pieces were finally coming together. I had to get moving. I texted DuPont, telling him that White Jesus was van Buren at FinCEN and had been working with Goodman. He sent a reply within seconds.

"Was planning to go today. Will call and make appointment with van Buren. Who told you?"

"My father. Goodman's account list came from him. Long story. Van Buren will fill you in."

^ ^ ^ ^

After parking at B&A headquarters, I phoned Fiona to let her know I was there. She met me at the front desk and waited while I checked in and received my visitor's badge. We went to one of the employee restaurants on the ground floor of the building to talk. It was more informal than her office, and we would be less likely to be overheard by her colleagues.

"I'm glad you're here," Fiona said. "I've been worried ever since we spoke. We need to talk."

After some small talk, Fiona told me about her meeting with Sue Cooper, going to Wilcox's home in St Margarets, and her encounter with the man who was with him. All I could do was shake my head. "What were you thinking?"

"In retrospect, I guess I wasn't thinking. I'm so glad you're here now."

"Any sign of the mystery man since then?"

"None. But I haven't been back to my house."

"Good. You need to stay with me at the Milestone."

"I was hoping you would say that. I checked out of the hotel in Sevenoaks. My bag's in the car. How are your father and Michelle?"

I filled her in on my father's meeting with Richard Moore in London, including my suspicion that Moore was a dangerous man. I also told her what my father said about Agent Goodman and about FinCEN, van Buren, White Jesus, and the list of accounts.

"Dad and Michelle are in Rome now. He said he would check in with me two or three times a day to let me know they're okay. My father is already in enough trouble with the feds. If Moore finds out he gave that list of accounts to a federal agent, he's a dead man walking. And there's one more thing."

"There's always one more thing with you, Jake. What is it?"

I told Fiona about going to Dennis Goodman's home, the flash drive, the wreck, and about being treated at the hospital. I think she took it pretty well.

"Are you all right?" she said.

"I'm 100 percent." That was a bit of a stretch. It was more like 80 percent. I still ached in places I didn't know I had.

"No you're not. You've been knocked unconscious. You shouldn't have left the hospital, and you certainly shouldn't be flying about."

"I'd be concerned about repeated brain injury leading to dementia if I thought I would live long enough to develop it."

"That's not funny."

32

AFTER RECEIVING JAKE'S cryptic text, DuPont called FinCEN's New York office and made an appointment with Branson van Buren. On the train ride to New York, DuPont did some online research into van Buren's background and made some calls to his contacts within FinCEN, asking about van Buren's experience and competence. It was time well spent. Soon after van Buren graduated from the Raymond A. Mason School of Business at the College of William and Mary in Williamsburg, Virginia, he landed an internship with FinCEN. Six months later, he was hired as an intelligence research specialist within the division supporting domestic and international law enforcement agencies in combating money laundering and other financial crimes. DuPont's FinCEN contacts told him that van Buren and been with FinCEN for three years and was a rising star within the agency, a reputation earned by working longer and harder than anyone they had ever seen. Van Buren, they said, had no social life from what they could see. On his time off, he played club rugby and worked out at a martial arts gym. Unlike most others in his position, he was quick to seek out opportunities to go into the field—the more dangerous the better.

Van Buren was sifting through some notes on his desk when DuPont walked into his office.

"So you're White Jesus."

"I'm afraid so. It's the hair," van Buren said, pointing to his shoulder-length, platinum-blond hair. "And you're HSI Agent Jim DuPont, the new case agent on the counterfeit medicine case that Agent Goodman and I were working on. You don't know how glad I am to meet you." Van Buren glanced at his watch. "You're early."

"If you're on time, you're late. That's my philosophy."

Branson van Buren was unlike any FinCEN forensic accountant that DuPont had ever seen. He was close to six feet tall and weighed about one hundred eighty pounds, most of which appeared to be muscle. His hair alone was enough to distinguish him from most accountants with whom DuPont had worked.

"We have a lot to discuss," DuPont said. "I'm especially interested in what you know about a list of financial accounts that Edward Palmer gave you and Goodman."

"It's a long story."

"So I understand."

"My supervisor came into my office one day and told me that I would be working with an HSI special agent on a counterfeit medicine case. It was a new area for me, so I was excited by the opportunity. Counterfeit medicine cases, my supervisor said, were often run through the FinCEN because they likely involved money laundering. Following a cursory review and analysis, most were eliminated or given a low priority. However, if something of substance was discovered during the initial screening, the case was tagged for further investigation. This case had all the makings of one of those."

"Is that when you met Dennis Goodman?"

"That's right. Agent Goodman had proof that the death of a Philadelphia child following a kidney transplant was associated with counterfeit Transpro. He was confident that the medicine had come into the country from Europe through the Port of New York, although it had probably been manufactured in India or Africa. He also noted the child was the nephew of the don of a New York Mafia family. Because the counterfeit version of the drug entered the US at the Port of New York and because he needed to work closely with FinCEN, Goodman spent much of his time working out of ICE's office here in New York, so much so that he believed they were trying to have him transferred here so they could get credit for the case."

"When did Edward Palmer enter the picture?" DuPont asked.

"Agent Goodman determined that HealthTech, a global drug distribution company, had distributed the counterfeit drug. Using FinCEN financial tracking technology and tools, I detected a high volume of account activity by Palmer Global Investments on behalf of HealthTech and its shell companies. Armed with that information, Agent Goodman and I paid an unannounced visit to Edward Palmer at PGI."

"So both of you went to PGI?"

"Correct. At that point, I had only touched the surface, so it was more of a fishing expedition than anything else. Goodman was awesome to watch. Edward Palmer was very calm and professional at first. Then, Goodman began to ramp up the pressure. The more pressure Goodman applied, the more Palmer squirmed in his chair. For me, it was a master class in interrogation. Believing that we already had enough evidence to put him away and thinking his only way out was to cooperate, Palmer caved. He agreed to help us build a case against Richard Moore, the owner and president of HealthTech, if we would wait until he returned from his honeymoon and if we promised him immunity from prosecution. Goodman didn't promise him anything but hinted that if the information he provided led to arrest of those responsible, the federal prosecutors would look favorably on his cooperation. Palmer said that he and his fiancée would be honeymooning in Europe, and he had a meeting scheduled with Richard Moore while there. He might be able to obtain more information. As a measure of good faith, Palmer downloaded the account information onto a flash drive and gave it to Agent Goodman. I have to say that Palmer was contrite. Moore had him do a couple of shady things, but that rapidly mushroomed. Once Palmer crossed the line, there was no going back, and before he knew it, he was in way over his head. There's a meeting on the books with Palmer after he returns from his honeymoon."

DuPont tapped his fingers on the arm of chair. Jake had talked to his father and knew most or all of what van Buren was telling him, at least from his father's perspective. *Why didn't he call me and tell me this instead of sending me that text?* "Right.

Let's keep that on the calendar for now, except it will be you and me meeting with him."

"After we left PGI, I pressed Goodman regarding his lack of concern about Edward Palmer being a flight risk. Goodman said the risk of Palmer fleeing was small because he wanted immunity and the only way to get that was by cooperating with us. Goodman said he had considered having Palmer work with an agent in our London office and wear a wire when he met with Moore, but decided that was too risky."

"What happened to the flash drive?" DuPont asked.

"When we returned to the office, I downloaded the information from the flash drive onto my computer and reviewed it. The earlier dated transfers were made using regional and community banks in the Northeast. They were glad to have the business and less likely to meet anti-money laundering standards. As I dug through the accounts, I detected a pattern. Initially, the transfers of money between the accounts and banks were frequent and small, less than ten thousand dollars each, keeping it under the federal reporting requirement radar. From what he could tell, Palmer Global Investments had established all of the accounts and passed money through them. Each deposit and withdrawal was less than $10,000, a process referred to as smurfing. The task was daunting, like unraveling a knotted ball of twine one thread at a time. Then Palmer Global Investments began to move large sums of money into corporate accounts, most of them located in the Cayman Islands. I confirmed and documented each transaction. Also I researched those companies and found that most were shell companies with little or no assets or operations. It was tedious work but exciting. Meanwhile, Goodman was working with the US Attorney's office to build a case against HealthTech."

"I have two lists of bank accounts related to the counterfeit medicine case," DuPont said. "One, a list of accounts from Liberty Bank in Philadelphia, appears to be a subset of those on a large spreadsheet, which we discovered on a flash drive in Goodman's safe deposit box."

"That is probably the same flash drive Edward Palmer gave us the day we met with him," van Buren said. "After we downloaded it onto our system, Goodman kept it. Oh, there's one more thing.

Goodman said he needed an experienced investigator to do some legwork, something I was pleased to hear. However, I was surprised when Goodman said the person he had in mind was Edward Palmer's son. I raised the issue of conflict of interest, but Goodman explained that he and Jake Palmer had worked together in the past and he owed Jake Palmer a favor. Goodman assured me everything would be fine because it wasn't Edward Palmer they were after. It was the person behind the entire operation, Richard Moore."

"Jake Palmer is working with me now. I believe Dennis may have had other reasons to bring Jake in, like to be certain his father did the right thing and to protect his father from harm."

"The last time I saw Agent Goodman, he left, saying he was meeting with Jake Palmer to convince him to work with HSI on this case. I haven't tried to contact Palmer since Goodman's death. A couple of days before Goodman was shot, he warned me to be careful. He seemed nervous as a cat. He felt certain someone was tailing him."

"He had good instincts," DuPont said.

"Can you send me the list of account numbers? I want to compare them to the ones I have to confirm it is indeed the same list."

"You'll have them as soon as I get back to the office," DuPont said.

"So what now?"

DuPont smiled. "Have you ever been to Italy?"

33

EDWARD PALMER AND Michelle Petrochelli's five-star hotel atop Rome's Spanish Steps was popular with celebrity guests. Not only was the location one of the best in Rome, the staff knew how to keep the admiring public and the paparazzi at bay. However, the hotel staff could only do so much. So, Michelle contacted her Italian agent, who had the security company used by the modeling agency assign two bodyguards to protect them. She was one of the agent's most important clients. Providing protection was cheap insurance.

Palmer had not looked forward to the Petrochelli family luncheon; part of him dreaded it. His wife had warned him that many of her extended family spoke little or no English. However, he had a fantastic time. The food was spectacular, and the overwhelming sense of family and love, both of which he realized were missing from his life, had surprised him. Their welcome was as warm and genuine as the bear hugs he received, and he had never seen Michelle so relaxed.

Back at the hotel, they took advantage of the sunny, crisp winter day to walk, accompanied by their bodyguards, through the Villa Borghese Gardens. Along the way, Michelle asked him, "Why did we leave London so abruptly, without checking out or telling Richard Moore goodbye?"

It was a question she had asked in London. He dismissed it then, saying it was because of a change in their flight schedule.

He had hoped she wouldn't raise the issue again. This time, she asked in a way that told him she had not believed the answer he had given her in London, and she wanted to know the truth, whatever the cost. He did not want her to know his company was in financial peril. Would she leave him? Would she believe he had married her for her money? Would she ask for a divorce? Regardless of the consequences, the time had come. He told her about Patrick's bad investments and the large losses his company had incurred. He described his business relationship with Richard Moore and HealthTech. He saved the worst for last, telling her about Dennis Goodman's murder.

She listened. "Is that all?" Michelle asked. "Have you told me everything?"

"Yes, that's all. I'm sorry I didn't tell you before the wedding. I was afraid you would leave me or call off the wedding. I kept telling myself that this wasn't a big deal and it would go away. But it's only gotten worse. I'm worried what Moore will do if he finds out I'm cooperating with the government investigation of him and HealthTech."

"I'm hurt that you didn't trust me enough to confide in me. I wouldn't have left you. I love you. We would have worked together to figure a way out. Is there any proof that Richard Moore had the federal agent murdered?"

"No."

"Is there any reason to believe that he would know you were contacted by a federal agent?"

"No. But Jake seemed very disturbed when I told him."

"You told your son before you told me?"

"I felt he should know in case anything happened. He's accustomed to dealing with such people. Agent Goodman had just met with Jake, at the hotel where Jake was staying in New York. When Goodman stepped outside the hotel, the gunman shot him."

"Why did he meet with Jake?"

"Goodman wanted him to work on the counterfeit medicine case. At the time, Jake didn't know about my involvement; and apparently, Goodman didn't tell him."

"Perhaps you are being paranoid. We have bodyguards. We'll go to the reception tonight and leave for Positano in the morning. In a few days, when we're back in New York, you'll demand protection and freedom from prosecution in exchange for your full cooperation. They need your testimony to convict Moore. They will not allow anything to happen to you."

The newlyweds finished their walk and returned to the hotel, saying little else to each other. They had a light dinner in their room and afterwards got ready to attend the reception. Michelle was the honored guest at one of the designer shops on the Via Condotti that sold the lingerie she modeled. The owners wanted to celebrate her wedding and sell some bras in the process. She would be the center of attention, as usual.

Michelle took almost two hours to get ready, giving Edward plenty of time to think after he was dressed. He sat in the living room and had a glass of Italian Barolo Riserva, hoping it would calm his nerves. He had not heard from Richard Moore since dinner the night before he and Michelle sneaked out of their London hotel. Maybe his fear of Moore was paranoia. And although Goodman was dead, the promise he made to work with the feds to bring Moore down hung over his head. He would have to face that when they returned to New York. What would it do to his company? He could not imagine a scenario where he would be allowed to work in the financial industry; much less continue as President of Palmer Global Investments. Perhaps Patrick could become president. He was innocent and unaware of the money laundering. But was he savvy enough to run the company?

When his wife emerged dressed and ready to go, he opened the door and summoned Gustafo, one of their bodyguards, who was sitting on a bench at the end of the hall reading a magazine.

"We're about ready to leave," Edward Palmer said. "Another ten or fifteen minutes."

"Yes sir. I'll let Tony know and advise our dispatcher." Tony was the other bodyguard. He was posted downstairs, watching the hotel entrance and lobby. Gustafo spoke into his communicator.

Edward Palmer closed the door and returned to the sitting room and sat next to his wife, who had poured him a final glass of wine from the bottle. She had none for fear of spilling some on her dress. He finished the wine and opened the door to tell Gustafo they were ready. The three of them took the elevator to the ground floor. Gustafo walked a couple of steps in front of the couple as they made their way to the main entrance.

Tony was standing outside the entrance to the hotel. He was dressed in a dark grey suit and wearing an overcoat with a scarf wrapped around his neck. The shop was only a short walk from the hotel; however, Michelle did not want to walk down the Spanish Steps, the one hundred thirty-five wide steps descending from the Trinita dei Monti, a sixteenth century church near their hotel, to the Piazza de Spagna.

"I confirmed the identity of the car company and the driver," Tony said. "We'll ride with you and I'll wait with the driver until you're ready to leave. Gustafo will be just outside the shop."

Tony and Gustafo escorted them to the waiting Mercedes van's open passenger door and stood outside until the couple was in the bench seat behind the driver. As they settled themselves for the short ride, Tony and Gustafo remained outside the van and talked quietly. When they were finished, Tony got into the front passenger seat, and Gustafo climbed into the third row seat.

On the way to the shop, Tony and the driver spoke in Italian. Palmer leaned close to Michelle and whispered, "What are they saying? Is there a problem?"

"They're mostly talking sports and arguing about the best route to the reception."

The driver maneuvered the van through the evening traffic on the congested, narrow streets, stopping in front of the shop on the Via Condotti, four blocks of high-end, designer shops that ran from the Piazza de Spagna to the Via del Corso. Tony asked them to wait. Gustafo went inside the store while Tony stood guard outside the van. Gustafo returned in a few minutes, telling them that everything was in order, and they were ready for Michelle's entrance. Tony handed Palmer a security company business card on which he had written his mobile phone number.

"We can't block the front entrance, so we'll have to move. Gustafo will wait outside the shop's door where he can observe who enters and leaves, while keeping an eye on the two of you. I'll be in the van parked nearby. Call or text me when you're ready to leave. We'll bring the van to the door, and then Gustafo will escort you from the door to the van."

∧∧∧∧

Mike Baxter had watched Edward Palmer and his wife arrive and saw their two security guards and driver. As soon as the van pulled away, he walked by the security guard posted outside and entered the shop with the self-confidence of any guest, looking every bit the part of a well-heeled invitee. Years of working with Viktor Utkin had taught Baxter when to be ruthless and when to be polite and courteous. Knowing the difference and pulling it off had been difficult for Baxter to master. He removed his overcoat and draped it over his arm. He introduced himself to the receptionist, who asked if he would like to check his coat. Baxter refused. He told the receptionist that he was with the Petrochelli's security team and needed to check the rear entrance. He pointed to a crowd, including a few paparazzi, gathered outside the front entrance, saying the team was concerned for her security and they might need to leave through the rear entrance.

"No worries, sir," she said. "She's very accustomed to having the paparazzi and crowds around. I assure you. In fact, it's good for her and her lingerie brand."

Baxter stood silent and glared at the receptionist.

"I'll have someone show you the rear entrance."

She motioned for one of the attendants to come over and whispered in his ear. The attendant nodded and asked Baxter to follow. Once outside the public area of the store, they entered a room bustling with caterers and waiters. On the opposite side was the rear entrance. He walked to the side street where the caterer's van was parked, as was the car waiting for him with the motor running. Baxter went back inside, thanked the attendant, and followed her back to where everyone was gathered. He snatched a glass of champagne off the tray when one of the servers offered it to him, drank it down and grabbed another when the server went by again. He watched Michelle Petrochelli and her husband Edward Palmer. Later, when they were standing alone and talking to each other, Baxter approached them.

"I'm with your security team. You need to follow me," Baxter whispered to avoid being overheard.

"I don't know you. Who are you?" Edward Palmer said.

"I've been called in to assist your two security men," Baxter said calmly in his British accent. "There's a situation. We need to leave immediately."

"We're not ready to leave. I need to say my goodbyes," Michelle insisted.

"No. We need to leave now."

"What's the urgency?" Michelle asked.

Baxter pointed toward the entrance. "There is a group of paparazzi outside. A large crowd has gathered. We'll be leaving out the back. Your van is waiting there."

Michelle glared at Baxter. "Where are Tony and Gustafo?"

"They're waiting for us outside the rear entrance."

She looked at her husband. "Call Tony," and then snapped at Baxter. "What is the name of my security firm?"

Her husband reached in his pocket for his phone.

"Leave the damn phone in your pocket." Baxter leaned toward. "I have a pistol in my hand under the overcoat. Come with me. Say anything, and you're dead. If someone speaks to you, answer in English, or I'll shoot you both and the person you're talking to."

The three of them moved toward the rear entrance, Edward and Michelle in front and Baxter close behind. Baxter caught her looking around the room but not before her eyes made contact with the store manager, who was talking to the receptionist. The manager approached them. The receptionist was walking toward the door.

"May I assist you? You're headed toward the room the caterers are using," the manager said in Italian.

Michelle responded in English. "I'm afraid there's a security concern outside. We need to leave by the rear entrance. I'm sure it's nothing. However, we must go. Thank you very much for the evening. It's been lovely."

"Please allow me to walk you to your car," she said.

"That's not necessary," Baxter said.

"I insist." Without waiting for a response, she led them through the crowd and into the employee-only area the caterers were using, where she had taken Baxter earlier.

As they approached the rear door, a man entered the room and shouted, "*Arresto*! Stop!"

Baxter recognized him. It was their security guard, the one who had been posted at the front door. The man rushed toward them, knocking down a server who was carrying a tray of dishes from the reception into the back room. The dishes crashed onto the floor, catching everyone's attention. The manager grabbed Baxter's arm. Baxter reached out with his pistol and struck her on the side of her head, knocking her to the floor. Blood was gushing onto her face from a deep gash.

Screams filled the room. The caterers ran toward the door leading into the shopping area, blocking the way for the security guard.

"Go! Go!" Baxter said, pushing them toward the door.

The unarmed guard shoved his way through the fleeing caterers and ran toward them.

Baxter aimed his pistol and fired twice. Both shots struck the guard in the chest.

34

LONDON IS A dark place in the winter with the sun not rising until almost eight o'clock and setting before four o'clock. Television meteorologists describe the weather in vague degrees of brightness or dullness rather than sunny or cloudy. Fiona and I walked from our hotel to a restaurant a block off busy Gloucester Road on what was one of the brighter days. The restaurant was nestled in a posh residential area on a corner of a three-way intersection among some small boutiques. If a restaurant in congested Kensington could be considered secluded, this was it.

We sat at a table for two and talked about a variety of things, all the while knowing it was only a momentary escape from what had brought us together this week. Inevitably, our conversation came around to more serious topics.

I was relieved to hear that Fiona had not seen or heard from the man she encountered in St. Margarets. Perhaps he had not identified her, or maybe he had. Leaving Sevenoaks Weald to stay in a hotel was the best decision she had made. I told her about my trip to Florida, Mother's funeral, and my work with Agent DuPont. She never raised the subject of our relationship or our future. Just as well. I was concerned that this was all too much for her, and I didn't want to steer the conversation in that direction.

We left the restaurant and walked, holding hands, along Gloucester Road. When we came to Kensington Road, we turned left. On our right was Kensington Gardens, which adjoined Hyde Park, stretching east to Park Lane and north to Hyde Park Corner. The Milestone Hotel was ahead, just opposite Kensington Palace. Fiona glanced over her shoulder in the direction of Hyde Park. She said nothing, but her eyes conveyed that she was thinking of the night she almost died in the park beside Serpentine Lake.

My mobile phone rang.

"Is this Mr. Jake Palmer?" the caller asked.

"Yes."

"I'm Eugenio Gianfranco, the head of the security firm assigned to protect Michelle Petrochelli and your father while they are in Italy. He had provided your mobile phone number in case of emergency. I'm afraid I have some bad news."

I stopped in my tracks. My heart sank. "What is it?"

"Your father and his wife have been abducted."

"How's that possible? What happened? Weren't you guarding them?" I asked, raising my voice.

"They were attending a reception at a store on the Via Condotti. During the reception, one of our bodyguards was posted outside the store and another was waiting in the van nearby. During the course of the evening, one of them went inside for a routine check. The receptionist told him that a man who identified himself as one of Petrochelli's security guards said there was a security issue outside the front entrance, and he needed to escort Petrochelli and her husband out the rear door. Our guard, Gustafo, looked around and spotted Ms. Petrochelli and your father walking toward the kitchen ahead of an unknown man. When Gustafo shouted for them to stop, the man fired twice, killing him."

"Were my father or Michelle injured?"

"Not as far as we know. The second bodyguard heard the gunshots and got there a moment after Gustafo was shot. He said they left in a car that was waiting nearby."

"Who abducted them?"

"We don't know. Witnesses said he was a white male of average height with dark hair and a British accent. That doesn't really narrow it down. The police are investigating, as are we. The police are reviewing video from the security cameras. As yet, no one has come forward with a ransom demand."

I talked for a while longer, Fiona's arm interlocked with mine. When I finished, I said, "Dad and Michelle have been abducted. I'm going to Rome."

"I'm going with you," she insisted.

I didn't protest. Fiona would be an asset. She was fluent in Italian and knew Rome as well as she did London. But was I once again placing her in harm's way? All things considered, I felt it was safer for her to be with me in Rome while I searched for my father and Michelle than for her to be in London.

When we got to the Milestone, Fiona said she would book our flight to Rome and arrange for a car to meet us there. I had asked her to schedule the flight in the afternoon; I had something to do before we left. Fiona also arranged for the owner of the security company and the lead detective working on the case to meet with us. Because of Michelle's celebrity status, a senior detective was assigned to investigate the abduction, and it was being treated with great urgency.

∧∧∧∧

After breakfast, I threw my clothes in my suitcase and told Fiona I would meet her at Heathrow for our flight to Rome, saying I needed to see someone before we left. Fiona said that was just as well because she had to go by the office before she went to the airport. She told me she would not board the plane until I met her at the gate.

A rush-hour taxi ride would have taken too long, so I walked to the Kensington High Street tube stop. Using the large map on the wall of the station, I found the best route to HealthTech's headquarters. I took the Central Line to the City of London's financial district and walked the remainder of the way. I did not have an appointment with Moore; I doubted he would have accepted one. It was better just to show up. When I got to the office building, I checked the board. HealthTech's offices were on the top two floors. Moore's office would probably be in the corner of the top floor, most likely the southwest corner with a view of the Thames. The bigger the job, the better the view. With the walk and appearance of someone who knew where he was going, I located Moore's office. It was where I had guessed it would be. The office door and walls were glass, so I could see he was in.

A secretary was stationed at her desk outside Moore's office, and a large man in a dark suit was standing nearby with his arms crossed over his chest. I approached her and said, "Richard Moore, please. I believe he's expecting me."

The secretary looked at me over the top of her glasses, her gaze locking onto my eyes for a moment longer than felt comfortable. She brushed back her hair. "Your name?"

"Jake Palmer."

"I don't see your name on his diary for today. Are you sure you have an appointment for this morning, Mr. Palmer?"

"I don't have an appointment. Tell him I'm here."

"Just a moment." Moore's secretary picked up the phone. "Mr. *Jake* Palmer, to see you." She nodded her head a couple of times, said "yes, sir," and hung up the phone. "I'm sorry. His schedule is fully booked today. He asked if you could come by tomorrow afternoon. He could see you at three. Would that be satisfactory?"

"No," I replied emphatically and walked past her toward the door.

The muscle in the suit stepped between me and the door, puffing out his chest, and extending his right arm to block my path. "She said Mr. Moore couldn't see you today."

I reached out, grabbed the man's forearm with both hands and twisted, spinning him around and putting his head into a chokehold.

The secretary yelled for me to stop and said she was calling security.

"Better be more than one of them," I said loud enough for her to hear.

I shoved the man onto the floor, opened the door to Moore's office and walked in.

Moore stood up, his chair rolling back and slamming into the credenza behind his desk. "For goodness sake, man. There's no need for violence."

Moore picked up the phone. "Tell security to stand down. I'm OK." He hung up the phone and said, "Jake Palmer, I presume. It's pleasure to meet you. I must say, you don't favor your father at all."

Richard Moore's corner office, like the rest of HealthTech's headquarters, was Euro-contemporary with soothing recessed lighting accenting the walls and had a view of the Thames and central London to the west. Moore had two briefcases on the glass table that served as his desk. Both cases were open. Several stacks of paper were neatly arranged along the front edge of the desk, and there was a crosscut shredder beside where his chair had been.

"Going somewhere?" I said.

"Our annual management retreat is this week at an executive residence and meeting facility near Bath. It begins tomorrow. My senior staff and I are preparing to leave. We'll be gone for a few days."

"Is that why your secretary told me to come back tomorrow at three?" I moved around the desk, inching toward Moore, who stood his ground. "She knew you'd be gone."

"You assaulted my employee and barged into my office. If you're looking for your father, I have no idea where he is."

"Why would you even ask that?" I said.

"Because I sent a car to take him and his wife to Heathrow for his flight to Rome. The driver phoned and told me they had already checked out. Caught an earlier flight, I presume. No big deal, although it was rude for him not let me know, so that I could cancel the car."

"How did you know they were going to Rome?"

"The driver needs to know the flight number. He checks before he picks them up. If there's a flight delay or cancellation, he contacts them to adjust the pick-up time accordingly."

"So you had nothing to do with their abduction in Rome?"

"Abduction? What are you talking about?"

"If you're responsible for this and either of them is harmed, I'll kill you," I said, pointing a finger at Moore.

The façade of the gentleman executive disappeared. Moore's eyes narrowed, his face reddened in suppressed anger, and through clenched teeth he said, "Don't dare threaten me. If you think I had anything to do with their abduction, if they were in fact abducted, you're insane."

"I have the list of your accounts. You know—the ones you've used to launder your money. I've turned the list over to the feds.

Your days as a free man are numbered."

He involuntarily clenched his fists, and his face turned a darker shade of red. "If you actually have a list of my accounts, you could have gotten it only from your father. Our corporate accounts are private information and giving them to you is a violation of my contract with him. His investment firm can go under for all I care. As for the money being laundered, your father manages my investments in the States. If my money's been laundered, he's responsible. He's the one who will be incarcerated. Now, get the hell out of here."

Moore was smart. He would have managed the arrangement with my father to have plausible deniability about the way my father's company managed the money. My father would have to provide evidence to prove otherwise.

"I'll be watching you," I said, moving toward the door. "And for your information, I didn't get the list of accounts from my father." That was true. I had gotten them from Goodman, who had gotten them from my father.

When I opened the door, four men in dark suits were standing nearby. They had been watching through the glass door, ready to burst in if things got ugly. I walked by them, silently wishing they would try to stop me.

I left feeling good. Mission accomplished. I had poked the bear. *It's your move, Mr. Moore. Show me what you've got.*

35

THE APARTMENT FIONA had booked was a couple of hundred feet from the Piazza de Spagna on Via della Carrozze, a narrow, pedestrian street lined with small shops and restaurants with tables that spilled onto the street. Our driver pulled to the curb on the south side of the grand piazza, at the end of the street and away from the tourists gathered near the Spanish Steps. Fiona said she had stayed at the apartment a few times in the past during the off-season when the daily rate was cheap. She liked the neighborhood grocery store and prepared most meals in the apartment. Not far away was the designer store on Via Condotti where Dad and Michelle had been abducted at gunpoint.

I tipped the driver and walked with Fiona to the entrance, pulling our luggage, which bounced behind me on the uneven, cobblestone street. The sun lit up the yellow patina of the buildings. Above an arched doorway, I spotted the number 14. We squeezed between two of the tables where people, taking advantage of the unseasonably warm and sunny December day, were having lunch. To the right of the large weathered doors was a call box with several buttons. Fiona pressed the one labeled "Anita Apartment."

"*Pronto*," an Italian female voice said.

"*Bourn journo. Questa é* Fiona Collins."

"*Bourn journo*, Fiona.*"* The door lock clicked and I opened it.

When we stepped inside and the door closed behind us, the windowless entryway and stairway ahead were dark. Fiona reached over and pushed a button by the door and a dim light came on at the top of the stairway, providing just enough light for us to see our way.

"It's on the first floor," Fiona said. "You Americans would call it the second floor."

"How stupid of us. Of course, the second floor of a building is the first floor."

"If the cases are too heavy for you, there's a lift."

"I can manage, thank you."

At the small landing at the top of the steps, the door to the apartment was open. The rental agent was waiting for us with the keys. She spoke in English with a strong Italian accent. After answering a few questions, the agent gave us the keys, collected the rent and left.

Fiona flopped onto the long white couch in the living room. "I wish all of this was behind us and we were here on holiday."

I sat and put my arm around her. "Someday it will be just the two of us without the problems. I promise."

She laid her head on my shoulder and cuddled nearer to me. "I'll hold you to that promise."

"I can't get my mind off my father and Michelle. When are we meeting with the representative of the security company and the investigating detective?"

"I need to call to confirm that."

Fiona made the call and jotted down some notes as I paced across the room. "We're meeting Eugenio Gianfranco, the head of the security company, and Inspector Virgilio Tammaro at a restaurant on Via Belsiana at two o'clock. That's just around the corner from here." She glanced at her wristwatch. "We have time for lunch. Let's go to one of the restaurants at Piazza del Popolo."

Fiona took me along the picturesque Via Margutta, a block over from the most direct route to the piazza and, for the most part, the traffic and street noise of Rome. She reached over and grasped my hand. "I love Rome," she said. "Whenever I'm here, I feel like I'm home. By the way, I brought the camisole. The one I wore in Verona."

"That was our first time. And as I recall, you didn't have it on very long."

"It was a night I will always remember for more reasons than that."

"Right. Earlier, we had run into someone else we were investigating," I said.

"There seems to be a pattern here."

We ordered a light lunch at a restaurant on the Piazza de Popolo, sitting outdoors at a table with a perfect view of the piazza and the Egyptian obelisk in the center.

"If your manufacturing group is leading the counterfeit Transpro investigation, how did you get approval to come to Rome?"

"I called in couple of favors and the senior vice president of manufacturing assigned me to the case. Plus, I speak Italian."

"What exactly is your remit?"

"My assignment is liaise with the Italian authorities investigating counterfeit medicines and assist them in finding the source of the counterfeit version of Transpro."

"That's pretty vague. Did you tell them I would be with you?"

Fiona smiled and shook her head. "I thought it would be less complicated if I omitted that piece of information."

"What do you know about Tammaro? Is he with the police or with their regulatory authority investigation unit, like the FDA's Criminal Investigation Division?"

"He's the lead investigator in the government's counterfeit medicines group. The NAS investigates healthcare cases, involving everything from food to drugs, including pharmaceutical crime. He works closely with the Italian regulatory authority He will bring us up to date on the abduction investigation, as well."

"Have you worked with him before?" I asked.

"No. The only time I've spoken with him was when I called and arranged to meet today."

"Everything points to the kidnapping being related to the money trail of the Transpro case. It doesn't make sense," I said.

"Why? A fortune is at stake."

"For one thing, counterfeit medicine cases are difficult to make stick. Even if the kingpin is found guilty, the penalties are light. The penalties for kidnapping, on the other hand, far outweigh those related to manufacture and distribution of counterfeit medicine. And kidnapping someone as well known as Michelle Petrochelli—that's just incomprehensible. Whoever did this would be aware of how much press and police attention it would attract."

My cell phone rang. "I'd better take this. It might be about Dad," I said.

"You enjoying a glass of wine over lunch?" the caller said.

"As a matter of fact, I am. You're up early?" I mouthed "DuPont" to Fiona and stepped out onto the piazza so no one could overhear me. "Anything on Richard Moore?"

"Not much you don't already know. HealthTech is a privately-held company, so there's no public disclosure information. Moore has residences all over the globe and a mega yacht that is owned by HealthTech. He also has use of a private G650 jet. So far, the people I've spoken with about this believe he's simply laundering the money to avoid paying tax. If that's the case, we'll send what we have to the IRS and the British Revenue and Customs and let them go after him."

"Where are the jet and yacht?"

"The jet is at the City of London airport, and the yacht left the slip at St. Katherine's dock in London a couple weeks ago for maintenance," DuPont said.

"I saw Moore yesterday. He said he was leaving town for a management retreat. I don't believe him. He is up to something."

"Men in his position are always leaving town. What's the word on your father and his wife?"

"Fiona and I are meeting with the head of the security firm and the investigator for the Italian counterfeit medicines group this afternoon. To our favor, Michelle is one of the most recognizable faces in Italy. If anyone spots her, they'll alert the police."

We finished our lunch and took the more direct route back to the apartment. Two o'clock would not come soon enough. I was eager to talk to both Gianfranco and Tammaro. I needed answers. Although I had not completely ruled out the possibility that Michelle had been kidnapped for ransom and my father was simply collateral damage, I doubted that was the case. As far as we knew, the kidnappers had not contacted anyone regarding a ransom demand. Witnesses said the man who abducted them was a white male of average height with a British accent. That was not Viktor Utkin, although it could be one of his men. Since the kidnapper killed someone in the process, the police would never give up looking for him, even if a ransom was paid and Dad and Michelle were released. Richard Moore was responsible for this. I couldn't prove it, but I was sure of it.

36

RISTORANTE AL 34 was a family-owned and operated Italian restaurant near the apartment where Fiona and I were staying. The name was also the address, *Via Mario de' Fiori 34,* a possible tribute to the owner's failure to come up with an original name for an Italian restaurant in Italy or a clever way to ensure guests remember its address. At two o'clock in the afternoon most tables were empty. I saw two men having coffee and talking at a table in the back. One man was large with wavy black hair. He was wearing a collared shirt and had his brown leather jacket draped over the back of the chair. The other was slender with short hair and wearing a sport coat with a shirt and tie. Both men appeared to be in their forties. I moved toward the table with Fiona beside me. The men eyed us and smiled as we approached.

"Inspector Tammaro?" Fiona asked, alternating her glance from one of them to the other.

Both of the men stood. "Yes, and you must be Ms. Collins and Mr. Palmer," said the man in the tie.

"This is Eugenio Gianfranco, the head of the security company that was protecting your father and his wife."

Fiona and I shook hands and the four of us sat down. I sat next to Gianfranco and across from Tammaro and Fiona.

"Please bring us up to speed on where you are," I said.

Tammaro and Gianfranco looked at each other. Tammaro nodded at Gianfranco, who then started talking.

"Two of my best men were assigned to this case. They've been with the company for years. They know their stuff. They had been with your father and his wife all day. They accompanied them to a family wedding reception outside Rome. Mr. Palmer notified them that they would also be attending an evening reception at one of the shops on the Via Condotti. It was a short walk to the shop. You could almost see the store from their hotel. However Ms. Petrochelli didn't want to go up and down the Spanish Steps in her heels, so a van picked them up. My men rode in the van with them. At the shop, one of my men, Gustafo, went inside and conducted a security check. Once the couple was inside, Gustafo waited outside the shop while my other man, Tony, and the driver waited in the van parked nearby. There were a lot of people in the shop for the reception and a small crowd, including paparazzi, had gathered outside. The receptionist came outside, and told Gustafo that a man, claiming to be with his security company, was taking the Mr. Palmer and Ms. Petrochelli out the back entrance and that the store manager was with them. Gustafo, who was unarmed, caught up with them in the area being used by the caterers. He shouted for the man to stop and charged toward him. The man pulled a pistol and shot him. He died on the spot."

"We have witness reports and surveillance footage from several security cameras," Tammaro said. "The man who abducted your father and his wife shoved them into a black Audi A8 that was waiting for them on an adjacent street. The video is not clear enough to make out the registration number. The police are analyzing the security videos taken inside and outside the store, as well as one from a store on the adjacent street where the Audi was waiting. They are also conducting ballistics tests on the bullets that killed the security guard. We should know more soon."

I shook my head. "Any prints from the rear door?"

"The door was a push bar type. He didn't have to touch the bar to open it, and even if he did, there were hundreds of prints on the bar. Our search is underway. We'll find them. Everyone in Italy knows Michelle Petrochelli."

"If they are still in Italy," I said. "We believe that the abduction is related to work my father was doing for HealthTech, a drug distribution company."

"Counterfeit medicines have entered HealthTech's distribution system in the US and Europe," Fiona said. "The extent of the company's involvement in the counterfeit medicine operation is not known."

I turned to Tammaro. "My father, Edward Palmer, was managing HealthTech's investments in the States. He became suspicious and recently turned over a list of their accounts to a US special agent who was murdered in New York. What do you know about HealthTech and its owner, Richard Moore?"

"I'm familiar with HealthTech," Tammaro said. "However, we don't inspect drug distributors on a regular basis. Our most recent inspection of HealthTech's Italian facilities found only minor violations. To my knowledge, all have been resolved—we're certainly not aware of any issues related to counterfeit drugs."

"Does HealthTech have offices in Rome?" Fiona said.

"No corporate office, however, its largest distribution center in Italy is in Civitavecchia. It's managed by Antonio Moretti."

"What's the address?" I said. My question came across as a demand rather than a request.

"You cannot go there. We have no evidence regarding HealthTech's non-compliance with our regulations and certainly do not suspect anyone at their facility in Civitavecchia was involved with the abduction of your father and his wife. Finding them and the person responsible is our highest priority."

I leaned toward Tammaro. "We're going to Civitavecchia. Are you coming or not?"

∧ ∧ ∧ ∧

Despite Inspector Virgilio Tammaro's insistence that Fiona and I stay away from HealthTech's distribution center in Civitavecchia, when it was clear we were going anyway, he decided to accompany us. We were, after all, civilians not under his direct authority, and Fiona reminded him that she had a business reason to visit the facility. She had a good point. Gianfranco said he had lost one of his best men, and if there was any chance this would lead to the killer, he was going. Debate over. Road trip.

We got into Tammaro's car, Gianfranco in the front and Fiona and I in back. I sat behind Gianfranco, turned sideways toward

Fiona. It was either that or have my knees jammed into the back of Gianfranco's seat. Tammaro stayed in the passing lane like he owned it, flashing his lights and hitting the siren if anyone dared block his way. The speedometer needle hovered around one hundred forty kilometers per hour, which is around eighty-six miles per hour. Fiona squeezed my hand hard a couple of times.

"I've noticed that lane markings and speed limits don't seem to concern Italian drivers," I said to Tammaro. "Do the Italian police ever give tickets for traffic violations?"

"Of course," he replied. "Traffic tickets account for a lot of revenue for local governments, just like in America."

He had missed my sarcasm, or maybe he didn't. He sped up to somewhere between ninety and one hundred miles per hour. I kept quiet after that. We arrived in Civitavecchia within an hour. It was the port of Rome, and as with all port cities, industrial buildings and warehouses were everywhere. I had noticed Tammaro was packing a 9mm Beretta in a shoulder holster. Gianfranco appeared to be unarmed and, therefore, would not be much help if we ran into trouble, unless it was a fist fight, where he looked like he could more than hold his own.

By the time we arrived, it was four o'clock, and the sun was low in the sky. Three cars were parked near the door. The Audi A8 was not one of them. Tammaro backed into in a space about fifty feet away and to the right of the center of the warehouse. The building was larger and much newer than Dr. Abercrombie's warehouse in Philadelphia. An efficient drug distributor would not need a massive space. Because of the limited shelf life of most medicines, the best strategy was to keep the outgoing volume roughly equal to the incoming, maintaining the smallest possible inventory. Straight ahead of where we had parked was an industrial sliding door large enough for a truck to pull inside. To the right of that was a standard entry door. The top half of the door was wire-reinforced glass with metal bars on the outside. Other than that, there were no windows.

I told Fiona to wait in the car, or maybe I just thought I told her that. Because without acknowledging that I'd said anything, she got out. Tammaro was marching to the main entrance door with Gianfranco beside him. Fiona and I were a few steps behind them.

"Wait a moment," I said as we neared the building. Chances were that this was not a dangerous situation. It was unlikely that my father and Michelle were even in the building. Even so, years of special warfare training, as well combat experience, had hardwired me to prepare for the worst. We should enter the building as if a man were waiting inside with a gun aimed at the door. "I've got this."

I pushed by Tammaro and Gianfranco, who did not resist, and stood, my back against the side of the building next to the door. I moved slowly and glanced inside. The center of the warehouse was open all the way through to the opposite end, where there was another large sliding door, like the one in the front. On the sides were storage shelves, working space, and offices. Two cars, a red Lamborghini Aventador and a black Audi A8, were parked near the center facing the front sliding door. *Bingo.*

I ducked below the glass portion of the door and made my way to the other side. I whispered, "Black Audi A8" and pointed at Tammaro and Gianfranco, then to my eyes with my index and middle finger, and then to the glass portion of the door. They in turn peeked inside and stepped away. I pointed to Fiona and then to the car. She shook her head.

Tammaro walked away from the door and pulled his cell phone from his pocket. He made a call, speaking in Italian. I tapped Fiona on the shoulder.

"Calling for backup," she interpreted for me.

Gianfranco's jaw was tightened; he was ready to charge through the door and surprise whoever was in there. I took a few steps back from the building and looked at the roofline. A surveillance camera was aimed at the door. I shook my head and pointed at it. Gianfranco muttered something in Italian and spit on the ground. It needed no interpretation.

"Let's go back to the car," Tammaro said after finishing his call. "I have something we need."

Tammaro used his key remote to pop open the trunk. Inside were two padded cases. He opened them to reveal a Franchi SPAS-12 pump action shotgun and a Heckler & Koch 416 assault rifle. I quickly reached for the H&K 416, leaving Gianfranco the Franchi. Tammaro looked at me and asked if I knew how to use it. I said, "Naval Special Warfare" and left it at that. He nodded and opened a box of ammo. I loaded my pockets with the extra magazines and Gianfranco stuffed his with as many shells as his pockets would hold.

I had fired an H&K 416 before, although that was over ten years ago. I felt the weight of the weapon in my hands, turned it side-to-side a couple of times. The German weapon was similar to the American M4, which I had used during my years with SEAL Team Two. With a firing capacity of over eight hundred rounds a minute, on full automatic I could go through the magazine in a few seconds. I switched it to semi-automatic and checked the safety. I was good to go.

"You should stay here, Ms. Collins," Tammaro said to Fiona.

I looked at her, waiting for her response. This time, she offered no resistance. Fiona, like many British people who have grown up in a country without personal firearms, was uneasy being around guns.

Tammaro handed her his car keys and said, "In case you need to drive away." Fiona's eyes widened. She climbed in the driver's seat of the car and slid down until she could just see the warehouse door through the windshield.

I led the way back to the door. Tammaro reached for the doorknob, but I held out my arm and stopped him. I spoke in a normal voice. "I'm sure they've seen us on the surveillance camera and know we're armed. The driver of the Audi is probably inside. We know he's armed and have to assume that anyone with him is armed. Three cars parked outside plus the Lamborghini inside. I'm assuming at least three more men, maybe more and all armed, are with the Audi driver. The Lamborghini probably belongs to the owner, Moretti. Tammaro, you lead. Eugenio and I will be behind you on either side."

"No. We should wait. I've called for backup," Tammaro said.

Waiting was not a good idea. "All they have to do is open the rear sliding door to the warehouse and drive off. We need to go in now. One of us should go to the other end and cut off their escape, if they open that door."

Gianfranco said, "I'll go around."

We gave Gianfranco time to get into position. I looked back to Tammaro's car. Fiona's head was visible over the dashboard. I blew her a kiss. She responded with a quick wave. We were ready. I braced the H&K into my shoulder, fired two rounds into the lock mechanism, and kicked open the door. As soon as we entered, motors engaged and the front and rear warehouse doors opened. That was not good. Fiona had a view into the warehouse and, although she could not see through to the other side. Still, she was in the line of fire.

I swept the H&K through the warehouse. Tammaro was one step behind me. The storage area was on two levels on both sides. I assumed someone would take the high ground on the upper levels, covering the open expanse in the center of the building where the truck rolled through. A single entry door was on the left rear of the building. Like the one at the front, it had impact resistant glass with bars on the outside. Gianfranco was peering around the large door at the back as it opened.

I stepped away from the wall and aimed the H&K at the storage area on the left side, sweeping the barrel back and forth, up and down. There was an open stairwell behind me, leading up to the storage area. Tammaro held the Beretta with both hands and extended it outward, hugged the wall on the right side, pointing the pistol upward to the opposite side. Gianfranco was now standing in the open with the shotgun, moving it from one side of the building to the other, handling the shotgun with confidence.

The creaking sound of steps on the floor above me and to my left caught my attention. I nodded toward Tammaro. Because none of us were wearing a uniform, Tammaro announced our presence. He shouted in Italian and then in English, "Mr. Moretti, this is Inspector Tammaro. We are here on police business. Please come forward." Tammaro's voice echoed in the open warehouse. Shouting again, he said, "We want to talk to you. Backup is on the way. Step out where I can see you."

There were more sounds of quick footsteps from the right side of the warehouse above where we were standing. They were getting into position to put up a fight. I moved to the far side of the warehouse near the wall, never taking my aim away from the storage areas. Tammaro, Gianfranco, and I inched toward the center of the warehouse. The man who abducted my father and Michelle would allow his henchmen to initiate and sustain contact with us while he and Moretti escaped during the firefight.

The first shot fired hit the wall a couple of feet from me. I returned fire, two shots in quick succession in the direction of the muzzle flash. Immediately, shots were fired from above me at Tammaro and Gianfranco. Both of them returned fire. I had to get to high ground. I ran to the steps that led up to the storage area, taking them two at a time. In my peripheral vision, I saw Gianfranco behind the Audi.

I was now at the top of the stairs. Knowing Gianfranco's position behind the Audi, I swept my rifle toward the Lamborghini and fired twice more, flattening both left side tires. From my new vantage point, I had a clear view of the storage area across from me. Staying out of the open, I worked my way along the upper level.

It was then all hell broke loose. A shot from behind me ricocheted off a steel support beam to my right. In the tight quarters, I swung the rifle up and squeezed off a couple of shots to keep the shooter down as I moved toward him. With the rifle stock pressed into my shoulder, I worked my way around until I was behind the shooter. I still did not have a clear shot. He fired at Tammaro who was now in a deadly crossfire. He exchanged fire with the gunman farthest from me. Both men went down. I took advantage of the noise from the gunshots to rush the man near me. He heard me at the last second and swung his gun around. Before he could bring it to bear, I struck him in the forehead with the butt of the rifle. He was out cold, maybe dead. I didn't care which. I picked up the man's rifle and checked for other weapons. The boom of Gianfranco's shotgun was deafening inside the metal building, as he exchanged fire with yet another shooter. As I moved toward the other end of the warehouse, I glanced back toward Tammaro's car and prayed Fiona ducked onto the floor of the car when the gunfire started.

The doors to both ends of the warehouse were wide open. Tammaro had gotten up and was holding his left side. He worked his way toward the Audi. Gianfranco was standing between the two cars using them for cover. One of the office doors on the ground level swung open.

"Hold your fire," someone inside the office shouted. "We're coming out."

I stopped and aimed at the open doorway. My father and

Michelle emerged from the office with their hands up. Behind them was a man with two pistols: one pressed against my father's head and the other against Michelle's. He was a white male of average height with dark hair, just like the witnesses described. I worked to find an open shot, but he was shifting back and forth between his two hostages. The man shouted for Gianfranco to move away from the cars. I steadied the rifle on the rail, attempting to find a clear head shot. Dad and Michelle were standing close together, and with their hands still in the air. It was a high-risk shot at best, not yet worth taking.

The man moved slowly and deliberately behind his human shields.

"You can't escape," Tammaro said.

"Drop your weapons, or I'll kill one of them," the man shouted.

Tammaro, who was holding what appeared to be a wound on his side, stooped down and laid his pistol on the warehouse floor. Gianfranco did the same with the shotgun. I laid the rifle I had taken from the shooter at my feet, leaning the H&K against my leg and out of sight of the gunman below.

"Hands over your heads," the man shouted.

We all raised our hands. The man jammed the pistols against my father and Michelle's heads until they were standing in front of the Audi's driver's door. He opened the rear door, pushed Michelle inside, and closed it. Then he stood behind my father, opened the driver's door, slid in the driver's seat, and started the car, never taking the gun off my father.

My mind raced. The man would not allow my father to live. He knew too much about Richard Moore's operation. Doing nothing was not an option. I lowered one hand and reached for the H&K rifle, calculating the time it would take me to get off a shot versus the time it would take for the man to shoot my father and drive away. My father looked up and our eyes met. He, almost imperceptibly nodded his head. Was he saying goodbye, everything's all right? Maybe he recognized he was to blame and wanted to die. Or was he signaling me?

Dad dropped to the floor like a dead weight, leaving the man exposed in the car. He aimed the pistol at my father as he stomped on the gas. Smoke rose from the Audi's tires as the cars wheels spun for a moment, enough time for me to bring the H&K up and shoot. The bullet struck him in the left shoulder, causing him to drop his gun. Before I could fire again, the car accelerated out of the warehouse. I couldn't risk shooting again. I might hit Michelle, who was in the back seat. I followed the Audi with my aim anyway.

The car was ten yards outside the entrance and still picking up speed when Tammaro's car plowed into its left front quarter panel. The impact spun the Audi around until it came to a stop with the front facing to the right of the warehouse. A woman's scream came from one of the cars. Was it Fiona or Michelle?

Gianfranco sprinted to the Audi, the business end of the pump action shotgun pointed at the driver's window. He flipped the shotgun around and smashed the driver's window with the butt and pushed the side airbag away. The driver was slumped back in the seat and blood ran down his head. Gianfranco felt his neck for a pulse. "He's dead," he said, turning to look at me. Michelle was screaming in the back seat. "I'll get her out. Go to Fiona."

Fiona was behind the steering wheel, leaning back against the headrest. The front air bag had deployed. Blood was dripping from her nose. She would have black eyes tomorrow. Without looking, Fiona reached over and unlocked the door.

"That looks a lot easier and less painful in the movies," she groaned.

I unlatched her seatbelt. My hands were shaking. I helped her out and wiped the blood from her face with my hand and wiped it off on my jacket. I hugged and kissed her, gently in case she had a broken a rib. My father and Michelle stood outside the Audi embracing, both in tears.

"Are you both okay?" I asked them.

My father embraced me. "I've never been so happy to see someone as when I saw you up there." He pointed back to the warehouse. "For the first time since we were abducted, I knew everything would be okay. I love you, son."

Michelle hugged Fiona and sobbed, thanking Fiona for saving her life.

Tammaro, who was putting some pressure on the gunshot wound on his side, broke up the love fest and asked my father and Michelle, "Is this the man who abducted you?"

"Yes," my father said. "The men called him Mike. No one ever used his last name."

"He had an English accent," Michelle added.

White male, average height, dark hair, with an English accent. I put my hands on Fiona's shoulders. "I hate to ask this. Do you think you could look at the body?"

"Why?" she asked. "I wouldn't know him."

"You might."

She looked at me. Her eyes widened and took a quick inhale of breath. I held her hand as we walked, Tammaro trailing along with us. Steam poured from under the hood. I went to the driver's side door and held him up against the seat.

Fiona leaned in around me. She didn't say anything for a moment. "I didn't get a good look at him in St. Margarets. But I'm almost certain it's the man I saw there, the one who was with James Wilcox." Her face paled. She stepped away and leaned against Tammaro's car.

While I had him pushed against the seat I took a closer look at the driver. He had a gunshot wound to his left shoulder. That was mine. And he had another one in the center of the neck, just above the top of the sternum. He would have died instantly. I looked around the darkening landscape and called Tammaro over. He leaned in where Fiona had been standing.

"He has two wounds; one in the shoulder, which was my shot, and another here in the center of the neck. Here." I pointed to the wound. "Have ballistics check that out. He couldn't have driven out of the warehouse with that wound. He would have died instantly. Someone shot him as he drove out, just before the crash."

Tammaro stood, peering at an area in the near distance, and nodded. "I'll let them know."

Backup arrived along with the paramedics. A couple of them quickly confirmed the Audi driver was dead before turning their attention to Tammaro's flesh wound and Fiona's bloody nose. The rest spent an inordinate amount of time with Michelle, considering she had no visible injuries. The police cleared the warehouse and brought the wounded men out for the paramedics to treat. They found Antonio Moretti hiding under the desk in his office.

^^^^

Viktor Utkin had been parked a quarter mile, about four hundred meters, from the warehouse when the gunfire erupted. There was little he could do but watch through a pair of binoculars. Baxter had abducted Palmer and Petrochelli. However, Utkin told Baxter not to interrogate them. Anyone could torture a man or a woman and obtain information. That was easy. The subject would say anything to stop the pain. Knowing whether the information gathered was truthful and complete required the hand and mind of a trained and experienced master of the dark art of interrogation.

Because Utkin had arrived too late, his primary concern was Mike Baxter, the only one who knew anything about him. He had to die. When the gunfire began, Utkin grabbed a case from the trunk and quickly assembled the rifle, a VSS Vintorez compact Russian Spetsnaz sniper rifle with a permanently affixed silencer. He set up position behind his car and looked through the telescopic sight. The sun was setting, but he had plenty of light, and the wind was not a factor. Baxter was getting into the car with Michelle Petrochelli. Another car darted away from where it had been parked and was on a collision course with the Audi as it left the warehouse. The driver would be a difficult target moving fast from his right to his left. Without hesitation, he steadied himself and fired a single shot a moment before the car collided with the Audi. He never doubted that his shot hit the mark.

Using the telescopic site, he swept the scene before him in the distance. Utkin gathered himself and took aim once more. He could get off one shot and perhaps two or three, but the wail of sirens approaching filled the air. Utkin set the rifle on the ground pushed it under the car with his foot. Four Italian police cars and two ambulances with sirens blaring and emergency lights flashing flew by, as he played the part of the innocent bystander. Once they were gone, he retrieved his gun, got into his car, and drove off.

37

THE NEXT DAY, the shootout at the HealthTech drug distribution warehouse in Civitavecchia and the rescue of Edward Palmer and Michelle Petrochelli—Italy's living treasure—were headlines in the local and international newspapers. Fiona read the Italian newspaper's account of the incident to me over breakfast at Caffé Greco near the apartment. She had done a good job concealing her black eyes with makeup, although they still looked a little puffy.

Inspector Tammaro was being called a national hero, a brave policeman wounded in the operation that had rescued Edward Palmer and Michelle Petrochelli and killed or captured the men who had abducted them. Fiona was mentioned as a B&A Pharmaceuticals auditor who was accompanying Tammaro to investigate the presence of counterfeit medicine at the warehouse. Gianfranco was referenced as the head of Petrochelli's security team, and I only as Edward Palmer's son. That was fine by me. The less my name was in the news, the better. The article went on to say that the Italian regulatory authorities were now investigating HealthTech's drug distribution center in Civitavecchia in connection with a global counterfeit medicine operation and stated that HealthTech was cooperating with the investigators.

Fiona's reading was interrupted by a phone call from B&A Pharmaceuticals' CEO, calling to make sure she was all right. The

BBC had picked up the story and was running it on the morning news. He told her to take a few days off and said he wanted to see her when she returned to work. Instead of the call pleasing her, she was concerned about what he wanted to see her about. Were they going to fire her? I laughed. They wouldn't fire someone who had received international attention for rescuing a celebrity couple and uncovering a counterfeit medicine operation at a drug distribution facility in Italy involving one of B&A's most important medicines. More likely, she would get another promotion and a big jump in pay. Still, the call worried her.

After breakfast, we went to the police station to give our official statements. My father and Michelle had just finished with theirs. The four of us were talking when Tammaro came over. He told us that man who had driven the car out of the warehouse had been identified as Mike Baxter, a British ne'er-do-well who was believed to be working with Viktor Utkin, a former Russian Spetsnaz operative. Utkin hired himself out to wealthy individuals who needed protection or needed a problem eliminated, which led us to believe that Moore had done just that. Tammaro told me that ballistics confirmed the rifle bullet that caused Baxter's fatal wound had not come from the weapons we used. The crime scene investigators had found the bullet. It had passed through Baxter and the back of the driver's seat and was lodged in the rear passenger seatback, missing Michelle by inches and only because she was lying down to protect herself from the gunfire. Using that information, they confirmed what I suspected; the shot had been fired from in front of the car as it left the warehouse.

I had no doubt that Viktor Utkin fired the shot that killed Baxter. I told Tammaro that Utkin was the prime suspect in the murder of two men in the US who were involved with this case and gave Tammaro DuPont's telephone number. Tammaro believed Utkin would be on the run and far away from Italy. I disagreed. Utkin would be after my father, the key witness against Richard Moore.

Before Fiona and I went with Tammaro to give our statements, my father told us that he and Michelle had decided to stay in Italy. With Baxter dead and their security cover increased, they felt safe. They wanted time to recover from their ordeal and Positano was good medicine for whatever ailed them. I warned Dad that they were not safe. On the contrary, he was in great danger. Even after what they had been through, I could not convince him of the risks.

That night, Fiona and I walked to a restaurant on Via Margutta near our apartment and had dinner. She was much quieter than usual. Her ever-present smile had disappeared and her eyes were downcast. They were into the first glass of their second bottle of wine when Fiona said, "I don't know how much more of this I can take. I'm serious, Jake. Is this what life with you would be like?"

"I feel horrible you got involved. I didn't want you in harm's way, but you insisted."

"Me representing B&A was the only justification for us going to the warehouse. I had to go."

"In the end, it was you who saved Michelle's life. I couldn't shoot into Baxter's car when he was driving off because Michelle was inside. Utkin saw you were going to ram Baxter's car and shot him to prevent him from being captured. Were it not for you, Baxter would have driven away and Michelle would be dead instead of him."

"Are you sure it was Utkin?" Fiona asked.

"It had to be him. A single precision shot at a target in a moving vehicle. Very few people could do that."

It was good that Fiona was talking about it. Those feelings had been gnawing at her. Who's to say? Maybe Utkin would have shot Baxter anyway. Regardless, Fiona had stopped him. If she hadn't, Michelle would have been killed, probably after being raped and tortured.

"You can't imagine what it was like—sitting in the car, hearing those gunshots. I was terrified, wondering if you had been shot or killed. Once the front door rolled opened, I could see almost everything that happened. When I saw that he might try get away with Michelle, I knew I had to stop him. I started Tammaro's car and rammed into that Audi without even thinking." As she spoke, her voice trembled.

"That was a very courageous thing to do. You were amazing."

"I saw Michelle get into the back seat on the driver's side. I kept telling myself that if I didn't do something, he would kill her. When the Audi came out, I floored the accelerator and braced for impact. I aimed for the front of the car."

"I couldn't have done any better."

I signaled the waiter for the check. As we were leaving the restaurant, Fiona grasped my hand and said, "I love you with all my heart, Jake. I truly do. In New York, I said that I loved you and all that came with it. I said I wouldn't run away from you or from the trouble that attaches itself to you. But after all that's occurred . . ." She hesitated and took a deep breath and exhaled. "I'm not so sure I can cope with the fear and stress."

Tears flooded her eyes. I put my arms around her.

"Every case will not be like this," I said. I paused, kissed her forehead before looking into her eyes. "I can't promise that there won't be other violent cases. I'm not cut out for a desk job or for working for someone else."

"I know. Believe me, the last thing I want to do is change you. The really odd thing is that much of what terrifies me is what I love about you."

"Are we breaking up?" I said.

"No, of course not. I want to be honest with you and needed you to know it's weighing on my mind. I need time to think through and sort out everything. That's all."

"Take all the time you need, Fiona. I'm not going anywhere."

"I'm so glad to hear you say that."

She put her arms around me and rested her head on my chest. We stood on the sidewalk like that, comforting each other, for a few moments before resuming our unhurried walk back to the hotel. I had to be patient with her and give her time to figure out if she liked me as much as she loved me. As Leo Tolstoy said, "The two most powerful warriors are patience and time." Maybe we both needed to step back.

After a few minutes of walking in silence, I continued with our earlier discussion. "With what Agent DuPont has learned and with Tammaro conducting a full investigation of the medicines at the warehouse in Civitavecchia, the counterfeit medicine case will be winding down. A communication spokesman for Richard Moore's company issued a statement saying that HealthTech was unaware that counterfeit medicines had entered their supply chain. They are cooperating fully with the authorities and have initiated an investigation of their own. That's a complete load of BS, of course. The authorities in the UK are looking for Moore. We know that Hristo Adonov killed Goodman, and then Viktor Utkin probably killed Adonov and Middleton, the bank manager. Maybe Tammaro's right; Utkin has fled the country."

"What about the money? Where's Moore's money going? You always say to follow the money."

"The FinCEN will sort that out soon enough. They have experts who do that for a living and advanced technology with which to do it."

"If your case is winding down and the CEO told me to take a few days off, maybe we should stay here for a few more days and relax."

"I have an idea," I said.

"Oh, no. What are you thinking?"

"What would you say to spending some time in Positano?"

Fiona smiled for the first time that day. "Is that to spend time with me, or so you can watch over your father and Michelle?"

"Does it matter? Can't it be both?"

"As long as I'm with you, I'd love it. It's one of my favorite places."

I was relieved that Fiona agreed to go to Positano. The trip would be good for us but not without risk. Utkin was in Italy; I was sure of it. If he found the location of Michelle's reception and told Baxter, he would have no trouble finding my father and Michelle in Positano. Men like Utkin are complicated and unpredictable. He had used Baxter to abduct my father and Michelle and hold them until he arrived. He probably had been a man Utkin trained and trusted to carry out an important assignment; however, I was certain he had killed Baxter without giving it a second thought. In his mind, he had no choice. Utkin would blame someone for having to shoot his friend and would seek to avenge his death. He would have watched everything from the same vantage point from which he shot Baxter. He saw Fiona and me, so we were now under as much threat as my father. Behind this all was Richard Moore, hiding behind his veil of respectability, position, and wealth. I could have told Fiona to return to London while I went to Positano with my father and Michelle. She would have refused and worse; she might have taken it the wrong way, thinking I wanted her out of the way. Quite the contrary, I wanted her near me. Utkin had other men like Baxter working for him, and until Utkin was captured or dead, we were all in danger. Positano was the best option. Or was it? *Fiona, my father, Michelle, and I will all be in the same location.*

^ ^ ^ ^

As we walked on, Fiona confessed that the call from the B&A CEO was still nagging at her. What did he want to talk her about? She decided to call her boss to get his take on it. They discussed the incident at the warehouse in Civitavecchia, and before he asked, she told him why she was there with the police, explaining the possible connection between counterfeit Transpro and the HealthTech distribution center in Civitavecchia. That was the easy part. She went on to explain why the police inspector was with her, and the head of Michelle Petrochelli's security company, and me. He understood and was pleasant enough, however, something in his voice was unsettling. This was no ordinary audit of a drug distribution warehouse, and she found it difficult to pass it off as one. He told her that she had been through a lot and encouraged her to take as much time off as she needed before she returned to work.

"He seemed too empathetic, even patronizing," Fiona said. "The CEO had spoken with him. I'm sure of it. The longer I take off, the longer they have to decide what they should do with me."

I smiled and sang, "How do you solve a problem like Fiona?"

"I'm not laughing."

Although she did smile.

38

I LET MY father know we would be coming and would stay in a hotel near them. He insisted we stay at their five-star hotel. I acquiesced. Fiona rented a car, saying she would drive because she had more experience driving in Italy and on the winding cliffside roads of the Amalfi coast. We drove by Naples and Mount Vesuvius and through a well-used mountain pass, stopping at a scenic overlook in Ravello when we arrived at the coast. The small town was a haven for American and European artists and writers, including the English writer Graham Greene, whom I had studied in college. Next, we stopped for lunch at the town of Amalfi, eating at a small restaurant on the town square.

Leaving Amalfi, Fiona focused on driving while I absorbed the scenery, the Mediterranean Sea on the left and the cliffs on my right. I was delighted that Fiona was smiling and talking a mile a minute, telling me every detail about her previous trips to the Amalfi Coast. She was the happiest she had been since we arrived in Italy. Before entering Positano, Fiona pulled over to another scenic overlook perched high on the cliff above the town. She described everything, pointing out where we would be staying and other places of note. The town was a maze of narrow streets and alleyways on a steep hillside, providing plenty of places for Utkin and his men to set up, leaving me unsettled.

"Is this road the only road in and out of the town?" I asked.

"Pretty much," Fiona said. "It's a nightmare in the summer. And when there's a major crash on this road, traffic backs up fast."

Evil was about to sweep into Positano, like a silent and unstoppable fog. Viktor Utkin was no ordinary thug. He was Spetsnaz, a highly-trained killer with the advantage of being on the offensive. He would be invisible unless he wanted to be seen, silent unless he wanted to be heard.

^^^^

When we arrived at the hotel, Fiona unpacked while I went to see my father and Michelle on the third floor and check out their security detail. On the way, I ran into Gianfranco. He shook my hand and pulled me in for a man hug, pounding my back a couple of times.

"You don't know how relieved I am to see you," I said. "Did Tammaro tell you they've identified the man we're looking for?"

"Yes. Viktor Utkin. I don't care who he is. That bastard is not getting through to them this time. I'm not letting them out of my sight until they are on the flight home. I have four members of my team with me."

"If you need me. I'll be nearby. I'll be happy to stand watch with your men or help out in any other way. We're in Room 107. Otherwise, Fiona and I can enjoy a little time to ourselves."

"We've got it covered. Fiona is quite a lady. A keeper, as I believe you Americans say. Have some fun and enjoy Positano, one of the most romantic places in the world."

"That's what I hear. Before I go, something's been bothering me," I said. "How did Utkin and Baxter know my dad and Michelle were attending the reception on the Via Condotti in Rome? Is it possible they were followed? Did you check out the driver?"

"No way they were followed. My men are trained to be alert for a tail, and Tony is one of my most experienced. I'd trust him with my life. Baxter killed Gustafo. Not something he would do if either of them had led him there. And the car company is one Michelle's agency has used for years. The driver didn't know where he was taking them until he picked them up. After that, one or both of my men were in the van, and they told the driver where to go and how to get there."

"How then?"

"I don't know. Let me talk to Tony. I want to run a couple of ideas by him."

When I got back to the room, Agent DuPont called. I sat on the sofa beside Fiona and told him I was putting him on speaker, so Fiona could listen.

"We raided Abercrombie's warehouse," DuPont said.

"What'd you find?" I asked.

"Most of the medicines were legit, but we found several types of counterfeit medicines in large quantities, including counterfeit Transpro. The best our people could determine, most were manufactured in China and India. An arrest warrant was issued. Abercrombie was arrested at his clinic and was out on bail before you could say pill pusher. It was like he knew it was coming and had planned for it. His attorney is claiming Abercrombie was not aware the drugs were counterfeit."

"Any other arrests?"

"We interviewed the warehouse workers. They didn't know arsenic from aspirin. Just doing their jobs."

I smiled. Moses Jefferson had taken my advice and was not around for the bust. He might have also warned Abercrombie. "They'll have a hard time proving Abercrombie knew some of the drugs were counterfeit. The last point in the distribution chain is usually unaware that counterfeit medicines have entered the system. Perhaps it is as simple as the price he paid for those drugs was the lowest."

"You're not defending him, are you?" DuPont said.

"He's certainly not guilt free. I'm just saying he may actually be doing some good for his community. I'd be surprised if he's convicted. The Medicaid Fraud Unit stands a better chance of putting him away. You mentioned that Moore had a private plane and a yacht.

"That's right. The plane is at the City of London airport, and the yacht is docked in London at St. Katherine Docks when it's in port. It left from here a couple of weeks ago and is due back in a few days."

"If he were to leave the country, he might take the yacht."

"Right," DuPont said. "Planes are too easy to locate and track, and they require flight plans be filed. So, Inspector Tammaro called me. What's this about a shootout at a drug distribution warehouse near Rome? Is that the one that shipped the Transpro to Abercrombie's warehouse?"

"Sure is," I said. I gave DuPont my take on the meeting with Inspector Tammaro and Gianfranco and our visit to the warehouse.

"Fiona rammed his car?" DuPont asked with a laugh.

"That's right, a perfect hit on the left front."

"Well, I'll be damned. You didn't tell me she was freakin' Wonder Woman."

I grinned. "Damn straight, Fiona is Wonder Woman. I wouldn't mess with her."

She punched me on the arm and mouthed, "Stop."

"I think Utkin is still in Italy. Moore wants my father out of the way so he can't testify against him. Utkin won't leave Italy until he's completed the assignment."

"You're probably right," DuPont said. "You be careful. Viktor Utkin is a nasty piece of work, with no moral compass. I met your White Jesus, Branson van Buren. Now that I'm the case agent, he and I are working together. He wants to meet with you and your father now, before they return to New York. I told him you were both moving around Italy and gave him your contact information."

"Good. We're in Positano on the Amalfi Coast. We're staying at the same hotel as my dad and stepmother." Referring to Michelle as stepmother was a tough adjustment. "Are you coming with him?"

"No. He'll swing by our attaché office in Rome and the HSI agent who's assigned to the task force will most likely accompany him to Positano."

After I finished the call, Fiona leaned her head on my shoulder and said, "I think we need to relax. Let's have dinner on the beach at Chez Black."

I phoned Gianfranco and let him know where we were going and asked if he had spoken with Tony. He said my father and Michelle were having dinner at the hotel restaurant. Tony was on another security detail in Rome and would phone him later that evening.

39

THE STORE IN the small village near Brighton on the south coast of England was a little over a mile from the cottage where Richard Moore was staying. He walked only because he needed to avoid using his car. The police were probably searching for it. However, the walk and the bite of the cold wind sweeping off the sea kept his mind sharp, enabling him to think through his current situation. Since leaving London, he had not used his personal or work mobile phones or a credit card. He paid cash and used contract phones to stay in touch with his personal attorney and with the head of HealthTech's Legal Department. Both advised him to lay low.

If the accusations were limited to the authorities finding counterfeit medicines in HealthTech's Civitavecchia warehouse, he would not be concerned. His legal and communications teams could manage that. However, Utkin's man, Mike Baxter, had abducted Edward Palmer and Michelle Petrochelli and was in a shootout with the police.

The incident was all over TV. Baxter was identified as an associate of Viktor Utkin, an international assassin. To make matters worse, Antonio Moretti had been arrested at the warehouse. Because he was a HealthTech employee, the company provided him with an attorney who stated to the police and the media that Moretti was a victim. He claimed Baxter and his men had forced their way into the warehouse to hide Palmer and Petrochelli and were holding him hostage, too. Moore shook his head. Of all the places, why had Baxter taken Palmer and his wife to one of his warehouses? Had Utkin told him to take them there?

Moore knew that sooner or later the police would find him. Maybe it would look better if he turned up at a police station, saying he had heard they were looking for him. If and when he emerged from his seclusion, his attorney would claim that he needed a physical and mental break from work and was shocked to learn of what had taken place in his absence. The attorney would claim that Moore was not aware of what had happened and say that HealthTech was cooperating fully with investigators. Proving Moore knew about the counterfeit medicines in HealthTech's inventory would be difficult; and after all, corporate executives were rarely indicted. But, prosecutors could establish motive. HealthTech had profited from the sale of the counterfeit Transpro, as well as other counterfeit drugs shipped to HealthTech by the Indian drug manufacturer.

The big problem for Moore was money laundering and income tax evasion. Many gangsters and corporate criminals had attempted to cover their financial tracks, creating a maze of fake companies and accounts nearly impossible to trace. But, eventually, it led to their downfall. If Edward Palmer was cooperating with US federal agents, they would have a list of the bank accounts Palmer Global Investments used to launder the money. In that case, Moore would claim that Edward Palmer was acting on his own. He would say that he had instructed Edward Palmer to manage his money and, to the extent legally possible, minimize his tax liability. No crime in that. But would a jury believe such a story? *Too risky. Edward Palmer needs to be eliminated. Immediately.*

Moore used a burner phone to call Viktor Utkin.

Utkin answered in Russian, "Da."

"What the hell happened in Civitavecchia?" Moore said. "Why did Baxter take Palmer and Petrochelli to my warehouse?"

"Where else could we take them? If I had gotten to the warehouse any sooner, I'd be dead, too. Baxter was with Palmer and his wife at the warehouse. Moretti was there, too. When I got close enough to the warehouse, I saw that the doors were open. Something was wrong. I stopped and got out of the car before I went any farther. That's when I heard gunshots. There was nothing I could do but watch from that distance. With Baxter and a couple of his men dead and Moretti in custody, your whole operation has turned to shit," Utkin said.

"It's time to take care of Edward Palmer and his son Jake," Moore said, taking a pause from his walk to the store. "I'll pay triple your fee."

"I'll kill them all. Jake Palmer, his girlfriend, and then his old man and his wife."

"I don't mind which order or how you do it. Just be certain Edward Palmer is dead. If he testifies against me, I'm done. Where are they now?"

"Positano."

"How do you know?"

"Someone owed me a favor."

"Don't delegate this, Utkin. You do it alone. I don't trust anyone else."

"Don't tell me how to do my job."

"Jake Palmer will be difficult. He's a former US Navy SEAL."

"Navy SEALs. Just hearing the name makes me want to puke. Maybe Palmer was tough when he was a SEAL. Now, he's just an out of shape has-been, basking in his past glory."

"Not from what I've seen. Don't take him lightly."

^^^

Utkin disconnected the cell phone and threw it against the wall. After he took care of Edward Palmer, he was finished with Moore. The only reason he was going to follow through at all was to avenge Baxter's death and further burnish his own reputation.

Utkin knew Positano well. A few years back, a drug kingpin paid him to take out a rival who was vacationing there. The rival and his girlfriend had no security because he was not suspecting a problem. Utkin followed them for days, until one day they went to a secluded beach. They were alone, sunning in lounge chairs and away from security cameras. He shot and killed the drug dealer and then his woman. Utkin was out of town before their bodies were discovered.

Utkin knew that Edward Palmer and his wife's security team would be strengthened, at least four or five men with them at all times, and he could not rely on the four targets to be in the same place at the same time. Therefore, in spite of what Moore had said, he would bring in some men to help, but the pleasure of killing Jake Palmer would be his and his alone.

40

FIONA AND I returned to our hotel after having dinner at Chez Black. An Italian Barolo wine had done wonders for our moods, and at least one of us was in the mood for love. We were in the hotel lobby on the way to our room when my cell phone rang. I didn't recognize the number and almost didn't answer it. Something told me I should.

"Jake Palmer?"

"Yes, who's calling?"

"Branson van Buren. I'm with the Financial Crimes Enforcement Network. Agent DuPont told me to call you. I'm working on the counterfeit medicine case that Agent Goodman spoke to you about."

"DuPont said you might contact me," I said.

"Yes, he gave me your number. I need to meet with you and your father as soon as possible. He said that it might be my best chance to talk to the two of you. I'm flying out tonight and will be in Rome tomorrow morning."

"Why the urgency? My father was going to meet with you and DuPont when he got back to New York."

"This case is moving fast. And—I don't know how to say this other than to be direct—your father's our prime witness, and there's already been one attempt on his life."

"You're right. The sooner the better."

"Where are you staying?" Van Buren asked.

I gave him the name and address of the hotel in Positano.

"Someone's picking me up at the airport. Before I come to Positano, I need to go to Rome to check in at the Homeland Security Investigations office and the Italian *Raggruppamento Operativo Speciale*. I'll see you sometime tomorrow, late afternoon or early evening. Let your father know."

"Will do."

"Who was that, and why were you giving out the name and address of our hotel?" Fiona asked.

"That was van Buren with FinCEN. He's coming to Positano to meet with Dad and me." I was determined to keep the interruption from spoiling our evening and made an attempt to deflect. "That was a great meal, wasn't it?"

The elevator door opened, and we stepped inside.

"You said this was all winding down. You said we could relax and enjoy our time in Positano."

"Van Buren's working with DuPont now, investigating the money laundering. He's a bean counter."

My phone rang again. These phone calls were ruining my buzz. After a bottle or two of wine, there's a small window of time between being excited about getting your girlfriend into bed and just being excited about going to bed. That window was about to slam shut. I answered and mouthed "Gianfranco" to Fiona.

Fiona crossed her arms over her chest and stepped away from me, as much it was possible in the small elevator.

"I talked to Tony," Gianfranco said. "He said that the only person who was aware of the hotel and the reception on Via Condotti was our dispatcher. The car company knew the hotel, of course, but knew nothing about the reception until the driver was given the destination. It's the same company that drove them to Positano. However, it wasn't like the reception was a big secret. The lingerie company and the store wanted the paparazzi there. All the more publicity for them."

"So you can't really tell if it was the dispatcher or not?"

"Correct. The dispatcher has been with us for less than a year. I had his background and security checks sent to me. There's nothing out of the ordinary. I called and asked the dispatcher if he told anyone. He insisted he didn't. Said he knew that was prohibited and he would be fired if he did. I also called the owner of the car company. They're reputable, and the driver's been with them for years."

"It could be immaterial. We have to assume Utkin knows Dad and Michelle are in Positano and where they're staying."

"I'll watch your father and Michelle. Take care of yourself and Fiona. Chances are he knows you're here, too."

"He'll go after my father before me. Without Dad's testimony, Moore has a good chance of getting off with some petty regulatory fines and penalties. If he were to take me out first, the police would come running and take Dad and Michelle to a very secure location."

"And where will these police come running from?" Gianfranco asked.

"What do you mean?" I asked.

"It's Positano, and it's off-season. Have you seen any police since you arrived?"

"As a matter of fact, I haven't. Regardless, Utkin will want us together, so it's the one thing we must avoid."

No police and, by plan or luck, Utkin had managed to get the four of us in Positano. Things were spinning out of control. While talking to Gianfranco, I had followed Fiona out of the elevator and down the hallway. She opened the door and stood by the window, looking outside with a blank expression.

"I'm sorry, Fiona. I've put you in the middle of it again."

"I'd say I was becoming accustomed to it, but I'd be lying. What are you going to do, Jake?"

"I need to think like him, an operative going after his target," I said. "He'll first assess his chances of getting Dad and me together. When he realizes that's not going to happen, he'll go after Dad and worry about me later. This is a small town with a single road leading in and out of it. How would he do it? When would be the best time and place? He'll know a security team is guarding them. An up close hit would be hard to pull off. Gianfranco's men will be watching the road into town. That won't help. Utkin's too smart. He'll find a way to get in and out of Positano without being noticed."

"How about a sniper rifle or some IED-like explosive?" Fiona said.

"Explosives are too messy and imprecise. In a town built on a hillside going down to the sea, a sniper has a lot of options. The best place to set up would be somewhere with a clear view of the hotel entrance. I'll check out those locations in the morning. Gianfranco will want to keep Dad's time outdoors to an absolute minimum. That's going to be difficult without making him and Michelle feel like prisoners."

^ ^ ^ ^

Traveling within Europe with a firearm is very risky. To circumvent this, Utkin stashed weapons, cash, and falsified passports in several major European cities, including a secure, climate-controlled storage facility near Rome.

Driving on the coastal road that passed through Positano never entered Utkin's mind. Instead, he and the four men he had recruited met in Amalfi and paid a truck driver one hundred euros to take them to Positano. His men were out of sight in the back of the truck with a large wooden case that held their weapons, ammunition, and explosives. Utkin got into the cab with the truck driver.

Concealed from the driver was Utkin's ankle holster, which held a PSM 5.45mm compact pistol loaded with eight 5.45x18mm 7N7 full metal jacket cartridges. On the floor at Utkin's feet was a metal case, not much larger than a briefcase. Inside was his VSS Vintorez compact Russian Spetsnaz sniper rifle with a permanently affixed silencer. The silencer reduced the sound of a gunshot to a *click*, although it also reduced the effective range to four hundred meters or less. Utkin used the weapon to kill Baxter at the warehouse in Civitavecchia. He had been close to the maximum range from Baxter when he fired the shot, calculating that the dry winter air and lack of wind would increase distance and accuracy.

The rifle was broken down into three major components. Each fitted snuggly into the cut out spaces in the padded case along with a telescopic sight, a night scope, and two twenty-round subsonic, tungsten-tipped cartridges—subsonic to eliminate the sonic boom and tungsten-tipped to penetrate body armor or military helmet. His men had a large, innocent-looking crate with the guns and ammunition they needed.

Locating Palmer and Petrochelli had been easy. Her plans and movements were in all the local tabloids and newspapers. Finding out they were leaving Rome and going to Positano had proved more difficult. Utkin told one of the hotel bellmen that he was a big fan of Petrochelli and offered him five hundred euros to tell him their plans. The bellman said no at first, but when Utkin handed him a thousand euros, the bellman said he had overheard that they were going to Positano. The bellman did not know where they were staying, but that was simple—the most expensive hotel in town.

The truck driver dropped Utkin and the men off where SS163 met the Via Cristoforo Columbo, a smaller road that wound into the town. From there they walked, Utkin in front, carrying his case, and his men following behind him at a distance, so they did not appear to be together. Two of the men lugged the wooden case carrying the munitions. They made their way into the town center at the bottom of the hill, near the five-star hotel where he believed Palmer and Petrochelli were staying. Utkin located a hotel with a view of that hotel and went inside. Before checking in, he asked the manager to see the rooms on the top floor. The third room Utkin was shown was near the stairs to the right of the elevator. He opened the curtains and raised the window. Two men wearing overcoats were pacing outside the nearby hotel entrance. Security men standing watch. Utkin smiled. Edward Palmer was there.

"I'll have this room," he told the manager. "And the other two rooms you showed me on the floor below mine for my friends to share."

They returned to the front desk. Utkin checked in with a false name and passport and paid cash for three rooms for a week. The men were waiting outside. He opened the door and waved them in. Utkin told the manager they did not want to be disturbed during their stay. The manager paid little attention to the men as they filed in.

Once in his room, Utkin unpacked the Vintorez. He cleaned and assembled it. The rifle had only been fired once recently, the shot that killed Baxter. No matter, it had to be cleaned anyway, along with his pistol.

It was possible the couple would enter and leave by the rear entrance of their hotel. The alleyway behind it was too narrow for a motor vehicle. That limited his options for setting up. However, the street's steep incline provided some advantages, such as placing himself above or below the target.

Utkin settled in for what could be a long wait. He had met with his men and laid out the plan, as well as alternative plans should they need to change on the fly. He told them to wait in their rooms and be ready. He would tell them when it was time. This time, there would be no escape for Edward Palmer. The security men were incompetent and could not hold them off. Utkin calculated they had fifteen minutes to kill Edward Palmer and his wife and get away. If the plan went afoul, Utkin would leave without the men. They were expendable, just like Baxter.

Sooner or later, Edward Palmer, Michelle Petrochelli, and their bodyguards would emerge. Even newlyweds need a break. *Why stay in Positano if you're prisoners inside a hotel?* Utkin smiled at the thought. *This is going to be easy.*

41

THE PERMANENT RESIDENTS of Positano were few in relation to the number of tourists who flocked to the town in the warmer months. Michelle selected the location because it was one of her favorite places and because she and my father could relax relatively free of harassment from the paparazzi and tourists who crowded around and snapped photos every moment they were out in public. Under normal circumstances, the attention was part of the job of being a model. Being in the limelight was good for her and good for the companies that designed and made the clothes and lingerie she modeled and the perfume she wore and promoted.

Now, however, she was just like any other bride on her honeymoon. She wanted a romantic, private escape from the distractions of life with her husband, and Positano provided it. The security team accompanied them whenever they left their room. Gianfranco, intent on preventing another abduction or worse, stationed someone inside the restaurant or shop with them, while others guarded the entrances and exits. Even though the heightened security constricted their movements, having come so close to death, Edward and Michelle had come to terms with their relative confinement in the five-star hotel.

I met with Gianfranco and went over the security arrangements. He said it was their last night in Italy, and they insisted on going out to dinner. The restaurant they chose was a ten-minute walk up the hill from their hotel. It was one of Michelle's favorites. It had a loyal, local clientele and did well in the off-season, unlike many restaurants that either closed or suffered through the winter months.

Gianfranco had visited the restaurant earlier in the day to assess the security risks. The manager showed him around. There were about twenty tables set for either two or four guests. He told the restaurant manager to expect VIP guests for dinner and explained the security arrangements and selected their table, one near the back of the restaurant and away from the windows. The manager told him that he expected only about half the tables to be taken and would seat no one near them.

Afterwards, Gianfranco had met with his team at the hotel and laid out the plan for the evening. He distributed photographs of Utkin, although none were recent. He would take the lead on the way to and from the restaurant, walking in front of the couple. Two men would follow close behind, with another posted well ahead of them. The fifth man with binoculars would be posted on the rooftop of a four-story building uphill from the hotel and near the restaurant. He would be there an hour before the dinner and would remain until notified that they were back inside their room at the hotel.

"Sounds good. I'll play free safety," I said.

A puzzled look swept over Gianfranco's face.

"In American football, the free safety hangs back on defense and watches the play develop. He observes the quarterback, receivers, and running backs, anticipating what is going to happen. The free safety has the size and skills to make the big hit on the ball carrier or receiver or intercept the pass, preventing a long gain or touchdown."

Gianfranco smiled and nodded his head. "Yes. Like the center back in soccer."

"Exactly. You might not see me or know where I am, but I'll be there," I said.

"Did your father tell you they are leaving for the US tomorrow morning?"

"He did. Tonight will be Utkin's best and last chance. Things become more difficult for him after that."

"You know we're not even sure that Utkin is in Italy, much less Europe," Gianfranco said.

"He's here."

"How can you be so sure?"

"I just am. Does anyone else know about the dinner or their plan to leave tomorrow?"

"No one, including our dispatcher. I've planned the security arrangements for their departure and travel to Rome, where they will stay for one night before returning to New York."

"Tell him. Let him know the plans."

"Are you crazy? He's the person we suspect of leaking the information."

"This will be our best chance to get Utkin. We need to dangle the bait in front of his face and anticipate his move. Tell him the name and location of the restaurant."

Gianfranco shook his head. "The bait you're speaking of is Michelle Petrochelli and your father. I'm paid to protect them, not to capture or kill Utkin."

"Forget it. I have an idea."

"Is that supposed to make me feel better?" Gianfranco said, laughing.

I walked from the hotel to the restaurant. When I got to the restaurant, I stood at the entrance and looked down the street, the direction from which my father and Michelle would come with Gianfranco and his men. I identified the buildings where Utkin would have the best shot on the way to the restaurant and at the entrance, taking into consideration what the conditions would be that evening for light and wind. My gaze eventually settled on one building as the most probable site. It was a hotel. I walked down the hill, went inside and stood in front of the reception desk.

"Can I help you, sir?" the desk clerk asked in English.

"My girlfriend and I are thinking about moving from our hotel. We plan on staying in Positano several more days, and while our hotel is very nice for a short stay, it's too expensive. May I see a couple of your rooms?"

"Certainly." The clerk got a master key from a drawer and came from behind the counter.

As we walked toward the elevator, I said, "We met a man in the restaurant last night, a large man. Sounded Eastern European or Russian. He said he was staying here and recommended it. Told us that you're reasonably priced and that his room was excellent. He checked in a couple of days ago. I believe he said he was staying on the street side on the top floor."

"Mr. Petroski. He checked in yesterday. Very quiet gentleman. We have a couple of rooms available near his. I'll show you those."

"That would be fantastic."

The rooms were small and clean, similar to those in many European hotels, especially the less expensive ones. I looked out the window and to right and left, concluding that Utkin would want a room on the top floor. The height would give him a firing angle above the security team that would surround Dad and Michelle. The entrance to the restaurant was visible without obstruction. There was a view of the street below; however, the angle from the window to the restaurant was ninety degrees. Utkin could get a shot off, however, it was far from ideal. The second room I was shown was at the end of the hall. I again looked from the window toward the restaurant and the hotel. It was at the end of the building farther away from the restaurant. The view was not perfect, but it was the best in the hotel.

The best shot would be when the party walked by this hotel, but the security team would be more likely to spot him or determine where the shot came from and converge on the building afterwards. Utkin would move out immediately after he fired.

"I'll take this room," I said.

We went to the lobby where I put down a one-night deposit on the room. The desk clerk gave me two keys.

When I got back to our hotel, Fiona was on the bed reading a book.

"Grab a suitcase. We're moving."

Fiona set straight up. "Moving? Why? I like it here."

"I think I've found where Utkin is staying. I've checked us into the room next to his."

"Why me? I could just stay here where it's safe."

"I needed to check in with you to look as innocent as possible. You know."

"No. I don't know." Fiona took a deep breath and exhaled. "It's all right. I'd rather be with you than by myself. It'll take me a few minutes to pack."

"Don't bother. We're not checking out of here. We'll take a couple of empty suitcases. I called my father and let him know."

"Do you even have a gun?"

"I'll get one from Gianfranco."

^ ^ ^ ^

On the way to the hotel, I told Fiona to check in for us. She spoke to the desk clerk in Italian. Both laughed at whatever they were discussing. I was a couple of steps to her side, but as far as the desk clerk was concerned, I might have just as well been in Philadelphia. He never took his eyes off Fiona. I picked up "Petroski" but little else. When Fiona and I got onto the elevator with our empty luggage, I asked her what they were talking about.

"I told him that we weren't married and were having a dirty weekend."

"Dirty weekend?"

"It's when a couple goes away to have wild, passionate sex."

"When do we start?"

"Tonight, after your father and Michelle are back in their hotel room, and we can relax enough to really enjoy it."

"Maybe it would be better to relax now."

Ignoring my comment, she continued. "I asked about Mr. Petroski, saying we wanted to see if he was free for dinner. He offered to call him for us, but I told him not to because we wanted to surprise him. He said his room was on the same floor as ours. He apologized for not giving me Petroski's room number, saying it was strictly forbidden to divulge a guest's room number. I told him I'd phone Petroski later. I asked if he was in. He said Petroski and his friends left for lunch, and he hadn't seen them since. You didn't tell me he had friends."

"That's because I didn't know. How many friends?"

"I told him we wanted to make reservations for all of us tonight and asked how many were with him. He said three or four, maybe five. He wasn't paying attention when they came in and went up to the two rooms they were sharing."

Just as I expected, Utkin had brought help. That changed everything. A man with a rifle was one thing. A man with a rifle and a few friends was quite another. How would he use them?

Utkin would want to kill my father himself in order to be certain he was dead. There would be no delegating this hit. Perhaps Utkin wanted the men to occupy the security team's attention while he went after my father and Michelle. If Utkin had the corner room on the top floor—the same floor as us—the men must be staying somewhere else. When we got to our room, I stood at the wall separating our room and Utkin's and listened. It was 4:00 p.m. Nothing.

I sat on the bed beside Fiona. "I need to see Gianfranco. I'll be right back."

"Get a gun," she said, "and lots of bullets."

"All this talk of guns and ammo is turning me on. Maybe I should stay."

"Out," she said, pointing at the door.

42

GIANFRANCO AND I pleaded with my father and Michelle to change their plans and have their meal in the hotel. They resisted, arguing there was no proof Utkin was even in Italy, much less Positano. I reminded my father that Tammaro had forensic evidence that the bullet that killed Baxter was not from any of our weapons. The fatal shot had been fired from a rifle straight ahead of the car as it sped out of the warehouse. My father replied, saying that did not prove Utkin had fired the shot. I also told him that an Eastern European man matching Utkin's description had checked into a hotel nearby along with a few of his friends. Michelle offered that none of it proved Utkin was there, saying that a lot of eastern Europeans visit the Amalfi Coast during the off-season when the rates are cheaper.

Frustrated and a little upset with the two of them, I left with Gianfranco. In the hallway outside the room, he told me the plan for moving to and from the hotel. Each of the team members, including him, would have a communicator and a photograph of Viktor Utkin, the most recent one available. A fifth team member would be on a rooftop with a full view of the route from the hotel to the restaurant. I asked which building. When he told me, I let him know that Fiona and I had moved and were staying there. I thought that's where Utkin and his men were staying. He threw up his hands and shouted something in Italian before he walked away. I didn't full comprehend what he said; however, I picked up *stupido* and *imbecile*.

∧∧∧∧

I returned to our room and waited along with Fiona, who was reading her book and doing her best to ignore me.

"I haven't heard a peep from next door since we checked in."

"Men like Utkin don't make noise. They are exceptionally good at being still and quiet for long periods of time."

"Aren't you a man like Utkin, former naval special warfare and all? I've not noticed you being quiet and still for long periods. You tend to be fidgety, like now."

The buzzing of my cell phone saved me from having to respond. It was Gianfranco. They would be leaving for the restaurant at half past eight.

"They're getting ready to leave for dinner. I can't stay here," I said. "Utkin and his men are in place by now, waiting for them to walk to the restaurant. After I leave, call the front desk and ask for Utkin—I mean Petroski. I'll be outside his room. The ring will confirm it's his room. When he answers, I'll bust in."

"You don't even have a gun, do you? You said you were going to get one from Gianfranco."

"Lock the door when I leave. If you hear gunshots, call the police."

Fiona drew me close and kissed me. "I'm going to be really cross with you if you don't come back."

Closing the door behind me, I hesitated until I heard the deadbolt engage. I stood outside Utkin's room, the one next to ours, and put my ear close to the door. Not a peep. Fiona was right. Neither of us had heard anything from the room since we checked in, and that wasn't because the walls were exceptionally well soundproofed. The room phone rang. I waited. Three rings, four rings. Even if he was in the room, he wasn't going to answer the phone. No one Utkin knew would call the room, including his men. They were already in position. Five rings, six rings—*screw it*.

I raised my right leg, drew it back to my chest, and extended it with full force near the handle of the old door. The door cracked around the lock and flew open. I rushed into the room. Empty. The bed was made. There was no luggage or books or newspapers. I checked the closet and bathroom. The sink and tub were clean. It was as if the room had never been occupied. A noise came from behind me. I swung around.

It was Fiona, tapping lightly on the broken door. "Jake," she whispered. "Jake," she said louder.

"Utkin's not here," I said. "This has to be his room. The phone was ringing."

"I know. I could hear it through the wall," Fiona said.

I stepped to the window. The security team, my father, and Michelle had emerged from the hotel and were walking to the restaurant. The window would have provided a good shot over their entire route, better than any other room in the hotel. But it wasn't perfect. Would Utkin settle for less than perfect?

I stared out the window, arms crossed over my chest. "Where could they be?"

"It's like he was never here," Fiona said after looking in the closet, bathroom, and under the bed. "Why would he do that? Where is he?"

I said nothing. No other hotel or room would provide the angle this one did. A rooftop shot would be possible, but one of Gianfranco's men was on the roof of this building. He would see Utkin—unless Utkin saw him first. *Damn it. He's on the roof.*

I placed my hands on Fiona's shoulders and looked her in the eyes. Regardless of which man Gianfranco put on the roof, he would be no match for Utkin.

"Go to the room and wait for me."

"I'm frightened," she said.

"Don't be. You'll be fine. Go back to our room and lock the door."

"I'm not frightened for me. I'm frightened for you. You're unarmed and going up against a murderer and four or five of his men."

"I've been in worse situations."

"When?"

I hugged her and ran up the flight of stairs to the hotel roof, taking two steps at a time.

^^^^

At the top of the stairs, I opened the door. The hotel's

heating, air conditioning, and air-handling equipment took up most of the space on the roof. The hum of the equipment was the only sound that broke the silence of the night. The streetlights below provided some ambient light but not a lot. Gianfranco's man would be close by and might have an itchy trigger finger.

"It's me, Jake Palmer." No answer. I shouted, "Jake Palmer here. Don't shoot."

The view would be perfect for Gianfranco's man and for Utkin. If Utkin wanted a place to set up with his rifle, this was ideal. Utkin's men could approach the group on the ground from different directions, corralling them and cutting off their escape. Utkin would have all the time in the world to pick them off. However, if he wanted to use this rooftop, Utkin had to take out Gianfranco's man.

I moved to one of the air-handling units and glanced around the corner. Seeing nothing, I ducked behind another unit ten feet to the right. A loud metallic clunk came from beside me. There was a bullet hole in the sheet metal a few inches from the corner and within my reach. I reached out and felt it. Two more bullets struck the sheet metal in quick succession, each nearer to me than the previous one.

I slid along the backside of unit and glanced around the corner. Gianfranco's man lay motionless near the edge of the roof, his rifle beside him. His black leather jacket was open, exposing a belt holster and pistol. I took two deep breaths and sprinted to the guard. Using his body as a shield, I grabbed the rifle and took the pistol from the holster. Two bullets thudded into the body, splattering blood onto me. The suppressed muzzle flash revealed his location on the roof of the adjacent building. There was a gap of a few feet between them. I brought the rifle's scope to my eye and fired several times where I had seen the flash. The sound of the unsuppressed rounds should have alerted Gianfranco.

I moved nearer to the gap, fired two more shots with the rifle and dropped it. Holding onto the pistol, an Austrian Glock 9mm, I sprinted toward the adjacent building and jumped. I cleared the gap with only a foot to spare, shoulder-rolled and popped up. I swept the rooftop with my pistol and moved around until I was certain Utkin was no longer there.

I flew down the steps until I reached the ground floor and
ran out a fire exit onto the street behind the building. No sign of
the shooter. I never saw him although I'm sure it was Utkin. He
had disappeared. I made my way over to the main street in time
to see Gianfranco and the security team hustling my father and
Michelle into the restaurant.

^ ^ ^ ^

When I got to the restaurant, two of the security team
members were posted at the restaurant door, their pistols drawn
and by their side. Neither had seen Utkin or his men. They said
they heard shots and closed in around my father and Michelle
and got them inside the restaurant. They said another man was
at the back entrance, and Gianfranco was inside. They had been
unable to raise their man on the roof. I told them he was dead.
Their faces tightened, jaws clenched.

I tucked the pistol in my belt and went inside. Gianfranco
was sitting at the small bar on the left side of the restaurant.
Only about half of the tables in the dimly lit restaurant were
occupied. Dad and Michelle were sitting at a table against the
far wall with no one seated near them.

"What the hell happened out there?" Gianfranco asked. "We
heard shots."

I sat on the barstool next to him. "Your man on the roof is
dead. I told your men outside."

"Damn it. How?"

"When I got to the rooftop, he was already dead. Someone
fired at me from the adjacent building. I got your man's rifle and
pistol and returned fire. I leapt across to the other building, but
the man was gone. I lost him. I have no idea where he is, but I'm
sure it was Utkin."

"Your father and Michelle are safe for now." Gianfranco
nodded toward their table. My father motioned for me to come
over. "Go ahead, I need to step outside and talk to my men."

Dad and Michelle were sitting across from each other at
a table for four, having cocktails—my father, a martini, and
Michelle, a Bellini. I sat at the seat to my father's left where I
had a clear view of the front entrance.

My father looked me up and down. "You're a mess," he said.

"What have you been doing?"

"Trying to prevent the two of you from getting killed."

"Why don't you join us for dinner? We haven't ordered yet."

"How can you sit here and order dinner as if nothing happened. Are you crazy? A Russian hit man is in Positano and is trying to kill you, and he's brought some of his thugs to help him do it. He already killed one of Gianfranco's men."

Michelle gasped. My father's expression changed ever so slightly. "We heard the shots," he said. "We're safer here than anywhere else. You and Gianfranco's men are guarding us."

"You're not at all safe here." I looked at Michelle. "Talk some sense into him."

"I tried and failed. Your father is a stubborn man."

"I can't stay."

My father tilted his head and said, "Where are you going?"

"Getting the two of us in the same place is exactly what Utkin wants," I said. "I need to check in with Fiona and find Utkin before he finds us. Continue sipping your martini, if you must. I need to talk to Gianfranco."

I was at the door when Gianfranco came back inside. "They're gone," Gianfranco whispered.

"Who's gone?"

"My men at the door," he whispered.

I pushed the door open enough to see outside. The two guards were gone.

"I can't raise anyone on the communicator," Gianfranco said. "I need to check on my man in the back. You stay here."

In a few minutes, Gianfranco returned. He shook his head as he approached.

"What is it?" I said.

Gianfranco's face was pale. "He's gone. They're all gone. So are their weapons."

"Any sign of blood?"

"None that was obvious. I didn't linger."

One man was dead on the rooftop, and three were missing. Utkin was closing in. We were trapped inside the restaurant. Utkin controlled the space outside.

I went to the maître d' and said, "Call the police. We're in danger."

"What!"

"You heard me. Tell them some men are trying to kill Edward Palmer and Michelle Petrochelli. They've already killed one of the security team, maybe all four of them."

"The police are not so quick to respond this time of year."

"I don't care. Call them."

The maître d' picked up the phone and dialed a number, his hands shaking. He spoke in Italian. After a rapid exchange, he hung up. "The police are coming. The nearest car is in Amalfi, tied up with a traffic fatality. The dispatcher called another unit. They'll be here as soon as they can, within the hour."

I called Fiona. No answer. I needed to find her. What if Utkin or his men had her? I shouldn't have left her alone, but I had no other choice. I went back to the table and told my father and Michelle that the three security guards outside the restaurant were missing. The other customers were watching him. They knew something was up, and whatever it was wasn't good.

"Should we go?" Michelle said.

"No," my father said. "We're not leaving until the police arrive. We're safer here than out there."

"He's right," I said. "If we leave the restaurant, Utkin would get what he wanted, the three of us together and out in the open. The police are on the way. We'll stay here."

Gianfranco and I needed to keep my father and Michelle safe for an hour. It was unlikely that Utkin would storm the restaurant. That wasn't his style.

"I don't like waiting," I said. "By the time the police arrive, Utkin will have vanished. He'll then pick his time and place to finish the job. I need to find him now, before the police arrive. You stay with them."

"Where are you going?" Michelle asked.

"To find Fiona and kill Viktor Utkin." I told Gianfranco where I was going and exited the front entrance of the restaurant, sprinting across the street. I expected to hear bullets sailing past me and ricocheting off the pavement. There were none. I made it to the other side of the street and had my back against the building across from the restaurant, moving along the structures until I felt it was safe to break into a run. Reaching our hotel, I went inside. The manager was not behind the desk.

When I got to our room, I used my key and opened the door. Not good. The deadbolt wasn't engaged. I drew the pistol from my belt and went inside. I cleared the room and bathroom. No sign of Fiona and no sign of a struggle. I went to Utkin's room. The door was still open from where I had kicked it in earlier. *Where the hell is Fiona? Do they have her?*

When I returned to the lobby, the manager who had checked us in was back behind the desk.

"Have you seen Mr. Petroski? Or Ms. Collins?" I said calmly.

"Ms. Collins left with three men a few minutes ago. They walked in that direction." The manager pointed in the direction of the restaurant.

My heart sank. "With Petroski?"

"No. He wasn't with them."

"Has Petroski checked out?"

"Not yet. He paid for a week in advance."

43

I DIDN'T KNOW which direction to turn. My strongest instinct was to find Fiona. Once again, I had put her in danger. If anything happened to her, I would never forgive myself. *God, let her be safe. I'll never let this happen again.*

I stood at the hotel desk and concentrated, attempting to put emotion aside and treat the situation as a mission gone horribly wrong. *What should I do?* The answer seemed obvious. I would protect the target. I should return to the restaurant to protect my father. Otherwise, I was simply being lured away from him by my burning desire to kill Utkin and my heartfelt urge to find and protect Fiona. Gianfranco and I had to keep Dad and Michelle safe until the police arrived, less than an hour. We could manage that. Logic dictated that Fiona would be used as a bargaining chip to get my father. That's one bridge I'd have to cross when I came to it.

"Mr. Palmer, are you all right?" said the hotel manager.

"I'm okay."

I left and walked at a deliberate pace down the middle of the street toward the restaurant. Although it was a stupid thing to do, I was desperate to draw Utkin and his henchmen out. It was almost ten o'clock, and the streets were deserted. The thought of losing my father and Fiona on the same night was more than I could bear. I had to calm myself and gain control of the situation.

When I got to the restaurant, I burst in. The table where my father and Michelle and been sitting with Gianfranco was empty, as were most of the others. I heard voices and swung my head around. Three men were drinking coffee at a table near the bar, two middle-aged men and a youngish man with long hair. I turned to the restaurant manager who was standing nearby.

"Where are they? Where is everyone?" I asked.

"The other customers became nervous. They asked for their bills even before finishing their meals and left. Everyone's gone except them." He nodded toward the men. Your family is in the storage room. Follow me."

I glanced back at the bar before going with the manager. The three men were watching us. When we got to the storage room, Gianfranco was standing outside the door. Before I could speak, he said, "I decided it was best to isolate them from the restaurant. Fiona's inside."

"What?"

I went inside the small storage room. My father, Michelle, and Fiona were standing together talking.

I grabbed and hugged Fiona. "I've never been so glad to see you. How did you get here? Who were the men with you when you left the hotel?"

"Branson."

A puzzled look came across my face. "Who?"

"Branson van Buren. You know. FinCEN. He was flying into Rome today. He doesn't look like any finance type I've ever seen. How did he find you?"

"He went to our first hotel. When we weren't in, he phoned your father. You had given DuPont contact information for him, including his Italian contract phone. Your father told him where we were staying."

"Right. That's good. That's actually great. I'm glad you're here."

"Gianfranco said the plan is to hunker down and wait for the police," Fiona said.

"Is that van Buren at the bar?" I asked. "The man with long hair."

"Yes and he has two men with him. I'm not sure who they are," Fiona said. "There's something I need to tell you. It's important."

"Tell me when I get back," I said as I left.

"Jake!" Fiona shouted.

I kept going. I went to the bar and introduced myself. Van Buren explained that he had checked in with the Homeland Security Investigations office and with the Italian *Raggruppamento Operativo Speciale*, or ROS, in Rome, when he arrived. The ROS, he explained, investigated organized crime and terrorism and worked with the Finance Ministry on terrorist financing. He told them why he was in Italy and said he needed to get to Positano to meet with my father and me. They told him he could not go alone, and someone would need to sit in on the interviews, so they brought him here. I looked at the other man, who looked like an American. Van Buren explained he was with HSI and based in Rome.

"A multiple car accident occurred on the road a few miles back. We just made it through. The road could be blocked for a while," van Buren said.

"We'll protect you until the police arrive," one of the men said. "We've called for backup as well."

"Do you know who's out there?" I said, motioning toward the door.

"Gianfranco said it was Viktor Utkin and his men," the HSI agent said.

At that moment, a crash came from the back of the restaurant. Two men barreled through the front entrance with guns drawn. Neither was Utkin. The restaurant manager dropped behind the desk.

I reached for my pistol. Van Buren's butt was glued to the chair. The ROS man and the HSI man with him drew their pistols and pointed them at the men. They shouted in Italian. "*Cada le vostre armi*, which I interpreted to mean drop your damn guns or kiss your ass goodbye.

No reply was expected and none came. The first shot came from one of two attackers who had entered the front door. It struck one of the ROS men in the hip, knocking him down. The second attacker shot the HSI man in the left arm. Still, he managed to get off a shot, hitting the attacker who had shot him. I fired my Glock twice, hitting one of them in the chest. He fell backward. Before the other one could swing his pistol around, I fired another three rounds, killing him. Van Buren was crouched on the floor, covering his head with his hands. The ROS man and HSI man were wounded but alive.

A third attacker ran in from the back door of the restaurant with a semi-automatic rifle and starting shooting. He stopped, aimed at van Buren and pulled the trigger. The rifle jammed. I jumped for a pistol on the floor beside the ROS man, sliding across the floor, as the attacker worked to clear the jam.

Before I could retrieve the pistol from the floor, van Buren leapt from his chair and rushed him, ramming his shoulder into the attacker's abdomen and knocking the rifle from his hands. The man attempted to get up and was gasping for air when van Buren struck him in the side of the neck with his fist. He was out.

"Wow. That was impressive for anyone, especially so for an accountant."

It had all happened in a matter of seconds. By the time Gianfranco arrived, it was over. He tore a tablecloth into pieces and tied up the attacker van Buren had slammed into, while I checked on the ROS and HSI agents. The ROS agent was dead, and the HSI agent was wounded and bleeding profusely. I called Gianfranco over. Using the remainder of the tablecloth, he worked to stop the bleeding.

The police and backup agents were on the way. The wreck on the cliffside road would slow them down. He had maybe a half hour, certainly no more than an hour. I guessed that Utkin ordered his three men to wound and kill as many of us as they could. As a result, one of us was dead; and another, injured. Two of Utkin's men were dead and one was injured. It was a chess match, sacrificing pawns to put some rooks and knights out of action. It was only the beginning, an initial incursion. Utkin was coming soon.

"Can you handle a gun?" I asked van Buren.

"Don't like guns. I've never fired one."

"Now might be a good time to learn."

^^^^

I peeked out the restaurant window, watching for any movement. How much longer could Utkin wait? The police would arrive soon. But would they arrive in time. The options were limited. It was Utkin and at least one more of his men against Gianfranco and me. I wasn't counting on van Buren unless we got into a fistfight, which was unlikely. Utkin could withdraw and regroup for an attack on the way to the airport tomorrow or in the US after they got back. By then, my father would have met with the feds and given a statement incriminating Richard Moore. No. It was now or never.

Having collected the pistols off the dead and wounded men in the restaurant, we had plenty of firepower to fend off another assault. I told Gianfranco to guard the rear entrance while I guarded the front. Van Buren seemed incapable of moving or speaking.

I held out a pistol for him. "Use it or you're no good to anyone. In that case, you should go to the storeroom with the others, where you'll be safe."

Van Buren took the pistol. His hand was shaking as he stared at it.

The pistol was loaded with a round in the chamber. I gave him a quick lesson. "Don't worry about changing the magazine. By the time you fire all the rounds, it'll be over. Got that?"

"Yeah. Keep firing until either it's empty or I'm dead."

Gianfranco and I moved the wounded HSI agent behind the bar. He was stable but in need of medical care. The bar provided some protection. It was away from the windows and door. The police should have cleared the wreck by now or found a way around it. Thirty minutes max. That was Utkin's window of opportunity. He wouldn't wait until the last minute. He was coming soon.

"How can you appear so calm?" Van Buren asked.

"You learn to control your emotions and focus on the task at hand. If fear overcomes you, the enemy has the advantage. Your objective is to make them fear you; theirs is to make you fear them."

"It difficult to make them fear us when we're the ones pinned down."

Van Buren was right. We were the ones on the defensive. Utkin was on the offensive and had the upper hand. He had sacrificed his men to inflict as much damage on us as possible. If his men had killed us, they would have stepped outside and told him it was over. They didn't, so he would assume they were dead. But he wouldn't know how many of us had been killed or wounded. It didn't matter. Whatever the outcome, it was a good tradeoff. Next time there would be no walking in the door with a pistol. Utkin will have saved the best for last. His sniper rifle would be relatively useless in close quarters. He would need a short barrel automatic rifle or maybe an explosive device, like a grenade or two.

My thoughts were jarred by the sound of bullets hitting the restaurant's front windows and striking inside the restaurant. Utkin wasn't trying to hit us as much as he was keeping us on edge.

"Incoming," I shouted to Gianfranco.

"He's softening us up," Gianfranco shouted back.

"Be ready."

Van Buren and I were crouched on the floor behind the bar. A couple of the rounds struck the mirror behind the bar where the liquor was displayed, shattering a few of the liquor bottles. Van Buren curled up in a tight ball.

"Wait here. I need to talk to Gianfranco," I said. "If you hear something crash through the window, duck down, close your eyes, and cover your ears. After the blast, start firing because Utkin will follow it in. Don't worry about aiming. You only want to get his attention." Before van Buren could protest, I was gone.

"It's me," I shouted, as I approached Gianfranco near the back entrance to the restaurant.

"Who's guarding the front?" Gianfranco said.

"Van Buren."

"With what?"

"I showed him how to use a pistol."

Gianfranco cocked his head and squinted. Then shook his head. "I figure Utkin's about ready."

"Right. Look, I've got to do something. Otherwise, he is going to have the upper hand. He'll probably have an automatic weapon and maybe a flashbang."

"If he lobs in a flashbang, which he probably will, he'll come in right behind it, knowing we'll be stunned," Gianfranco said.

"Keep watch on the back door. I'm going to talk to the manager. I need to see if there's another way out, a less obvious one than the rear door you're guarding. If there is, I'll call your cell phone when I'm there."

Both switched their cell phones to vibrate. "Good luck. Been nice knowing you if this doesn't end well," Gianfranco said.

"Same here."

With that, I was off to the storage room. Fiona ran up and hugged me. She held me tight in her arms as I explained what I wanted to do and asked the manager about any other exits or entrances. Dad and Michelle listened intently, as did Fiona. The manager told me how to get to the floor two levels above, where there were windows but no fire escape. I gave Fiona a quick hug and kiss and took off.

I had two pistols, both with partially loaded magazines. That was enough for what I had to do. The pending face-off would not result in a prolonged exchange of gunfire. It would be a quick and violent end, one way or the other. I made it to the third level. The structure was once a residence, but from the look of it, had not been used in quite some time.

The windows were covered with dusty, tattered curtains. I walked around, looked out each of the windows. My best chance at avoiding detection was to leave out the side window. The adjoined building was a single level. I unlatched the window and pushed. It had not been raised in years and took effort to break the layers of paint that glued it shut. The drop from the window to the rooftop of the other building was about ten feet. Before I climbed out the window, I made certain both pistols were snug in my belt. I flipped around and held on to the windowsill with my hands and let my legs hang down. The windowsill creaked, and then the rotten wood cracked and gave way. I crashed onto the rooftop with a thud.

I had landed on an uneven place in the roof and rolled my right ankle. A mouthful of unspoken expletives filled my mind. I stood and tested the ankle, wincing in pain. Although it hurt like hell, I told myself that sometimes, walking off a bad sprain is the best thing to do. Sometimes it isn't.

The rooftop was flat. There was a four-foot parapet wall with a small coping on the top. I limped to the back of the building and looked down over the wall to the alleyway. The alley was dimly lit, but I could see a man holding an automatic rifle and standing behind a trash receptacle. Beside him was a dark pile—the security guards' bodies. Utkin had probably instructed the man to wait until he heard gunfire and then charge through the rear entrance for a simultaneous frontal and rear assault.

I had a fairly easy, although unconventional, shot. The only thing standing in my way was the fact that the gunshot would give away my position and might prompt Utkin to strike. On the other hand, if I didn't shoot him, Gianfranco had little chance against the automatic rifle. And if the man killed Gianfranco, everyone else was as good as dead.

I hobbled over to the front of the building and looked over the edge. The street was empty. A fire ladder was attached to the side of the building, one that was inaccessible from the ground. Assuming it was still functional, I could climb onto the ladder and my weight would extend the ladder to the ground. However, that could make enough noise to attract the attention of both Utkin and the man in the alley. I made my decision, called Gianfranco, and told him the plan. Gianfranco said he would go to the front of the restaurant with van Buren after he heard the shot.

Moving to the back edge of the building, I leaned over the parapet wall. The man was fifteen to twenty feet directly below and shifting nervously back and forth. I took one of the pistols from my belt and aimed downward, steadying my hands and the pistol against the wall, waiting for him to stop. The only kill shot was the top of the man's head, probably seven or eight inches in length and six or so inches across, about the size of a center bull's-eye on a pistol range target. I had fired the same type of pistol before but not this particular one. Having not sighted it in, I could not trust its accuracy. The pain in my ankle was breaking my concentration. I took the weight off it just as he became still. I pulled the trigger, and he went down like a rock.

I shoved the pistol into my waistband in the back and climbed onto the ladder. Within seconds, I was on the ground, running in the alleyway to the street. In spite of the cool weather, I broke out in a sweat. As I rounded the corner, a concussion grenade exploded in the restaurant. The sound was unmistakable. The M4 stun grenade explodes with a flash of over one million candela and almost two hundred decibels. Gianfranco and van Buren would be disoriented and have temporary blindness, deafness, and loss of balance. Utkin was right behind it, running across the street toward the front entrance. He would have seen me, had the incredible sound and shock wave from the grenade not still been in the air. I slammed into him just before he got to the door.

The force of the collision knocked an automatic rifle from Utkin's hands. It tumbled to a stop several feet away. The impact also knocked one of the pistols from my waistband. Both of us bounced onto our feet. Utkin saw my pistol on the ground and flashed a wide smile.

"Jake Palmer."

"Give it up, Utkin. It's done. Your men are dead." The two-tone wail of the sirens in the distance was not getting any louder. "The police are coming. Shouldn't you be going?"

"I have enough time to kill you and your father. It won't take long. Besides, we left a little roadblock, on the highway each side of the town. Traffic may be a problem."

I reached for my other pistol. As I did, Utkin charged and hit me with the full force of his large frame. I landed on my back, my holstered pistol smashing into my spine. Utkin, now on top of me, grabbed my throat with both hands. I tried to push his hands away, but Utkin was a beast.

I couldn't breathe. I searched for leverage, finding none. If I didn't do something quick, Utkin would crush my windpipe. *Where the hell is Gianfranco?* I tried to slap Utkin's ears, but Utkin blocked with his elbows. I tried to go through Utkin's arms to get to his neck, but Utkin straightened his arms.

Utkin looked toward the restaurant door. Gianfranco was staggering out, shaking his head. He was still reeling from the flash bang. A pistol in his hand hung limply by his leg. Utkin released one of his hands from my throat, reached behind him and threw a knife at Gianfranco. The move was so quick, I could hardly see it. The blade hit Gianfranco in the chest, near the heart. He stumbled back, looked at the knife in disbelief, and then to me, before falling onto the street.

With one of Utkin's hands freed from my throat, I slapped Utkin's ear and then hit his nose with the palm of my hand. Blood spurted and he groaned, putting both hands again on my throat. Out of the corner of my eye, I saw someone else exit from the restaurant. It was van Buren. He moved toward Utkin, shuffling his feet on the pavement, like an old man. His pistol was unsteady but aimed in Utkin's general direction.

"Shoot the bastard," I grunted.

Utkin smiled at van Buren.

"Pull the trigger, or we both die," I shouted.

Utkin laughed. "You'd better be quick kid or he's right. You'll both die tonight."

Van Buren, his hands shaking and the pistol pointed at Utkin, was now close enough to touch.

"Pull the damn trigger, or he'll grab your gun," I shouted.

Without any emotion on his face, Van Buren lurched at Utkin, striking him on the side of the head with the butt of the pistol. The blow was too high and too light.

Utkin's right fist connected with van Buren's temple. Van Buren went down like a tree falling, the back of his head hitting the street and bouncing.

I pushed and rolled Utkin on his side and then reached for the pistol in my waistband. Utkin grabbed my wrist with his right hand and pushed. When he did, I rose and bit into his nose. Blood gushed from Utkin's nose. He screamed and pulled back, tearing away. I spit blood and skin onto his face.

I moved the pistol's barrel toward Utkin's chest. His eyes were wide with fury, not fear. With blood dripping from his nose, he pushed my arm away.

"Drop the gun, Mr. Palmer," a man with a Russian accent shouted. I jerked my head around. A man with a pistol aimed at my head stood just out of reach. Weren't all of Utkin's men dead? Of course—Utkin held one man in reserve in case things went wrong, or maybe he was the one who had organized the roadblock and had just returned to the party. I relaxed my grip on the gun. Utkin took it and stood over me.

"You'll never get away, Utkin," I said.

"So long, Jake Palmer. After you're dead, I'll kill your father, his wife, and your girlfriend."

"*Arresto!*" said a male voice. "Stop!" he repeated with an Italian accent.

Three men moved toward Utkin and his man. Each had a pump shotgun pressed into his shoulder. *Who the hell were they?*

Utkin and his man backed away, swinging their pistols toward the men. Utkin's man muttered something in Russian. Utkin, wiping blood from his face, stepped sideways toward an alleyway. A shotgun blast knocked Utkin's man off his feet. Utkin took off toward the alleyway. The third man discharged his shotgun at him. Utkin flinched and kept running.

One of the men walked over to me, "You okay?"

"Yes. Not to seem ungrateful, but who are you?"

"*Amici*. Friends. Where is Fiona?"

They knew Fiona? Fiona! I ran into the restaurant and to the storage room, asking myself how they knew Fiona? I found her and the others huddled into a corner of the room. Seeing Utkin's blood and bits of nose tissue on me was more than Fiona could take. She burst into tears. Michelle covered her face and turned away. My father took a couple of steps backwards, recovered, and then rushed to my side. The restaurant manager stood back, muttering something in Italian and crossing himself. The sirens were finally getting louder.

"I'll be right back," I said to Fiona.

"Don't leave," she pleaded. "Where are you going?"

"To find Utkin."

When I got outside, the three shotgun-toting men were gone. Van Buren's pistol was still on the street. I grabbed it as I ran by. I could tell by the weight and the fact the barrel was cold, that he had not fired it. I checked the magazine anyway.

Chances were Utkin was long gone. Knowing the police would seal off the road into and out of Positano, his plan had to be to escape by sea. I had seen a dock near the restaurant where Fiona and I had eaten lunch. If Utkin got there first and a boat was waiting, it would be too late to catch him. If, on the other hand, the shotgun wound and my bite off of his nose had slowed him down, I might just get there before him, even with my bad ankle.

I ran at full speed to the dock. My ankle was killing me, but I refused to allow the pain to slow me. A man was smoking a cigarette near the far end of the dock. A high-speed motor yacht was tied up beside him. I'd done it. I had beaten Utkin there. Maybe he was bleeding out in one of the side streets. With the pistol by my side, I walked on the dock toward the yacht.

The man flicked his cigarette into the water and said something in Italian. The boat's motor roared to life. The man on the dock untied the bow and stern lines and stepped aboard the boat. They had been waiting for someone. If Utkin were onboard, they would have already left.

"Viktor Utkin. I'm looking for Viktor Utkin," I shouted.

The boat's motor roared and revved up. *Odd, unless*—I spun around. Utkin was standing behind me. The sound of the motor had covered his approach. On the well-lit dock, I could clearly see his wounds. The man was a frightful sight. His face was a bloody mess, as was his left side. Utkin had been too far away for the shotgun blast to be fatal, but the pellets had done their damage, and he was losing blood.

Before I could bring my pistol to bear, Utkin sprang forward and threw a punch that landed on the side of my face, knocking me to my knees. The pistol flew out of my hand and slid on the dock, stopping inches from the edge. I couldn't allow Utkin to get on top of me again. As bad off as Utkin appeared, he was still strong as an ox and could easily kill me. Utkin drew his leg back; his foot hit me like a sledgehammer in the stomach. I doubled over.

Utkin kicked again. I rolled out of the way, feeling his foot brush through my hair. As his foot sailed by, I grabbed it, pushed up and twisted, causing Utkin to lose his balance. His back hit the concrete dock. I popped up to my feet.

"Stay down, Utkin. You're done."

"I'm never done," Utkin said. He reached toward his foot.

A gun in an ankle holster or another knife? I grabbed his arm. He grabbed mine in return. He pulled, and I resisted. I wasn't going to let him get me down again. He gripped my arm with his massive hands and used my weight to pull himself up. I took my free hand and struck him in what remained of his nose. He retreated a couple of steps to the edge of the dock. As he did, the back of his foot knocked my pistol into the water. I shoved him and we both fell in.

Once under the surface, I saw my pistol sinking below us. I swam toward it. Utkin grabbed my leg with one hand and used his free hand to reach for his ankle. Whether it was small pistol or a knife, I didn't care. Either way I was in trouble. I kicked the leg he was holding, pushed away from Utkin, and swam toward the pistol, grabbing it just before it vanished from my sight. Rolling onto my back, I saw Utkin. He was in the water above me, silhouetted by dock lights. Utkin was raising his arm to get his pistol in a position to fire. I kicked my legs, propelling me toward him. I had to get as close to him as possible for the shot to be effective. With our arms outstretched, the gun barrels were about five feet apart, close enough for a bullet fired underwater to be lethal. Utkin and I both fired.

Kicking to the surface, I came up gasping for air, my ears ringing. Utkin popped up beside me face down. I grabbed his motionless body around the neck in a lifeguard rescue hold and swam the short distance to the shore. I laid him on his back at the edge of the water. The round from my pistol had hit Utkin in the forehead. Utkin's bullet had missed me. I sat beside Utkin's lifeless body, as the motor yacht disappeared into the night. It was over.

44

UTKIN'S KNIFE HAD missed Gianfranco's heart and major blood vessels by less than an inch. The paramedics examined him at the scene; and with the knife still in his chest, they transported him to the hospital for treatment, where he was expected to recover. Utkin's fist had knocked van Buren out cold. He was semi-alert and suffering the lingering effects of the flashbang grenade but refused to go to the hospital. Tough kid. The Italian ROS man, who accompanied van Buren to Positano, was dead, and the HSI agent was hospitalized with multiple gunshot wounds. The police identified Utkin and all of his men, each of whom had an extensive criminal record.

Fiona told me she had phoned Anthony Calabrese and let him know we were in Positano, and in serious trouble. She had kept the card he had given me in New York with nothing but his phone number on it. She gave him the addresses of our hotel and the restaurant. Calabrese said he would take care of it and hung up. He had sent the three men who showed up in the alleyway with shotguns, the men who saved my life. Now I was indebted to Calabrese, a debt that would need to be paid upon his request and without question, regardless of what I was told to do. Those were the rules; at least those were his rules. I don't like being told to do something without having a say in what it is. I added that to my list of bridges to cross at a later date, when I saw him.

The Italian press and television news reported the story, which was picked up by the international media. Once again, Fiona was more than happy to serve as a translator. Gianfranco, Fiona, and I received numerous requests to be interviewed. Gianfranco spoke from his hospital bed, only to be certain his men's sacrifices were fully appreciated. Fiona declined the requests, saying only that she worked for B&A Pharmaceuticals and all questions should be referred to B&A's legal department. As for me, stating I was working with US Homeland Security Investigations might cause some hard feelings at home with people I would work with in the future. Instead, I said Fiona and I were romantically involved, and I had accompanied her to Italy to meet up with my father and Michelle Petrochelli.

Moore's attorneys insisted my father was responsible for the money laundering, and Moore was unaware that counterfeit medicines were in HealthTech's supply chain. The official HealthTech statement expressed concern about the counterfeit medicines and their negative impact on health and on society. It also stated that HealthTech would assess its internal controls and make any changes required to ensure its distribution channels were free of counterfeit medicines. It was all corporate communications bullshit, of course.

The full investigation by the local and national Italian police took several days. The local police whisked away my father and Michelle and placed them under protective custody at their hotel in Positano until van Buren and a Rome-based HSI agent escorted them to New York. Tammaro and a detective interrogated Fiona and me. After a few days, Tammaro told Fiona and me that we were free to leave Italy.

∧∧∧∧

When we returned to England, I stayed with Fiona at her house in Sevenoaks Weald. Her peaceful village was good therapy. We bundled up and went on long, country walks in the Kent countryside, stopping for lunch in quiet pubs, warmed by log fires. The night before I was to leave, we made love. It was more passionate and uninhibited than usual, as if our two bodies had become one. Afterwards, I was lying on my back. Fiona rolled on top and kissed me deeply. Her tears dropped from her eyes onto my cheek.

"Was it that bad?" I whispered with a smile.

"No. It was wonderful."

"Why the tears then?"

"It felt like the final time," Fiona said, sniffling.

"How about again tomorrow morning before I leave?"

When she didn't answer, I became worried. "Fiona, what is it? Talk to me."

"I can't. Not now. Tomorrow morning before you leave. I promise."

I didn't sleep much that night. Her comment brought me to only one conclusion.

When I woke the next morning, I reached for Fiona before opening my eyes. She wasn't there. I got dressed and followed the smell of coffee brewing in the kitchen. After we finished an early breakfast, she cleared the table and sat back down with a cup of tea.

"I love you. You know that, don't you?" Fiona said.

"I do. I love you, too."

"Then you must know how hard it is for me to say that I can't go on like this. No matter how hard I try, I can't un-see you covered with blood. It's there every time I close my eyes. I need to get on with my life, Jake. My normal work and social life—dinner with girlfriends after a long day at work, going to the cinema, seeing a play, visiting a new exhibit at the museum, going to the opera. You told me once that the adrenaline rush is addictive, and it's hard to return to the mundane day-to-day job after you've been in the thick of the fight. I get it. It happened before. I returned to work, settled into my routine, and realized I was bored by the relative monotony of it. Maybe it will happen again. I'll be bored to death and find I can't live without you. But I must try."

"I understand. Believe me, I do. I can't continue to put you through this. I care for you too much to do that," I said.

"Don't get me wrong. Our relationship has been romantic, exciting, and at times, terrifying. That's affected me in ways I can't begin to describe. I need some time to sort out my conflicting thoughts and feelings."

"This isn't the end, is it? We'll still keep in touch and see each other, right?"

She smiled and punched me lightly on the arm. "Yes, you silly man. I just need a little time."

That was a *yes*; however, the smile on her face didn't match what her eyes told me. Seeing me might kindle more bad memories than good and if she had PTSD, might cause her to regress. I've watched several of my friends struggle with it, trying counseling, antidepressants, marijuana, alcohol, or yoga to overcome the devastating effect of living with a violent past. When she was ready, if ever, I would be waiting. Did she want me to talk her out of this? Should I say more? Whatever I said would most likely come out all wrong, and it was doubtful anything I said would change her mind. Maybe she just needed a short break from me.

"I do understand, Fiona. I'll let you be the judge of when. No matter how long that takes, I'll be waiting."

^ ^ ^ ^

I was in the boarding gate at Heathrow when my cell phone rang. *Fiona?* Without looking at the phone, I answered, excited that she had called. It was van Buren.

I walked over to a relatively quiet corner of the lounge, where I could talk to him without being overheard. Van Buren said meetings with my father regarding his involvement with Richard Moore and HealthTech had been productive. In exchange for his full cooperation, it was likely that the US Attorney would not charge my father. I smiled, picturing Dad and Michelle in the witness protection program. That would never happen. I couldn't envision them holed up in Podunk, Idaho, with false identities, living an unassuming life in an eighteen hundred square-foot home.

Van Buren told me that Homeland Security Investigations and FinCEN resources had been applied to track the HealthTech money my father had laundered. Most of the banks had probably not violated any laws. Liberty Banking & Trust, on the other hand, may have been aware and more directly involved, especially as it related to the incident at the bank regarding the contents of Goodman's safe deposit box and the subsequent wreck.

Ray Addison, the Liberty Banking & Trust senior vice president, was being investigated. FinCEN believed Saudi Sheikh Khalifa Isma'il El-Hashem, a major investor in HealthTech and a recipient of laundered cash from the company, was funneling money through some sketchy Muslim charities to Islamic extremists. This was nothing new. Saudis donated to Muslim charities as a means to fund terrorist organizations. It would be almost impossible to implicate Sheikh El-Hashem or any other donor who did not want to be identified.

"The higher ups are running around like ADHD college kids off their meds," van Buren said. "You've really impressed the top brass. I've heard they want you to work with us or HSI."

"I'm flattered, but no," I said.

"Just giving you a heads up."

"Thanks. I'll be sure not to answer my phone if the caller ID is a clandestine government agency. By the way kid, you did great in Positano. Had you not tapped Utkin on the head things could have turned out differently than they did. I owe you."

"I thought I was a tough guy, rugby player, martial arts and all. I discovered I'm not so tough. When the bullets started flying, I lost it. I may have actually wet myself. After the concussion grenade exploded, I was out of it. I hardly remember going outside. Then Utkin knocked me out like he was swatting a fly. I've got to get back to the gym."

∧∧∧∧

My father had insisted on upgrading me to first class on the flight to Philadelphia. I didn't argue. The episode had brought us closer together. Whether or not his investment company would survive was still in question. Even if the company went under, I was certain both Dad and Patrick had fat rainy-day funds squirrelled away, ones that would carry them through comfortable, although not extravagant, retirements.

The plane took off on time, soon rising to the thick clouds that covered southern England. After bumping through the cloud layer, we emerged into sunshine and the perfect blue sky. I stared blankly out the window. Like Fiona, I was looking forward to getting on with my normal life. Unlike her, I had difficulty imagining what that would look like.

45

THE DAY AFTER returning to Philadelphia, I met with Agent DuPont over a cup of coffee. He said Dr. Abercrombie's warehouse had been raided and some counterfeit medicines, including Transpro, were found. The FDA inspectors cited Abercrombie with several violations, most of which would be corrected before the inspectors were back behind their desks in Bethesda, Maryland.

HSI had traced the counterfeit Transpro to a manufacturing plant near Bangalore, India. Local law enforcement, accompanied by a local HSI agent, went to the site, only to discover the building was empty. DuPont told me that my father was a valuable asset in the case against Richard Moore and HealthTech. HSI was working with the US Internal Revenue Service, the UK HM Revenue & Customs, and the Italian Revenue Agency to indict Moore on international money laundering and tax evasion. My father's testimony, along with that of Antonio Moretti in Italy, would bring Moore down. The Italian investigators could not prove whether Moretti was involved with Utkin and Baxter at the warehouse in Civitavecchia or was a victim, as he claimed. However, Moretti had distanced himself from the HealthTech attorney who was representing him and had hired his own lawyer. Moretti was now cooperating with the authorities' counterfeit medicine investigation of Richard Moore and

HealthTech. Of course, Moore argued that my father and the HealthTech finance department were in collusion, and he had no direct involvement or knowledge of the money laundering or the counterfeit medicines. Because Viktor Utkin and Mike Baxter were dead and the surviving gunmen knew nothing about Moore, evidence that he had any connection to the deaths of Dennis Goodman, Hristo Adonov, Rick Middleton, and the men at Positano would be circumstantial at best.

Not long after returning to New York, Dad announced his retirement from Palmer Global Investments and turned the business over to Patrick. He told me that he wanted out while he served as a state witness against Richard Moore and HealthTech. He feared that when news of what he had done for HealthTech became public, it would destroy the company. News of HealthTech's possible involvement in the distribution of counterfeit medicines, Dad's retirement, and PGI's possible involvement in money laundering was enough to panic investors. Many of them were already closing their PGI accounts. I doubted Patrick would be able to keep the company afloat. On a personal note, Dad and Michelle were getting along well. I was wrong about her. She had a good heart and stood by him when others would have walked away. Although Dad and I had become much closer, he still did not understand what I did for a living, and that was okay with me.

^^^^

One morning, I left my condo to go for a run and found a black Mercedes S-Class waiting outside with the motor running. The front passenger window went down and a man said Mr. Calabrese wanted to see me. I sat beside Calabrese in the back seat, as I had done before. He thanked me for what I had accomplished; and likewise, I thanked him for saving my life, as well as those of Fiona, Michelle, and my father. In a few well-chosen words, he confessed that he might have played a part in the importation and distribution of counterfeit drugs, including the drug that killed his nephew. His brother was unaware of it, and he planned to keep it that way. Calabrese said he was finished with that unsavory business and would revert to other ways of making money, ones that let him sleep at night. I didn't ask what those were. I was certain there was very little that kept Anthony Calabrese awake from worry or guilt. He looked me in the eyes and shook my hand, saying he would be in touch. I couldn't describe it, but something about his expression and tone made me believe that Richard Moore was a dead man walking.

Eventually, I received a call from a Special Agent in Charge at the Office of Homeland Security Investigations, the call van Buren warned me about. He said that the deputy director wanted to meet with me regarding a full-time position. I told him I had no interest in having a boss or having any job I couldn't walk away from but might consider some contract work.

The next day, while at home, my cell phone rang again— another D.C. area code, with no caller ID. I hesitated before curiosity got the best of me, and I answered. A man said, "Mr. Palmer, please hold for the President of the United States." I stifled a laugh, thinking it was a spoof of some kind; however, in a few seconds, I heard the distinctive voice of the president. He thanked me for my service in Naval Special Warfare and for what I had done recently with Homeland Security Investigations and FinCEN, as well as breaking up the terrorist cell in Virginia a couple of years ago. He said he had been informed that I was not interested in working for Homeland Security or anyone else. He tugged on my emotions and patriotism, saying I had once answered the call to duty, and he was asking I do it again. The country needed me, and someone from Joint Special Operations Command would be in touch. I couldn't say no to the president, so I said only that I looked forward to the call. I'd see what JSOC had to say.

Maybe it was a premonition or a coincidence that Fiona was on my mind when she called later that afternoon. More likely, it was because she was never out of my thoughts for long. She spoke so fast that I could barely get a word in. Where was the glum, downhearted Fiona I had kissed goodbye when she dropped me off at Heathrow?

"I met with the CEO when I returned to work after you left," Fiona said. "He offered me a position as the global director of audit across all divisions."

"That's fantastic, Fiona. And you were afraid he would fire you."

"You'll find this interesting. He told me regardless of whether I took the position or kept my current one, I must avoid any further entanglements that would reflect poorly on B&A. Some people, he said, were not happy having an employee running around like an action hero. He gave me until the end of the month to decide."

"Am I the entanglement?"

"That's how I interpreted it," she said.

"Did you tell him that was no longer an issue because you were done with me?"

"Of course, not. Now, you're going to think I'm really crazy."

"I already do. It's a good crazy. The kind of crazy I love."

"I've turned down the job."

"Let me guess—because you couldn't promise him you'd never get entangled with me again?"

"No, because I've accepted a job with MI6, the UK Secret Intelligence Service."

"What? MI6! Your CIA? Why? What happened?"

"After my meeting with the CEO, I thought about the position he offered me and realized I wasn't as excited about it as I should have been. It wasn't the job. It was that after all that's happened, I was ready to move on, turn the page. Don't get me wrong. I'm proud of what I've done with B&A, and the company's been good to me. But I needed a job that would reinvigorate me and provide some excitement in my life."

"I'm, as you would say, gob smacked." I said. "I thought you were over all the excitement and wanted a return to your normal life."

Fiona laughed. "Anyway, I began looking for another position, one in another industry. Nothing seemed to fill the bill, when, on a whim, I went to the MI6 website and found a job opening for an intelligence officer. After going through some initial screening, I was contacted by phone. The person I spoke with said how pleased they were to receive my application. They were aware of my small part in breaking up the terrorist cell in Virginia a couple of years ago, as well as my involvement in the raid on the drug distribution warehouse in Civitavecchia and, as he called it, the recent unpleasantness in Positano. Actually, they knew everything about me: my background, experience, relationship with you—literally everything."

"It's MI6. They have the means to find out anything they want to know about anyone of interest to them. And because the UK has over six million surveillance cameras in operation, if you like, they can send you a video of your life."

Fiona hesitated. I could almost hear her heart thumping.

"I went into MI6 headquarters a couple of days ago for my face-to-face interviews. Before I left, they offered me a job as an MI6 intelligence officer. I start next month. Can you believe it?"

No. I couldn't. Nothing Fiona could have said would have surprised me more. My head was a whirlwind. It would be dangerous. I wouldn't be there to protect her. Why was she even considering it? We had broken up because of what I did for a living. What did this mean for our relationship? Were we a couple again?

"So you're going to be a spy?" With all the questions I had, that was what came out.

She laughed. "Not really. Broadly speaking, the job is to gather, deliver, and utilize intelligence. I may do all of them during my career. To begin with, I'll have an induction period, after which they'll assign me to the aspect of the job that best suits me. I'll be based in London, but because of my knowledge of the Italian language and culture, I'd spend quite a bit of time in Italy. I'm on paid leave from B&A until the end of this month. I'd really like to see you before then."

"Same here. I have so many questions. I don't know where to begin. I'm between cases now. I can leave on the evening flight and be there tomorrow morning." My mind was racing with all I needed to do before leaving and which flight I should catch. Then it hit me. "Are you at home? Where are you?"

"Outside your door."

ACKNOWLEDGMENTS

First and foremost, thanks are due to my loyal readers. They motivate me to keep writing. Also, I am deeply indebted to my wife, Mildred, former director of medical education for GlaxoSmithKline and adjunct associate professor at the Campbell University School of Pharmacy, for her willingness to read and edit countless versions of this manuscript, as she has done for my previous two books.

Thank you to my amazing beta readers who provided constructive feedback on what I euphemistically called a final draft. Without doubt, the revisions made based on their comments greatly improved the manuscript. Thanks once again to my sister Judith Armfield, a lifelong teacher of English and journalism and brother-in-law Bob Armfield, Agent (Ret.) Raleigh-Wake CCBI, for being beta readers. Thanks also to my first time beta readers Betty Ann Samson, Amor Moffat and Maggi Davis. A special note of gratitude is due to beta reader Randy Anderson, US Customs Service Special Agent and member of the Joint Terrorism Task Force (Ret.), who provided technical advice.

Lastly, I want to thank Koehler Studios and my awesome editors, Joe Coccaro and Randi Sachs, for their work on my manuscript, and Kellie Emery for the cover design. She knocked it out of the park.

All characters are fictitious and resemblance to anyone living or dead is unintended. I have used names of four people I know and respect. Jim DuPont has been a friend since childhood. I hope he enjoys the book and the character who shares his name. Sue Cooper is a former coworker and lives in Italy. Peter Rees and I worked together in the UK. He and his wife Norma are enjoying retirement in North Yorkshire.

CPSIA information can be obtained
at www.ICGtesting.com
Printed in the USA
LVOW12s2133061216
516120LV00001B/80/P